THE HOLLOW NEEDLE

The riddle of the Hollow Needle hides a secret that the rulers of France have handed down to each other since ancient times — a royal fortune made up of the most fabulous treasure ever imagined. Arsène Lupin believes he has found the key to unravelling the mystery. However, two opponents are dogging his footsteps. Once again, Lupin's path has crossed with that of his old nemesis Holmlock Shears. And now Isidore Beautrelet — a mere sixth-form schoolboy, but a brilliant amateur detective — is also seeking to cross swords with the notorious gentleman burglar . . .

published in France in 1909 as *L'Aiguille Creuse*

This Large Print Edition
published 2016

A catalogue record for this book is available
from the British Library.

ISBN 978–1–4448–3083–5

Published by
F. A. Thorpe (Publishing)
Anstey, Leicestershire

Set by Words & Graphics Ltd.
Anstey, Leicestershire
Printed and bound in Great Britain by
T. J. International Ltd., Padstow, Cornwall

This book is printed on acid-free paper

MAURICE LEBL

Firs

THE HOLLO
NEEDLE

Translated from the French b
Alexander Teixeira de Mattos

Complete and Unabridged

ULVERSCROFT
Leicester

Contents

Contents

1

The Shot

Raymonde listened. The noise was repeated twice over, clearly enough to be distinguished from the medley of vague sounds that formed the great silence of the night and yet too faintly to enable her to tell whether it was near or far, within the walls of the big country-house, or outside, among the murky recesses of the park.

She rose softly. Her window was half open: she flung it back wide. The moonlight lay over a peaceful landscape of lawns and thickets, against which the straggling ruins of the old abbey stood out in tragic outlines, truncated columns, mutilated arches, fragments of porches and shreds of flying buttresses. A light breeze hovered over the face of things, gliding noiselessly through the bare motionless branches of the trees, but shaking the tiny budding leaves of the shrubs.

And, suddenly, she heard the same sound again. It was on the left and on the floor below her, in the living rooms, therefore, that occupied the left wing of the house. Brave

1

and plucky though she was, the girl felt afraid. She slipped on her dressing gown and took the matches.

'Raymonde — Raymonde!'

A voice as low as a breath was calling to her from the next room, the door of which had not been closed. She was feeling her way there, when Suzanne, her cousin, came out of the room and fell into her arms:

'Raymonde — is that you? Did you hear — ?'

'Yes. So you're not asleep?'

'I suppose the dog woke me — some time ago. But he's not barking now. What time is it?'

'About four.'

'Listen! Surely, some one's walking in the drawing room!'

'There's no danger, your father is down there, Suzanne.'

'But there is danger for him. His room is next to the boudoir.'

'M. Daval is there too — '

'At the other end of the house. He could never hear.'

They hesitated, not knowing what course to decide upon. Should they call out? Cry for help? They dared not; they were frightened of the sound of their own voices. But Suzanne, who had gone to the window, suppressed a scream:

2

'Look! — A man! — Near the fountain!'

A man was walking away at a rapid pace. He carried under his arm a fairly large load, the nature of which they were unable to distinguish: it knocked against his leg and impeded his progress. They saw him pass near the old chapel and turn toward a little door in the wall. The door must have been open, for the man disappeared suddenly from view and they failed to hear the usual grating of the hinges.

'He came from the drawing room,' whispered Suzanne.

'No, the stairs and the hall would have brought him out more to the left — Unless — '

The same idea struck them both. They leant out. Below them, a ladder stood against the front of the house, resting on the first floor. A glimmer lit up the stone balcony. And another man, who was also carrying something, bestrode the baluster, slid down the ladder and ran away by the same road as the first.

Suzanne, scared to the verge of swooning, fell on her knees, stammering:

'Let us call out — let us call for help — '

'Who would come? Your father — and if there are more of them left — and they throw themselves upon him — ?'

'Then — then — we might call the servants

— Your bell rings on their floor.'

'Yes — yes — perhaps, that's better. If only they come in time!'

Raymonde felt for the electric push near her bed and pressed it with her finger. They heard the bell ring upstairs and had an impression that its shrill sound must also reach any one below.

They waited. The silence became terrifying and the very breeze no longer shook the leaves of the shrubs.

'I'm frightened — frightened,' said Suzanne.

And, suddenly, from the profound darkness below them, came the sound of a struggle, a crash of furniture overturned, words, exclamations and then, horrible and ominous, a hoarse groan, the gurgle of a man who is being murdered —

Raymonde leapt toward the door. Suzanne clung desperately to her arm:

'No — no — don't leave me — I'm frightened — '

Raymonde pushed her aside and darted down the corridor, followed by Suzanne, who staggered from wall to wall, screaming as she went. Raymonde reached the staircase, flew down the stairs, flung herself upon the door of the big drawing room and stopped short, rooted to the threshold, while Suzanne sank in a heap by her side. Facing them, at three

4

steps' distance, stood a man, with a lantern in his hand. He turned it upon the two girls, blinding them with the light, stared long at their pale faces, and then, without hurrying, with the calmest movements in the world, took his cap, picked up a scrap of paper and two bits of straw, removed some footmarks from the carpet, went to the balcony, turned to the girls, made them a deep bow and disappeared.

Suzanne was the first to run to the little boudoir which separated the big drawing-room from her father's bedroom. But, at the entrance, a hideous sight appalled her. By the slanting rays of the moon, she saw two apparently lifeless bodies lying close to each other on the floor. She leaned over one of them:

'Father! — Father! — Is it you? What has happened to you?' she cried, distractedly.

After a moment, the Comte de Gesvres moved. In a broken voice, he said:

'Don't be afraid — I am not wounded — Daval? — Is he alive? — The knife? — The knife? — '

Two men-servants now arrived with candles. Raymonde flung herself down before the other body and recognized Jean Daval, the count's private secretary. A little stream of blood trickled from his neck. His face already wore the pallor of death.

5

Then she rose, returned to the drawing room, took a gun that hung in a trophy of arms on the wall and went out on the balcony. Not more than fifty or sixty seconds had elapsed since the man had set his foot on the top rung of the ladder. He could not, therefore, be very far away, the more so as he had taken the precaution to remove the ladder, in order to prevent the inmates of the house from using it. And soon she saw him skirting the remains of the old cloister. She put the gun to her shoulder, calmly took aim and fired. The man fell.

'That's done it! That's done it!' said one of the servants. 'We've got this one. I'll run down.'

'No, Victor, he's getting up . . . You had better go down by the staircase and make straight for the little door in the wall. That's the only way he can escape.'

Victor hurried off, but, before he reached the park, the man fell down again. Raymonde called the other servant:

'Albert, do you see him down there? Near the main cloister? — '

'Yes, he's crawling in the grass. He's done for — '

'Watch him from here.'

'There's no way of escape for him. On the right of the ruins is the open lawn — '

'And, Victor, do you guard the door, on the

6

left,' she said, taking up her gun.

'But, surely, you are not going down, miss?'

'Yes, yes,' she said, with a resolute accent and abrupt movements; 'let me be — I have a cartridge left — If he stirs — '

She went out. A moment later, Albert saw her going toward the ruins. He called to her from the window:

'He's dragged himself behind the cloister. I can't see him. Be careful, miss — '

Raymonde went round the old cloisters, to cut off the man's retreat, and Albert soon lost sight of her. After a few minutes, as he did not see her return, he became uneasy and, keeping his eye on the ruins, instead of going down by the stairs he made an effort to reach the ladder. When he had succeeded, he scrambled down and ran straight to the cloisters near which he had seen the man last. Thirty paces farther, he found Raymonde, who was searching with Victor.

'Well?' he asked.

'There's no laying one's hands on him,' replied Victor.

'The little door?'

'I've been there; here's the key.'

'Still — he must — '

'Oh, we've got him safe enough, the scoundrel — He'll be ours in ten minutes.'

The farmer and his son, awakened by the

7

shot, now came from the farm buildings, which were at some distance on the right, but within the circuit of the walls. They had met no one.

'Of course not,' said Albert. 'The ruffian can't have left the ruins — We'll dig him out of some hole or other.'

They organized a methodical search, beating every bush, pulling aside the heavy masses of ivy rolled round the shafts of the columns. They made sure that the chapel was properly locked and that none of the panes were broken. They went round the cloisters and examined every nook and corner. The search was fruitless.

There was but one discovery: at the place where the man had fallen under Raymonde's gun, they picked up a chauffeur's cap, in very soft buff leather; besides that, nothing.

The gendarmerie of Ouville-la-Riviere were informed at six o'clock in the morning and at once proceeded to the spot, after sending an express to the authorities at Dieppe with a note describing the circumstances of the crime, the imminent capture of the chief criminal and 'the discovery of his headgear and of the dagger with which the crime had been committed.'

At ten o'clock, two hired conveyances came down the gentle slope that led to the house.

One of them, an old-fashioned calash, contained the deputy public prosecutor and the examining magistrate, accompanied by his clerk. In the other, a humble fly, were seated two reporters, representing the *Journal de Rouen* and a great Paris paper.

The old chateau came into view — once the abbey residence of the priors of Ambrumesy, mutilated under the Revolution, both restored by the Comte de Gesvres, who had now owned it for some twenty years. It consists of a main building, surmounted by a pinnacled clock-tower, and two wings, each of which is surrounded by a flight of steps with a stone balustrade. Looking across the walls of the park and beyond the upland supported by the high Norman cliffs, you catch a glimpse of the blue line of the Channel between the villages of Sainte-Marguerite and Varengeville.

Here the Comte de Gesvres lived with his daughter Suzanne, a delicate, fair-haired, pretty creature, and his niece Raymonde de Saint-Veran, whom he had taken to live with him two years before, when the simultaneous death of her father and mother left Raymonde an orphan. Life at the chateau was peaceful and regular. A few neighbours paid an occasional visit. In the summer, the count took the two girls almost every day to Dieppe.

He was a tall man, with a handsome, serious face and hair that was turning grey. He was very rich, managed his fortune himself and looked after his extensive estates with the assistance of his secretary, Jean Daval.

Immediately upon his arrival, the examining magistrate took down the first observations of Sergeant Quevillon of the gendarmes. The capture of the criminal, imminent though it might be, had not yet been effected, but every outlet of the park was held. Escape was impossible.

The little company next crossed the chapter-hall and the refectory, both of which are on the ground floor, and went up to the first story. They at once remarked the perfect order that prevailed in the drawing room. Not a piece of furniture, not an ornament but appeared to occupy its usual place; nor was there any gap among the ornaments or furniture. On the right and left walls hung magnificent Flemish tapestries with figures. On the panels of the wall facing the windows were four fine canvases, in contemporary frames, representing mythological scenes. These were the famous pictures by Rubens which had been left to the Comte de Gesvres, together with the Flemish tapestries, by his maternal uncle, the Marques de Bobadilla, a Spanish grandee.

M. Filleul remarked:

'If the motive of the crime was theft, this drawing room, at any rate, was not the object of it.'

'You can't tell!' said the deputy, who spoke little, but who, when he did, invariably opposed the magistrate's views.

'Why, my dear sir, the first thought of a burglar would be to carry off those pictures and tapestries, which are universally renowned.'

'Perhaps there was no time.'

'We shall see.'

At that moment, the Comte de Gesvres entered, accompanied by the doctor. The count, who did not seem to feel the effects of the attack to which he had been subjected, welcomed the two officials. Then he opened the door of the boudoir.

This room, which no one had been allowed to enter since the discovery of the crime, differed from the drawing room inasmuch as it presented a scene of the greatest disorder. Two chairs were overturned, one of the tables smashed to pieces and several objects — a traveling-clock, a portfolio, a box of stationery — lay on the floor. And there was blood on some of the scattered pieces of note-paper.

The doctor turned back the sheet that covered the corpse. Jean Daval, dressed in his usual velvet suit, with a pair of nailed boots on his feet, lay stretched on his back, with one arm folded beneath him. His collar and tie had been removed and his shirt opened, revealing a large wound in the chest.

'Death must have been instantaneous,' declared the doctor. 'One blow of the knife was enough.'

'It was, no doubt, the knife which I saw on the drawing-room mantelpiece, next to a leather cap?' said the examining magistrate.

'Yes,' said the Comte de Gesvres, 'the knife was picked up here. It comes from the same trophy in the drawing room from which my niece, Mlle. de Saint-Veran, snatched the gun. As for the chauffeur's cap, that evidently belongs to the murderer.'

M. Filleul examined certain further details in the room, put a few questions to the doctor and then asked M. de Gesvres to tell him what he had seen and heard. The count worded his story as follows:

'Jean Daval woke me up. I had been sleeping badly, for that matter, with gleams of consciousness in which I seemed to hear noises, when, suddenly opening my eyes, I saw Daval standing at the foot of my bed, with his candle in his hand and fully dressed — as he is now, for he often worked late into the night. He seemed greatly excited and said, in a low voice: 'There's some one in the drawing room.' I heard a noise myself. I got up and softly pushed the door leading to this boudoir. At the same moment, the door over there, which opens into the big drawing room, was thrown back and a man appeared who leaped at me and stunned me with a blow on the temple. I am telling you this without any details, Monsieur le Juge d'Instruction, for the simple reason that I remember only the principal facts, and that these facts followed upon one another with extraordinary swiftness.'

'And after that? — '

'After that, I don't know — I fainted. When I came to, Daval lay stretched by my side, mortally wounded.'

'At first sight, do you suspect no one?'

'No one.'

'You have no enemy?'

'I know of none.'

'Nor M. Daval either?'

'Daval! An enemy? He was the best creature that ever lived. M. Daval was my secretary for twenty years and, I may say, my confidant; and I have never seen him surrounded with anything but love and friendship.'

'Still, there has been a burglary and there has been a murder: there must be a motive for all that.'

'The motive? Why, it was robbery pure and simple.'

'Robbery? Have you been robbed of something, then?'

'No, nothing.'

'In that case — ?'

'In that case, if they have stolen nothing and if nothing is missing, they at least took something away.'

'What?'

'I don't know. But my daughter and my niece will tell you, with absolute certainty, that they saw two men in succession cross the park and that those two men were carrying fairly heavy loads.'

'The young ladies — '

'The young ladies may have been dreaming, you think? I should be tempted to believe it, for I have been exhausting myself in inquiries and suppositions ever since this morning. However, it is easy enough to question them.'

The two cousins were sent for to the big drawing room. Suzanne, still quite pale and trembling, could hardly speak. Raymonde, who was more energetic, more of a man, better looking, too, with the golden glint in her brown eyes, described the events of the night and the part which she had played in them.

'So I may take it, mademoiselle, that your evidence is positive?'

'Absolutely. The men who went across the park were carrying things away with them.'

'And the third man?'

'He went from here empty-handed.'

'Could you describe him to us?'

'He kept on dazzling us with the light of his lantern. All that I could say is that he is tall and heavily built.'

'Is that how he appeared to you, mademoiselle?' asked the magistrate, turning to Suzanne de Gesvres.

'Yes — or, rather, no,' said Suzanne, reflecting. 'I thought he was about the middle height and slender.'

M. Filleul smiled; he was accustomed to differences of opinion and sight in witnesses to one and the same fact:

'So we have to do, on the one hand, with a man, the one in the drawing room, who is, at the same time, tall and short, stout and thin, and, on the other, with two men, those in the park, who are accused of removing from that drawing room objects — which are still here!'

M. Filleul was a magistrate of the ironic school, as he himself would say. He was also a very ambitious magistrate and one who did not object to an audience nor to an occasion to display his tactful resource in public, as

15

was shown by the increasing number of persons who now crowded into the room. The journalists had been joined by the farmer and his son, the gardener and his wife, the indoor servants of the chateau and the two cabmen who had driven the flies from Dieppe.

M. Filleul continued:

'There is also the question of agreeing upon the way in which the third person disappeared. Was this the gun you fired, mademoiselle, and from this window?'

'Yes. The man reached the tombstone which is almost buried under the brambles, to the left of the cloisters.'

'But he got up again?'

'Only half. Victor ran down at once to guard the little door and I followed him, leaving the second footman, Albert, to keep watch here.'

Albert now gave his evidence and the magistrate concluded:

'So, according to you, the wounded man was not able to escape on the left, because your fellow-servant was watching the door, nor on the right, because you would have seen him cross the lawn. Logically, therefore, he is, at the present moment, in the comparatively restricted space that lies before our eyes.'

'I am sure of it.'

'And you, mademoiselle?'

'Yes.'

'And I, too,' said Victor.

The deputy prosecutor exclaimed, with a leer:

'The field of inquiry is quite narrow. We have only to continue the search commenced four hours ago.'

'We may be more fortunate.'

M. Filleul took the leather cap from the mantel, examined it and, beckoning to the sergeant of gendarmes, whispered:

'Sergeant, send one of your men to Dieppe at once. Tell him to go to Maigret, the hatter, in the Rue de la Barre, and ask M. Maigret to tell him, if possible, to whom this cap was sold.'

The 'field of inquiry,' in the deputy's phrase, was limited to the space contained between the house, the lawn on the right and the angle formed by the left wall and the wall opposite the house, that is to say, a quadrilateral of about a hundred yards each way, in which the ruins of Ambrumesy, the famous mediaeval monastery, stood out at intervals.

They at once noticed the traces left by the fugitive in the trampled grass. In two places, marks of blackened blood, now almost dried up, were observed. After the turn at the end of the cloisters, there was nothing more to be seen, as the nature of the ground, here covered with pine-needles, did not lend itself to the imprint of a body. But, in that case, how had the wounded man succeeded in escaping the eyes of Raymonde, Victor and Albert? There was nothing but a few brakes, which the servants and the gendarmes had beaten over and over again, and a number of tombstones, under which they had explored. The examining magistrate made the gardener, who had the key, open the chapel, a real gem of carving, a shrine in stone which had been respected by time and the revolutionaries, and which, with the delicate sculpture work of its porch and its miniature population of statuettes, was always looked upon as a marvellous specimen of the Norman-Gothic style. The chapel, which was very simple in the interior, with no other ornament than its marble altar, offered no hiding-place. Besides, the fugitive would have had to obtain admission. And by what means?

The inspection brought them to the little door in the wall that served as an entrance for the visitors to the ruins. It opened on a sunk road running between the park wall and a copsewood containing some abandoned quarries. M. Filleul stooped forward: the dust of the road bore marks of anti-skid pneumatic tires. Raymonde and Victor remembered that, after the shot, they had seemed to hear the throb of a motor-car.

The magistrate suggested:

'The man must have joined his confederates.'

'Impossible!' cried Victor. 'I was here while mademoiselle and Albert still had him in view.'

'Nonsense, he must be somewhere! Outside or inside: we have no choice!'

'He is here,' the servants insisted, obstinately.

The magistrate shrugged his shoulders and went back to the house in a more or less sullen mood. There was no doubt that it was an unpromising case. A theft in which nothing had been stolen; an invisible prisoner: what could be less satisfactory?

It was late. M. de Gesvres asked the officials and the two journalists to stay to lunch. They ate in silence and then M. Filleul returned to the drawing room, where he questioned the servants. But the sound of a horse's hoofs came from the courtyard and, a moment after, the gendarme who had been sent to Dieppe entered.

'Well, did you see the hatter?' exclaimed the magistrate, eager at last to obtain some positive information.

'I saw M. Maigret. The cap was sold to a cab-driver.'

'A cab-driver!'

'Yes, a driver who stopped his fly before the shop and asked to be supplied with a yellow-leather chauffeur's cap for one of his customers. This was the only one left. He paid for it, without troubling about the size, and drove off. He was in a great hurry.'

'What sort of fly was it?'

'A calash.'

'And on what day did this happen?'

'On what day? Why, to-day, at eight o'clock this morning.'

'This morning? What are you talking about?'

'The cap was bought this morning.'

'But that's impossible, because it was found last night in the park. If it was found there, it must have been there; and, consequently, it must have been bought before.'

'The hatter told me it was bought this morning.'

There was a moment of general bewilderment. The nonplussed magistrate strove to understand. Suddenly, he started, as though struck with a gleam of light:

'Fetch the cabman who brought us here this morning! The man who drove the calash! Fetch him at once!'

The sergeant of gendarmes and his

subordinate ran off to the stables. In a few minutes, the sergeant returned alone.

'Where's the cabman?'

'He asked for food in the kitchen, ate his lunch and then — '

'And then — ?'

'He went off.'

'With his fly?'

'No. Pretending that he wanted to go and see a relation at Ouville, he borrowed the groom's bicycle. Here are his hat and greatcoat.'

'But did he leave bare-headed?'

'No, he took a cap from his pocket and put it on.'

'A cap?'

'Yes, a yellow leather cap, it seems.'

'A yellow leather cap? Why, no, we've got it here!'

'That's true, Monsieur le Juge d'Instruction, but his is just like it.'

The deputy sniggered:

'Very funny! Most amusing! There are two caps — One, the real one, which constituted our only piece of evidence, has gone off on the head of the sham flyman! The other, the false one, is in your hands. Oh, the fellow has had us nicely!'

'Catch him! Fetch him back!' cried M. Filleul. 'Two of your men on horseback, Sergeant Quevillon, and at full speed!'

'He is far away by this time,' said the deputy.

'He can be as far as he pleases, but still we must lay hold of him.'

'I hope so; but I think, Monsieur le Juge d'Instruction, that your efforts should be concentrated here above all. Would you mind reading this scrap of paper, which I have just found in the pocket of the coat?'

'Which coat?'

'The driver's.'

And the deputy prosecutor handed M. Filleul a piece of paper, folded in four, containing these few words written in pencil, in a more or less common hand:

'Woe betide the young lady, if she has killed the governor!'

The incident caused a certain stir.

'A word to the wise!' muttered the deputy. 'We are now forewarned.'

'Monsieur le Comte,' said the examining magistrate, 'I beg you not to be alarmed. Nor you either, mademoiselle. This threat is of no importance, as the police are on the spot. We shall take every precaution and I will answer for your safety. As for you, gentlemen. I rely on your discretion. You have been present at this inquiry, thanks to my excessive kindness toward the Press, and it would be making me an ill return — '

He interrupted himself, as though an idea had struck him, looked at the two young men, one after the other, and, going up to the first, asked:

'What paper do you represent, sir?'

'The *Journal de Rouen*.'

'Have you your credentials?'

'Here.'

The card was in order. There was no more to be said. M. Filleul turned to the other reporter:

'And you, sir?'

'I?'

'Yes, you: what paper do you belong to?'

'Why, Monsieur le Juge d'Instruction, I write for a number of papers — all over the place —

'Your credentials?'

'I haven't any.'

'Oh! How is that?'

'For a newspaper to give you a card, you have to be on its regular staff.'

'Well?'

'Well, I am only an occasional contributor, a free-lance. I send articles to this newspaper and that. They are published or declined according to circumstances.'

'In that case, what is your name? Where are your papers?'

'My name would tell you nothing. As for

papers, I have none.'

'You have no paper of any kind to prove your profession!'

'I have no profession.'

'But look here, sir,' cried the magistrate, with a certain asperity, 'you can't expect to preserve your incognito after introducing yourself here by a trick and surprising the secrets of the police!'

'I beg to remark, Monsieur le Juge d'Instruction, that you asked me nothing when I came in, and that therefore I had nothing to say. Besides, it never struck me that your inquiry was secret, when everybody was admitted — including even one of the criminals!'

He spoke softly, in a tone of infinite politeness. He was quite a young man, very tall, very slender and dressed without the least attempt at fashion, in a jacket and trousers both too small for him. He had a pink face like a girl's, a broad forehead topped with close-cropped hair, and a scrubby and ill-trimmed fair beard. His bright eyes gleamed with intelligence. He seemed not in the least embarrassed and wore a pleasant smile, free from any shade of banter.

M. Filleul looked at him with an aggressive air of distrust. The two gendarmes came forward. The young man exclaimed, gaily:

'Monsieur le Juge d'Instruction, you clearly

suspect me of being an accomplice. But, if that were so, would I not have slipped away at the right moment, following the example of my fellow-criminal?'

'You might have hoped — '

'Any hope would have been absurd. A moment's reflection, Monsieur le Juge d'Instruction, will make you agree with me that, logically speaking — '

M. Filleul looked him straight in the eyes and said, sharply:

'No more jokes! Your name?'

'Isidore Beautrelet.'

'Your occupation?'

'Sixth-form pupil at the Lycee Janson-de-Sailly.'

M. Filleul opened a pair of startled eyes.

'What are you talking about? Sixth-form pupil — '

'At the Lycee Janson, Rue de la Pompe, number — '

'Oh, look here,' exclaimed M. Filleul, 'you're trying to take me in! This won't do, you know; a joke can go too far!'

'I must say, Monsieur le Juge d'Instruction, that your astonishment surprises me. What is there to prevent my being a sixth-form pupil at the Lycee Janson? My beard, perhaps? Set your mind at ease: my beard is false!'

Isidore Beautrelet pulled off the few curls

that adorned his chin, and his beardless face appeared still younger and pinker, a genuine schoolboy's face. And, with a laugh like a child's, revealing his white teeth:

'Are you convinced now?' he asked. 'Do you want more proofs? Here, you can read the address on these letters from my father: '*To Monsieur Isidore Beautrelet, Indoor Pupil, Lycee Janson-de-Sailly.*''

Convinced or not, M. Filleul did not look as if he liked the story. He asked, gruffly:

'What are you doing here?'

'Why — I'm — I'm improving my mind.'

'There are schools for that: yours, for instance.'

'You forget, Monsieur le Juge d'Instruction, that this is the twenty-third of April and that we are in the middle of the Easter holidays.'

'Well?'

'Well, I have every right to spend my holidays as I please.'

'Your father — '

'My father lives at the other end of the country, in Savoy, and he himself advised me to take a little trip on the North Coast.'

'With a false beard?'

'Oh, no! That's my own idea. At school, we talk a great deal about mysterious adventures; we read detective stories, in which people disguise themselves; we imagine any amount of terrible and intricate cases. So I thought I would amuse myself; and I put on this false beard. Besides, I enjoyed the advantage of being taken seriously and I pretended to be a Paris reporter. That is how, last night, after an uneventful period of more than a week, I had the pleasure of making the acquaintance of my Rouen colleague; and, this morning, when he heard of the Ambrumesy murder, he very kindly suggested that I should come with him and that we should share the cost of a fly.'

Isidore Beautrelet said all this with a frank and artless simplicity of which it was impossible not to feel the charm. M. Filleul himself, though maintaining a distrustful reserve, took a certain pleasure in listening to him. He asked him, in a less peevish tone:

'And are you satisfied with your expedition?'

'Delighted! All the more as I had never been present at a case of the sort and I find that this one is not lacking in interest.'

'Nor in that mysterious intricacy which you prize so highly — '

'And which is so stimulating, Monsieur le Juge d'Instruction! I know nothing more exciting than to see all the facts coming up out of the shadow, clustering together, so to speak, and gradually forming the probable truth.'

'The probable truth! You go pretty fast, young man! Do you suggest that you have your little solution of the riddle ready?'

'Oh, no!' replied Beautrelet, with a laugh.

'Only — it seems to me that there are certain points on which it is not impossible to form an opinion; and others, even, are so precise as to warrant — a conclusion.'

'Oh, but this is becoming very curious and I shall get to know something at last! For I confess, to my great confusion, that I know nothing.'

'That is because you have not had time to reflect, Monsieur le Juge d'Instruction. The great thing is to reflect. Facts very seldom fail to carry their own explanation!'

'And, according to you, the facts which we have just ascertained carry their own explanation?'

'Don't you think so yourself? In any case, I have ascertained none besides those which are set down in the official report.'

'Good! So that, if I were to ask you which were the objects stolen from this room — '

'I should answer that I know.'

'Bravo! My gentleman knows more about it than the owner himself. M. de Gesvres has everything accounted for: M. Isidore Beautrelet has not. He misses a bookcase in three sections and a life-size statue which nobody

28

ever noticed. And, if I asked you the name of the murderer?'

'I should again answer that I know it.'

All present gave a start. The deputy and the journalist drew nearer. M. de Gesvres and the two girls, impressed by Beautrelet's tranquil assurance, listened attentively.

'You know the murderer's name?'

'Yes.'

'And the place where he is concealed, perhaps?'

'Yes.'

M. Filleul rubbed his hands.

'What a piece of luck! This capture will do honour to my career. And can you make me these startling revelations now?'

'Yes, now — or rather, if you do not mind, in an hour or two, when I shall have assisted at your inquiry to the end.'

'No, no, young man, here and now, please.'

At that moment Raymonde de Saint-Veran, who had not taken her eyes from Isidore Beautrelet since the beginning of this scene, came up to M. Filleul:

'Monsieur le Juge d'Instruction — '

'Yes, mademoiselle?'

She hesitated for two or three seconds, with her eyes fixed on Beautrelet, and then, addressing M. Filleul:

'I should like you to ask monsieur the

reason why he was walking yesterday in the sunk road which leads up to the little door.'

It was an unexpected and dramatic stroke. Isidore Beautrelet appeared nonplussed:

'I, mademoiselle? I? You saw me yesterday?'

Raymonde remained thoughtful, with her eyes upon Beautrelet, as though she were trying to settle her own conviction, and then said, in a steady voice:

'At four o'clock in the afternoon, as I was crossing the wood, I met in the sunk road a young man of monsieur's height, dressed like him and wearing a beard cut in the same way — and I received a very clear impression that he was trying to hide.'

'And it was I?'

'I could not say that as an absolute certainty, for my recollection is a little vague. Still — still, I think so — if not, it would be an unusual resemblance — '

M. Filleul was perplexed. Already taken in by one of the confederates, was he now going to let himself be tricked by this self-styled schoolboy? Certainly, the young man's manner spoke in his favour; but one can never tell!

'What have you to say, sir?'

'That mademoiselle is mistaken, as I can easily show you with one word. Yesterday, at the time stated, I was at Veules.'

'You will have to prove it, you will have to. In any case, the position is not what it was. Sergeant, one of your men will keep monsieur company.'

Isidore Beautrelet's face denoted a keen vexation.

'Will it be for long?'

'Long enough to collect the necessary information.'

'Monsieur le Juge d'Instruction, I beseech you to collect it with all possible speed and discretion.'

'Why?'

'My father is an old man. We are very much attached to each other — and I would not have him suffer on my account.'

The more or less pathetic note in his voice made a bad impression on M. Filleul. It suggested a scene in a melodrama. Nevertheless, he promised:

'This evening — or to-morrow at latest, I shall know what to think.'

The afternoon was wearing on. The examining magistrate returned to the ruins of the cloisters, after giving orders that no unauthorized persons were to be admitted, and patiently, methodically, dividing the ground into lots which were successively explored, himself directed the search. But at the end of the day he was no farther than at the start; and he declared, before an army of reporters who, during that time, had invaded the chateau:

'Gentlemen, everything leads us to suppose that the wounded man is here, within our reach; everything, that is, except the reality, the fact. Therefore, in our humble opinion, he must have escaped and we shall find him outside.'

By way of precaution, however, he arranged, with the sergeant of gendarmes, for a complete watch to be kept over the park and, after making a fresh examination of the two drawing rooms, visiting the whole of the chateau and surrounding himself with all the necessary information, he took the road back to Dieppe, accompanied by the deputy prosecutor.

Night fell. As the boudoir was to remain locked, Jean Daval's body had been moved to another room. Two women from the neighbourhood sat up with it, assisted by Suzanne and Raymonde. Downstairs, young Isidore Beautrelet slept on the bench in the old oratory, under the watchful eye of the village policeman, who had been attached to his person. Outside, the gendarmes, the farmer and a dozen peasants had taken up their position among the ruins and along the walls.

All was still until eleven o'clock; but, at ten minutes past eleven, a shot echoed from the other side of the house.

'Attention!' roared the sergeant. 'Two men remain here: you, Fossier — and you, Lecanu — The others at the double!'

They all rushed forward and ran round the house on the left. A figure was seen to make away in the dark. Then, suddenly, a second shot drew them farther on, almost to the borders of the farm. And, all at once, as they arrived, in a band, at the hedge which lines the orchard, a flame burst out, to the right of the farmhouse, and other flames also rose in a thick column. It was a barn burning, stuffed to the ridge with straw.

'The scoundrels!' shouted the sergeant. 'They've set fire to it. Have at them, lads! They can't be far away!'

But the wind was turning the flames toward the main building; and it became necessary, before all things, to ward off the danger. They all exerted themselves with the greater ardour inasmuch as M. de Gesvres, hurrying to the scene of the disaster, encouraged them with the promise of a reward. By the time that they had mastered the flames, it was two o'clock in the morning. All pursuit would have been vain.

'We'll look into it by daylight,' said the sergeant. 'They are sure to have left traces: we shall find them.'

'And I shall not be sorry,' added M. de Gesvres, 'to learn the reason of this attack. To set fire to trusses of straw strikes me as a very useless proceeding.'

'Come with me, Monsieur le Comte: I may be able to tell you the reason.'

Together they reached the ruins of the cloisters. The sergeant called out:

'Lecanu! — Fossier!'

The other gendarmes were already hunting for their comrades whom they had left standing sentry. They ended by finding them at a few paces from the little door. The two men were lying full length on the ground, bound and gagged, with bandages over their eyes.

'Monsieur le Comte,' muttered the sergeant, while his men were being released; 'Monsieur le Comte, we have been tricked like children.'

'How so?'

'The shots — the attack on the barn — the fire — all so much humbug to get us down there — a diversion. During that time they were tying up our two men and the business was done.'

'What business?'

'Carrying off the wounded man, of course!'

'You don't mean to say you think — ?'

'Think? Why, it's as plain as a pikestaff! The

idea came to me ten minutes ago — but I'm a fool not to have thought of it earlier. We should have nabbed them all.' Quevillon stamped his foot on the ground, with a sudden attack of rage. 'But where, confound it, where did they go through? Which way did they carry him off? For, dash it all, we beat the ground all day; and a man can't hide in a tuft of grass, especially when he's wounded! It's witchcraft, that's what it is! — '

Nor was this the last surprise awaiting Sergeant Quevillon. At dawn, when they entered the oratory which had been used as a cell for young Isidore Beautrelet, they realized that young Isidore Beautrelet had vanished.

On a chair slept the village policeman, bent in two. By his side stood a water-bottle and two tumblers. At the bottom of one of those tumblers a few grains of white powder.

On examination, it was proved, first, that young Isidore Beautrelet had administered a sleeping draught to the village policeman; secondly, that he could only have escaped by a window situated at a height of seven or eight feet in the wall; and lastly — a charming detail, this — that he could only have reached this window by using the back of his warder as a footstool.

2

Isidore Beautrelet, Sixth-Form Schoolboy

From the *Grand Journal*.

DOCTOR DELATTRE KIDNAPPED
A MAD PIECE OF CRIMINAL DARING

At the moment of going to press, we have received an item of news which we dare not guarantee as authentic, because of its very improbable character. We print it, therefore, with all reserve.

Yesterday evening, Dr. Delattre, the well-known surgeon, was present, with his wife and daughter, at the performance of Hernani at the Comedie Francaise. At the commencement of the third act, that is to say, at about ten o'clock, the door of his box opened and a gentleman, accompanied by two others, leaned over to the doctor and said to him, in a low voice, but loud enough for Mme. Delattre to hear:

36

'Doctor, I have a very painful task to fulfil and I shall be very grateful to you if you will make it as easy for me as you can.'

'Who are you, sir?'

'M. Thezard, commissary of police of the first district; and my instructions are to take you to M. Dudouis, at the prefecture.'

'But — '

'Not a word, doctor, I entreat you, not a movement — There is some regrettable mistake; and that is why we must act in silence and not attract anybody's attention. You will be back, I have no doubt, before the end of the performance.'

The doctor rose and went with the commissary. At the end of the performance, he had not returned. Mme. Delattre, greatly alarmed, drove to the office of the commissary of police. There she found the real M. Thezard and discovered, to her great terror, that the individual who had carried off her husband was an impostor.

Inquiries made so far have revealed the fact that the doctor stepped into a motor car and that the car drove off in the direction of the Concorde.

Readers will find further details of this

incredible adventure in our second edition.

Incredible though it might be, the adventure was perfectly true. Besides, the issue was not long delayed and the *Grand Journal*, while confirming the story in its midday edition, described in a few lines the dramatic ending with which it concluded:

ISIDORE BEAUTRELET

THE STORY ENDS
AND
GUESS-WORK BEGINS

Dr. Delattre was brought back to 78, Rue Duret, at nine o'clock this morning, in a motor car which drove away immediately at full speed.

No. 78, Rue Duret, is the address of Dr. Delattre's clinical surgery, at which he arrives every morning at the same hour. When we sent in our card, the doctor, though closeted with the chief of the detective service, was good enough to consent to receive us.

'All that I can tell you,' he said, in reply to our questions, 'is that I was treated with the greatest consideration.

My three companions were the most charming people I have ever met, exquisitely well-mannered and bright and witty talkers: a quality not to be despised, in view of the length of the journey.'

'How long did it take?'

'About four hours and as long returning.'

'And what was the object of the journey?'

'I was taken to see a patient whose condition rendered an immediate operation necessary.'

'And was the operation successful?'

'Yes, but the consequences may be dangerous. I would answer for the patient here. Down there — under his present conditions — '

'Bad conditions?'

'Execrable! — A room in an inn — and the practically absolute impossibility of being attended to.'

'Then what can save him?'

'A miracle — and his constitution, which is an exceptionally strong one.'

'And can you say nothing more about this strange patient?'

'No. In the first place, I have taken an oath; and, secondly, I have received a present of ten thousand francs for my free surgery. If I do not keep silence, this sum will be taken from me.'

'You are joking! Do you believe that?'

'Indeed I do. The men all struck me as being very much in earnest.'

This is the statement made to us by Dr. Delattre. And we know, on the other hand, that the head of the detective service, in spite of all his insisting, has not yet succeeded in extracting any more precise particulars from him as to the operation which he performed, the patient whom he attended or the district traversed by the car. It is difficult, therefore, to arrive at the truth.

This truth, which the writer of the interview confessed himself unable to discover, was guessed by the more or less clear-sighted minds that perceived a connection with the facts which had occurred the day before at the Chateau d' Ambrumesy, and which were reported, down to the smallest detail, in all the newspapers of that day. There was evidently a coincidence to be reckoned with in the disappearance of a wounded burglar and the kidnapping of a famous surgeon.

The judicial inquiry, moreover, proved the correctness of the hypothesis. By following the track of the sham flyman, who had fled on a bicycle, they were able to show that he had reached the forest of Arques, at some ten miles' distance, and that from there, after throwing his bicycle into a ditch, he had gone to the village of Saint-Nicolas, whence he had dispatched the following telegram:

A. L. N., Post-office 45, Paris. Situation desperate. Operation urgently necessary. Send celebrity by national road fourteen.

The evidence was undeniable. Once apprised the accomplices in Paris hastened to make their arrangements. At ten o'clock in the evening they sent their celebrity by National Road No. 14, which skirts the forest of Arques and ends at Dieppe. During this time, under cover of the fire which they themselves had caused, the gang of burglars carried off their leader and moved him to an inn, where the operation took place on the arrival of the surgeon, at two o'clock in the morning.

About that there was no doubt. At Pontoise, at Gournay, at Forges, Chief-inspector Ganimard, who was sent specially from Paris, with Inspector Folenfant, as his assistant, ascertained that a motor car had passed in the course of the previous night. The same on the road from Dieppe to Ambrumesy. And, though the traces of the car were lost at about a mile and a half from the chateau, at least a number of footmarks were seen between the little door in the park wall and the abbey ruins. Besides, Ganimard remarked that the lock of the little door had been forced.

So all was explained. It remained to decide which inn the doctor had spoken of: an easy piece of work for a Ganimard, a professional ferret, a patient old stager of the police. The number of inns is limited and this one, given the condition of the wounded man, could only be one quite close to Ambrumesy. Ganimard and Sergeant Quevillon set to work. Within a circle of five hundred yards, of a thousand yards, of fifteen hundred yards, they visited and ransacked everything that could pass for an inn. But, against all expectation, the dying man persisted in remaining invisible.

Ganimard became more resolved than ever. He came back to sleep at the chateau, on the Saturday night, with the intention of making his personal inquiry on the Sunday. On Sunday morning, he learned that, during the night, a posse of gendarmes had seen a figure gliding along the sunk road, outside the wall. Was it an accomplice who had come back to investigate? Were they to suppose that the leader of the gang had not left the cloisters or the neighbourhood of the cloisters?

That night, Ganimard openly sent the

squad of gendarmes to the farm and posted himself and Folenfant outside the walls, near the little door.

A little before midnight, a person passed out of the wood, slipped between them, went through the door and entered the park. For three hours, they saw him wander from side to side across the ruins, stooping, climbing up the old pillars, sometimes remaining for long minutes without moving. Then he went back to the door and again passed between the two inspectors.

Ganimard caught him by the collar, while Folenfant seized him round the body. He made no resistance of any kind and, with the greatest docility, allowed them to bind his wrists and take him to the house. But, when they attempted to question him, he replied simply that he owed them no account of his doings and that he would wait for the arrival of the examining magistrate. Thereupon, they fastened him firmly to the foot of a bed, in one of the two adjoining rooms which they occupied.

At nine o'clock on Monday morning, as soon as M. Filleul had arrived, Ganimard announced the capture which he had made. The prisoner was brought downstairs. It was Isidore Beautrelet.

'M. Isidore Beautrelet!' exclaimed M.

Filleul with an air of rapture, holding out both his hands to the newcomer. 'What a delightful surprise! Our excellent amateur detective here! And at our disposal too! Why, it's a windfall! — M. Chief-inspector, allow me to introduce to you M. Isidore Beautrelet, a sixth-form pupil at the Lycee Janson-de-Sailly.'

Ganimard seemed a little nonplussed. Isidore made him a very low bow, as though he were greeting a colleague whom he knew how to esteem at his true value, and, turning to M. Filleul:

'It appears, Monsieur le Juge d'Instruction, that you have received a satisfactory account of me?'

'Perfectly satisfactory! To begin with, you were really at Veules-les-Roses at the time when Mlle. de Saint-Veran thought she saw you in the sunk road. I dare say we shall discover the identity of your double. In the second place, you are in very deed Isidore Beautrelet, a sixth-form pupil and, what is more, an excellent pupil, industrious at your work and of exemplary behaviour. As your father lives in the country, you go out once a month to his correspondent, M. Bernod, who is lavish in his praises of you.'

'So that — '

'So that you are free, M. Isidore Beautrelet.'

'Absolutely free?'

'Absolutely. Oh, I must make just one little condition, all the same. You can understand that I can't release a gentleman who administers sleeping-draughts, who escapes by the window and who is afterward caught in the act of trespassing upon private property. I can't release him without a compensation of some kind.'

'I await your pleasure.'

'Well, we will resume our interrupted conversation and you shall tell me how far you have advanced with your investigations. In two days of liberty, you must have carried them pretty far?' And, as Ganimard was preparing to go, with an affectation of contempt for that sort of practice, the magistrate cried, 'Not at all, M. Inspector, your place is here — I assure you that M. Isidore Beautrelet is worth listening to. M. Isidore Beautrelet, according to my information, has made a great reputation at the Lycee Janson-de-Sailly as an observer whom nothing escapes; and his schoolfellows, I hear, look upon him as your competitor and a rival of Holmlock Shears!'

'Indeed!' said Ganimard, ironically.

'Just so. One of them wrote to me, 'If Beautrelet declares that he knows, you must believe him; and, whatever he says, you may be sure that it is the exact expression of the truth.' M. Isidore Beautrelet, now or never is the time to vindicate the confidence of your friends. I beseech you, give us the exact expression of the truth.'

Isidore listened with a smile and replied:

'Monsieur le Juge d'Instruction, you are very cruel. You make fun of poor schoolboys who amuse themselves as best they can. You are quite right, however, and I will give you no further reason to laugh at me.'

'The fact is that you know nothing, M. Isidore Beautrelet.'

'Yes, I confess in all humility that I know nothing. For I do not call it 'knowing anything' that I happen to have hit upon two or three more precise points which, I am sure, cannot have escaped you.'

'For instance?'

'For instance, the object of the theft.'

'Ah, of course, you know the object of the theft?'

'As you do, I have no doubt. In fact, it was the first thing I studied, because the task struck me as easier.'

'Easier, really?'

'Why, of course. At the most, it's a question of reasoning.'

'Nothing more than that?'

'Nothing more.'

'And what is your reasoning?'

'It is just this, stripped of all extraneous comment: on the one hand, *there has been a theft*, because the two young ladies are agreed and because they really saw two men running away and carrying things with them.'

'There has been a theft.'

'On the other hand, *nothing has disappeared*, because M. de Gesvres says so and he is in a better position than anybody to know.'

'Nothing has disappeared.'

'From those two premises I arrive at this inevitable result: granted that there has been a theft and that nothing has disappeared, it is because the object carried off has been replaced by an exactly similar object. Let me hasten to add that possibly my argument may not be confirmed by the facts. But I maintain that it is the first argument that ought to occur to us and that we are not entitled to waive it until we have made a serious examination.'

'That's true — that's true,' muttered the magistrate, who was obviously interested.

'Now,' continued Isidore, 'what was there in this room that could arouse the covetousness of the burglars? Two things. The tapestry first. It can't have been that. Old tapestry cannot be imitated: the fraud would have been palpable at once. There remain the four Rubens pictures.'

'What's that you say?'

'I say that the four Rubenses on that wall are false.'

'Impossible!'

'They are false *a priori*, inevitably and without a doubt.'

'I tell you, it's impossible.'

'It is very nearly a year ago, Monsieur le Juge d'Instruction, since a young man, who gave his name as Charpenais, came to the Chateau d'Ambrumesy and asked permission to copy the Rubens pictures. M. de Gesvres gave him permission. Every day for five months Charpenais worked in this room from morning till dusk. The copies which he made, canvases and frames, have taken the place of the four original pictures bequeathed to M. de Gesvres by his uncle, the Marques de Bobadilla.'

'Prove it!'

'I have no proof to give. A picture is false because it is false; and I consider that it is not even necessary to examine these four.'

M. Filleul and Ganimard exchanged glances of unconcealed astonishment. The inspector no longer thought of withdrawing. At last, the magistrate muttered:

'We must have M. de Gesvres's opinion.'

And Ganimard agreed:

'Yes, we must have his opinion.'

And they sent to beg the count to come to the drawing room.

The young sixth-form pupil had won a real victory. To compel two experts, two professionals like M. Filleul and Ganimard to take account of his surmises implied a testimony of respect of which any other would have been proud. But Beautrelet seemed not to feel those little satisfactions of self-conceit and, still smiling without the least trace of irony, he placidly waited.

M. de Gesvres entered the room.

'Monsieur le Comte,' said the magistrate, 'the result of our inquiry has brought us face to face with an utterly unexpected contingency, which we submit to you with all reserve. It is possible — I say that it is possible — that the burglars, when breaking into the house, had it as their object to steal your four pictures by Rubens — or, at least, to replace them by four copies — copies which are said to have been made last year by a painter called Charpenais. Would you be so good as to examine the pictures and to tell us if you recognize them as genuine?'

The count appeared to suppress a movement of annoyance, looked at Isidore Beautrelet and at M. Filleul and replied, without even troubling to go near the pictures:

'I hoped, Monsieur le Juge d'Instruction,

that the truth might have remained unknown. As this is not so, I have no hesitation in declaring that the four pictures are false.'

'You knew it, then?'

'From the beginning.'

'Why didn't you say so?'

'The owner of a work is never in a hurry to declare that that work is not — or, rather, is no longer genuine.'

'Still, it was the only means of recovering them.'

'I consider that there was another and a better.'

'Which was that?'

'Not to make the secret known, not to frighten my burglars and to offer to buy back the pictures, which they must find more or less difficult to dispose of.'

'How would you communicate with them?'

As the count did not reply, Isidore answered for him:

'By means of an advertisement in the papers. The paragraph inserted in the agony column of the *Journal*, the *Echo de Paris* and the *Matin* runs, 'Am prepared to buy back the pictures.''

The count agreed with a nod. Once again, the young man was teaching his elders. M. Filleul showed himself a good sportsman.

'There's no doubt about it, my dear sir,' he

exclaimed. 'I'm beginning to think your school-fellows were not quite wrong. By Jove, what an eye! What intuition! If this goes on, there will be nothing left for M. Ganimard and me to do.'

'Oh, none of this part was so very complicated!'

'You mean to say that the rest was more so? I remember, in fact, that, when we first met you seemed to know all about it. Let me see, a far as I recollect, you said that you knew the name of the murderer.'

'So I do.'

'Well, then, who killed Jean Daval? Is the man alive? Where is he hiding?'

'There is a misunderstanding between us, Monsieur le Juge d'Instruction, or, rather, you have misunderstood the facts from the beginning The murderer and the runaway are two distinct persons.'

'What's that?' exclaimed M. Filleul. 'The man whom M. de Gesvres saw in the boudoir and struggled with, the man whom the young ladies saw in the drawing-room and whom Mlle. de Saint-Veran shot at, the man who fell in the park and whom we are looking for: do you suggest that he is not the man who killed Jean Daval?'

'I do.'

'Have you discovered the traces of a third

accomplice who disappeared before the arrival of the young ladies?'

'I have not.'

'In that case, I don't understand. — Well, who is the murderer of Jean Daval?'

'Jean Daval was killed by — '

Beautrelet interrupted himself, thought for a moment and continued:

'But I must first show you the road which I followed to arrive at the certainty and the very reasons of the murder — without which my accusation would seem monstrous to you. — And it is not — no, it is not monstrous at all. — There is one detail which has passed unobserved and which, nevertheless, is of the greatest importance; and that is that Jean Daval, at the moment when he was stabbed, had all his clothes on, including his walking boots, was dressed, in short, as a man is dressed in the middle of the day, with a waistcoat, collar, tie and braces. Now the crime was committed at four o'clock in the morning.'

'I reflected on that strange fact,' said the magistrate, 'and M. de Gesvres replied that Jean Daval spent a part of his nights in working.'

'The servants say, on the contrary, that he went to bed regularly at a very early hour. But, admitting that he was up, why did he disarrange his bedclothes, to make believe that he had gone to bed? And, if he was in bed, why, when he heard a noise, did he take the trouble to dress himself from head to foot, instead of slipping on anything that came to hand? I went to his room on the first day, while you were at lunch: his slippers were at the foot of the bed. What prevented him from putting them on rather than his heavy nailed boots?'

'So far, I do not see — '

'So far, in fact, you cannot see anything, except anomalies. They appeared much more suspicious to me, however, when I learned that Charpenais the painter, the man who copied the Rubens pictures, had been introduced and recommended to the Comte de Gesvres by Jean Daval himself.'

'Well?'

'Well, from that to the conclusion that Jean Daval and Charpenais were accomplices required but a step. I took that step at the time of our conversation.'

'A little quickly, I think.'

'As a matter of fact, a material proof was wanted. Now I had discovered in Daval's room, on one of the sheets of the blotting-pad on which he used to write, this address: 'Monsieur A.L.N., Post-office 45, Paris.' You will find it there still, traced the reverse way on the blotting-paper. The next day, it was discovered that the telegram sent by the sham flyman from Saint-Nicolas bore the same address: 'A.L.N., Post-office 45.' The material proof existed: Jean Daval was in correspondence with the gang which arranged the robbery of the pictures.'

M. Filleul raised no objection.

'Agreed. The complicity is established. And what conclusion do you draw?'

'This, first of all, that it was not the runaway who killed Jean Daval, because Jean Daval was his accomplice.'

'And after that?'

'Monsieur le Juge d'Instruction, I will ask you to remember the first sentence uttered by Monsieur le Comte when he recovered from fainting. The sentence forms part of Mlle. de Gesvres' evidence and is in the official report: 'I am not wounded. — Daval? — Is he alive? — The knife?' And I will ask you to compare it with that part of his story, also in the report, in which Monsieur le Comte describes the assault: 'The man leaped at me and felled me with a blow on the temple!' How could M. de Gesvres. who had fainted, know, on waking, that Daval had been stabbed with a knife?'

Isidore Beautrelet did not wait for an answer to his question. It seemed as though he were in a hurry to give the answer himself and to avoid all comment. He continued straightway:

'Therefore it was Jean Daval who brought the three burglars to the drawing room. While he was there with the one whom they call their chief, a noise was heard in the boudoir. Daval opened the door. Recognizing M. de Gesvres, he rushed at him, armed with the knife. M. de Gesvres succeeded in snatching the knife from him, struck him with it and himself fell, on receiving a blow from the man whom the two girls were to see a few minutes after.'

Once again, M. Filleul and the inspector exchanged glances. Ganimard tossed his head in a disconcerted way. The magistrate said:

'Monsieur le Comte, am I to believe that this version is correct?'

M. de Gesvres made no answer.

'Come, Monsieur le Comte, your silence would lead us to suppose — I beg you to speak.' Replying in a very clear voice, M. de Gesvres said:

'The version is correct in every particular.'

The magistrate gave a start.

'Then I cannot understand why you misled the police. Why conceal an act which you were lawfully entitled to commit in defence of your life?'

'For twenty years,' said M. de Gesvres,

'Daval worked by my side. I trusted him. If he betrayed me, as the result of some temptation or other, I was, at least, unwilling, for the sake of the past, that his treachery should become known.'

'You were unwilling, I agree, but you had no right to be.'

'I am not of your opinion, Monsieur le Juge d'Instruction. As long as no innocent person was accused of the crime, I was absolutely entitled to refrain from accusing the man who was at the same time the culprit and the victim. He is dead. I consider death a sufficient punishment.'

'But now, Monsieur le Comte, now that the truth is known, you can speak.'

'Yes. Here are two rough drafts of letters written by him to his accomplices. I took them from his pocket-book, a few minutes after his death.'

'And the motive of his theft?'

'Go to 18, Rue de la Barre, at Dieppe, which is the address of a certain Mme. Verdier. It was for this woman, whom he got to know two years ago, and to supply her constant need of money that Daval turned thief.'

So everything was cleared up. The tragedy rose out of the darkness and gradually appeared in its true light.

'Let us go on,' said M. Filluel after the count had withdrawn.

'Upon my word,' said Beautrelet, gaily, 'I have said almost all that I had to say.'

'But the runaway, the wounded man?'

'As to that, Monsieur le Juge d'Instruction, you know as much as I do. You have followed his tracks in the grass by the cloisters — you have — '

'Yes, yes, I know. But, since then, his friends have removed him and what I want is a clue or two as regards that inn — '

Isidore Beautrelet burst out laughing:

'The inn! The inn does not exist! It's an invention, a trick to put the police on the wrong scent, an ingenious trick, too, for it seems to have succeeded.'

'But Dr. Delattre declares — '

'Ah, that's just it!' cried Beautrelet, in a tone of conviction. 'It is just because Dr. Delattre declares that we mustn't believe him. Why, Dr. Delattre refused to give any but the vaguest details concerning his adventure! He refused to say anything that might compromise his patient's safety! — And suddenly he calls attention to an inn! — You may be sure that he talked about that inn because he was told to. You may be sure that the whole story which he dished up to us was dictated to him under the threat of terrible reprisals. The

doctor has a wife. The doctor has a daughter.
He is too fond of them to disobey people of
whose formidable power he has seen proofs.
And that is why he has assisted your efforts
by supplying the most precise clues.'

'So precise that the inn is nowhere to be
found.'

'So precise that you have never ceased
looking for it, in the face of all probability,
and that your eyes have been turned away
from the only spot where the man can be, the
mysterious spot which he has not left, which
he has been unable to leave ever since the
moment when, wounded by Mlle. de
Saint-Veran, he succeeded in dragging himself to it, like a beast to its lair.'

'But where, confound it all? — In what
corner of Hades — ?'

'In the ruins of the old abbey.'

'But there are no ruins left! — A few bits of
wall! — A few broken columns!'

'That's where he's gone to earth. Monsieur
le Juge d'Instruction!' shouted Beautrelet.
'That's where you will have to look for him!
It's there and nowhere else that you will find
Arsène Lupin!'

'Arsène Lupin!' yelled M. Filleul, springing
to his feet.

There was a rather solemn pause, amid
which the syllables of the famous name

58

seemed to prolong their sound. Was it possible that the vanquished and yet invisible adversary, whom they had been hunting in vain for several days, could really be Arsène Lupin? Arsène Lupin, caught in a trap, arrested, meant immediate promotion, fortune, glory to any examining magistrate!

Ganimard had not moved a limb. Isidore said to him:

'You agree with me, do you not, M. Inspector?'

'Of course I do!'

'You have not doubted either, for a moment have you, that he managed this business?'

'Not for a second! The thing bears his signature. A move of Arsène Lupin's is as different from a move made by another man as one face is from another. You have only to open your eyes.'

'Do you think so? Do you think so?' said M. Filleul.

'Think so!' cried the young man. 'Look, here's one little fact: what are the initials under which those men correspond among themselves? 'A. L. N.,' that is to say, the first letter of the name Arsène and the first and last letters of the name Lupin.'

'Ah,' said Ganimard, 'nothing escapes you! Upon my word, you're a fine fellow and old Ganimard lays down his arms before you!'

Beautrelet flushed with pleasure and pressed the hand which the chief-inspector held out to him. The three men had drawn near the balcony and their eyes now took in the extent of the ruins. M. Filleul muttered:

'So he ought to be there.'

'*He is there*,' said Beautrelet, in a hollow voice. 'He has been there ever since the moment when he fell. Logically and practically, he could not escape without being seen by Mlle. de Saint-Veran and the two servants.'

'What proof have you?'

'His accomplices have furnished the proof. On the very morning, one of them disguised himself as a flyman and drove you here — '

'To recover the cap, which would serve to identify him.'

'Very well, but also and more particularly to examine the spot, find out and see for himself what had become of the 'governor.''

'And did he find out?'

'I presume so, as he knew the hiding-place. And I presume that he became aware of the desperate condition of his chief, because, under the impulse of his alarm, he committed the imprudence to write that threat: 'Woe betide the young lady, if she has killed the governor!''

'But his friends were able to take him away afterward?'

'When? Your men have never left the ruins. And where could they have moved him to? At most, a few hundred yards away, for one doesn't let a dying man travel — and then you would have found him. No, I tell you, he is there. His friends would never have removed him from the safest of hiding-places. It was there that they brought the doctor, while the gendarmes were running to the fire like children.'

'But how is he living? How will he keep alive? To keep alive you need food and drink.'

'I can't say. I don't know. But he is there, I will swear it. He is there, because he can't help being there. I am as sure of it as if I saw as if I touched him. He is there.'

With his finger outstretched toward the ruins, he traced in the air a little circle which became smaller and smaller until it was only a point. And that point his two companions sought desperately, both leaning into space, both moved by the same faith in Beautrelet and quivering with the ardent conviction which he had forced upon them. Yes, Arsène Lupin was there. In theory and in fact, he was there: neither of them was now able to doubt it.

And there was something impressive and tragic in knowing that the famous adventurer was lying in some dark shelter, below the ground, helpless, feverish and exhausted.

'And if he dies?' asked M. Filleul, in a low voice.

'If he dies,' said Beautrelet. 'and if his accomplices are sure of it, then see to the safety of Mlle. de Saint-Veran. Monsieur le Juge d'Instruction, for the vengeance will be terrible.'

* * *

A few minutes later and in spite of the entreaties of M. Filleul, who would gladly have made further use of this fascinating auxiliary, Isidore Beautrelet, whose holidays ended that day, went off by the Dieppe Road. He stepped from the train in Paris at five o'clock and, at eight o'clock, returned to the Lycee Janson together with his schoolfellows.

Ganimard, after a minute, but utterly useless exploration of the ruins of Ambrumesy, returned to Paris by the fast night-train. On reaching his apartment in the Rue Pergolese, he found an express letter awaiting him:

Monsieur l'Inspecteur Principal:

Finding that I had a little time to spare at the end of the day, I have succeeded in collecting a few additional particulars which are sure to interest you.

Arsène Lupin has been living in Paris for twelve months under the name of Etienne de Vaudreix. It is a name which you will often come across in the society notes or the sporting columns of the newspapers. He is a great traveller and is absent for long periods, during which, by his own account, he goes hunting tigers in Bengal or blue foxes in Siberia. He is supposed to be in business of some kind, although nobody is able to say for certain what his business is.

His present address is 38, Rue Marbeuf; and I will call your attention to the fact that the Rue Marbeuf is close to Post-office Number 45. Since Thursday the twenty-third of April, the day before the burglary at Ambrumesy, there has been no news at all of Etienne de Vaudreix.

With very many thanks for the kindness which you have shown me, believe me to be, Monsieur l'Inspecteur Principal,

Yours sincerely,
ISIDORE BEAUTRELET.

P.S. — Please on no account think that it cost me any great trouble to obtain this information. On the very morning of the crime, while M. Filleul was pursuing his examination before a few privileged persons, I had the fortunate inspiration to glance at the runaway's cap, before the sham flyman came to change it. The hatter's name was enough, as you may imagine, to enable me to find the clue that led to the identification of the purchaser and his address.

The next morning, Ganimard called at 36, Rue Marbeuf. After questioning the concierge, he made him open the door of the ground-floor flat on the right, a very comfortable apartment, elegantly furnished, in which, however, he discovered nothing beyond some cinders in the fireplace. Two friends had come, four days earlier, to burn all compromising papers.

But, just as he was leaving, Ganimard passed the postman, who was bringing a letter for M. de Vaudreix. That afternoon, the public prosecutor was informed of the case and ordered the letter to be given up. It bore an American postmark and contained the following lines, in English:

DEAR SIR:

I write to confirm the answer which I gave your representative. As soon as you have M. de Gesvres's four pictures in your possession, you can forward them as arranged.

You may add the rest, if you are able to succeed, which I doubt.

An unexpected business requires my presence in Europe and I shall reach Paris at the same time as this letter. You will find me at the Grand Hotel.

Yours faithfully,
EPHRAIM B. HARLINGTON.

That same day, Ganimard applied for a warrant and took Mr. E. B. Harlington, an American citizen, to the police-station, on a charge of receiving and conspiracy.

★ ★ ★

Thus, within the space of twenty-four hours, all the threads of the plot had been unravelled, thanks to the really unforeseen clues supplied by a schoolboy of seventeen. In twenty-four hours, what had seemed inexplicable became simple and clear. In twenty-four hours, the scheme devised by the accomplices to save their leader was baffled; the capture of Arsène Lupin, wounded and dying, was no longer in doubt, his gang was disorganized, the address of his establishment in Paris and the name which he assumed were known and, for the first time, one of his cleverest and most carefully elaborated feats was seen through before he had been able to ensure its complete execution.

An immense clamour of astonishment, admiration and curiosity arose among the public. Already, the Rouen journalist, in a very able article, had described the first examination of the sixth-form pupil, laying stress upon his personal charm, his simplicity of manner and his quiet assurance. The indiscretions of Ganimard and M. Filleul, indiscretions to which they yielded in spite of themselves, under an impulse that proved stronger than their professional pride, suddenly enlightened the public as to the part played by Isidore Beautrelet in recent events. He alone had done everything. To him alone the merit of the victory was due.

The excitement was intense. Isidore Beautrelet awoke to find himself a hero; and the crowd, suddenly infatuated, insisted upon the fullest information regarding its new favourite. The reporters were there to supply it. They rushed to the assault of the Lycee Janson-de-Sailly, waited for the day-boarders to come out after school hours and picked up all that related, however remotely, to Beautrelet. It was in this way that they learned the reputation which he enjoyed among his schoolfellows, who called him the rival of Holmlock Shears. Thanks to his powers of logical reasoning, with no further data than those which he was able to gather from the papers, he had, time after time, proclaimed the solution of very complicated cases long before they were cleared up by the police.

It had become a game at the Lycee Janson to put difficult questions and intricate problems to Beautrelet; and it was astonishing to see with what unhesitating and analytical power and by means of what ingenious deductions he made his way through the thickest darkness. Ten days before the arrest of Jorisse, the grocer, he showed what could be done with the famous umbrella. In the same way, he declared from the beginning, in the matter of the Saint-Cloud mystery, that the concierge was the only possible murderer.

But most curious of all was the pamphlet which was found circulating among the boys at the school, a typewritten pamphlet signed by Beautrelet and manifolded to the number of ten copies. It was entitled, *Arsène Lupin and his method, showing in how far the latter is based upon tradition and in how far original. Followed by a comparison between English humour and French irony.*

It contained a profound study of each of

the exploits of Arsène Lupin, throwing the illustrious burglar's operations into extraordinary relief, showing the very mechanism of his way of setting to work, his special tactics, his letters to the press, his threats, the announcement of his thefts, in short, the whole bag of tricks which he employed to bamboozle his selected victim and throw him into such a state of mind that the victim almost offered himself to the plot contrived against him and that everything took place, as it were, with his own consent.

And the work was so just, regarded as a piece of criticism, so penetrating, so lively and marked by a wit so clever and, at the same time, so cruel that the lawyers at once passed over to his side, that the sympathy of the crowd was summarily transferred from Lupin to Beautrelet and that, in the struggle engaged upon between the two, the schoolboy's victory was loudly proclaimed in advance.

Be this as it may, both M. Filleul and the Paris public prosecutor seemed jealously to reserve the possibility of this victory for him. On the one hand, they failed to establish Mr. Harlington's identity or to furnish a definite proof of his connection with Lupin's gang. Confederate or not, he preserved an obstinate silence. Nay, more, after examining his handwriting, it was impossible to declare that he was the author of the intercepted letter. A Mr. Harlington, carrying a small portmanteau and a pocket-book stuffed with banknotes, had taken up his abode at the Grand Hotel: that was all that could be stated with certainty.

On the other hand, at Dieppe, M. Filleul lay down on the positions which Beautrelet had won for him. He did not move a step forward. Around the individual whom Mlle. de Saint-Veran had taken for Beautrelet, on the eve of the crime, the same mystery reigned as heretofore. The same obscurity also surrounded everything connected with the removal of the four Rubens pictures. What had become of them? And what road had been taken by the motor car in which they were carried off during the night?

Evidence of its passing was obtained at Luneray at Yerville, at Yvetot and at Caudebec-en-Caux, where it must have crossed the Seine at daybreak in the steam-ferry. But, when the matter came to be inquired into more thoroughly, it was stated that the motor car was an uncovered one and that it would have been impossible to pack four large pictures into it unobserved by the ferryman.

It was very probably the same car; but then the question cropped up again: what had become of the four Rubenses?

These were so many problems which M. Filleul unanswered. Every day, his subordinates searched the quadrilateral of the ruins. Almost every day, he came to direct the explorations. But between that and discovering the refuge in which Lupin lay dying — if it were true that Beautrelet's opinion was correct — there was a gulf fixed which the worthy magistrate did not seem likely to cross.

And so it was natural that they should turn once more to Isidore Beautrelet, as he alone had succeeded in dispelling shadows which, in his absence, gathered thicker and more impenetrable than ever. Why did he not go on with the case? Seeing how far he had carried it, he required but an effort to succeed.

The question was put to him by a member of the staff of the *Grand Journal*, who had obtained admission to the Lycee Janson by assuming the name of Bernod, the friend of Beautrelet's father. And Isidore very sensibly replied:

'My dear sir, there are other things besides Lupin in this world, other things besides stories about burglars and detectives. There is, for instance, the thing which is known as taking one's degree. Now I am going up for my examination in July. This is May. And I don't want to be plucked. What would my worthy parent say?'

'But what would he say if you delivered Arsène Lupin into the hands of the police?'

'Tut! There's a time for everything. In the next holidays — '

'Whitsuntide?'

'Yes — I shall go down on Saturday the sixth of June by the first train.'

'And, on the evening of that Saturday, Lupin will be taken.'

'Will you give me until the Sunday?' asked Beautrelet, laughing.

'Why delay?' replied the journalist, quite seriously.

This inexplicable confidence, born of yesterday and already so strong, was felt with regard to the young man by one and all, even though, in reality, events had justified it only up to a certain point. No matter, people believed in him! Nothing seemed difficult to him. They expected from him what they were entitled to expect at most from some phenomenon of penetration and intuition, of experience and skill. That day of the sixth of June was made to sprawl over all the papers. On the sixth of June, Isidore Beautrelet would take the fast train to Dieppe: and Lupin would be arrested on the same evening.

'Unless he escapes between this and then,' objected the last remaining partisans of the adventurer.

'Impossible! Every outlet is watched.'

'Unless he has succumbed to his wounds, then,' said the partisans, who would have preferred their hero's death to his capture.

And the retort was immediate:

'Nonsense! If Lupin were dead, his confederates would know it by now, and Lupin would be revenged. Beautrelet said so!'

* ★ *

And the sixth of June came. Half a dozen journalists were looking out for Isidore at the Gare Saint-Lazare. Two of them wanted to accompany him on his journey. He begged them to refrain.

He started alone, therefore, in a compartment to himself. He was tired, thanks to a series of nights devoted to study, and soon fell asleep. He slept heavily. In his dreams, he had an impression that the train stopped at different stations and that people got in and out. When he awoke, within sight of Rouen, he was still alone. But, on the back of the opposite seat, was a large sheet of paper, fastened with a pin to the grey cloth. It bore these words:

'Every man should mind his own business. Do you mind yours. If not, you must take the consequences.'

'Capital!' he exclaimed, rubbing his hands

with delight. 'Things are going badly in the adversary's camp. That threat is as stupid and vulgar as the sham flyman's. What a style! One can see that it wasn't composed by Lupin.'

The train threaded the tunnel that precedes the old Norman city. On reaching the station, Isidore took a few turns on the platform to stretch his legs. He was about to re-enter his compartment, when a cry escaped him. As he passed the bookstall, he had read, in an absent-minded way, the following lines on the front page of a special edition of the *Journal de Rouen*; and their alarming sense suddenly burst upon him:

STOP-PRESS NEWS

We hear by telephone from Dieppe that the Chateau d'Ambrumesy was broken into last night by criminals, who bound and gagged Mlle. de Gesvres and carried off Mlle. de Saint-Veran. Traces of blood have been seen at a distance of five hundred yards from the house and a scarf has been found close by, which is also stained with blood. There is every reason to fear that the poor young girl has been murdered.

Isidore Beautrelet completed his journey to Dieppe without moving a limb. Bent in two, with his elbows on his knees and his hands plastered against his face, he sat thinking.

At Dieppe, he took a fly. At the door of Ambrumesy, he met the examining magistrate, who confirmed the horrible news.

'You know nothing more?' asked Beautrelet.

'Nothing. I have only just arrived.'

At that moment, the sergeant of gendarmes came up to M. Filleul and handed him a crumpled, torn and discoloured piece of paper, which he had picked up not far from the place where the scarf was found. M. Filleul looked at it and gave it to Beautrelet, saying:

'I don't suppose this will help us much in our investigations.'

Isidore turned the paper over and over. It was covered with figures, dots and signs and presented the exact appearance reproduced below:

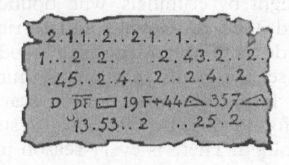

3

The Corpse

At six o'clock in the evening, having finished all he had to do, M. Filluel, accompanied by M. Bredoux, his clerk, stood waiting for the carriage which was to take him back to Dieppe. He seemed restless, nervous. Twice over, he asked:

'You haven't seen anything of young Beautrelet, I suppose?'

'No, Monsieur le Juge d'Instruction, I can't say I have.'

'Where on earth can he be? I haven't set eyes on him all day!'

Suddenly, he had an idea, handed his portfolio to Bredoux, ran round the chateau and made for the ruins. Isidore Beautrelet was lying near the cloisters, flat on his face, with one arm folded under his head, on the ground carpeted with pine-needles. He seemed drowsing.

'Hullo, young man, what are you doing here? Are you asleep?'

I'm not asleep. I've been thinking.'

'Ever since this morning?'

'Ever since this morning.'

'It's not a question of thinking! One must see into things first, study facts, look for clues, establish connecting links. The time for thinking comes after, when one pieces all that together and discovers the truth.'

'Yes, I know. — That's the usual way, the right one, I dare say. — Mine is different. — I think first, I try, above all, to get the general hang of the case, if I may so express myself. Then I imagine a reasonable and logical hypothesis, which fits in with the general idea. And then, and not before, I examine the facts to see if they agree with my hypothesis.'

'That's a funny method and a terribly complicated one!'

'It's a sure method, M. Filleul, which is more than can be said of yours.'

'Come, come! Facts are facts.'

'With your ordinary sort of adversary, yes. But, given an enemy endowed with a certain amount of cunning, the facts are those which he happens to have selected. Take the famous clues upon which you base your inquiry: why, he was at liberty to arrange them as he liked. And you see where that can lead you, into what mistakes and absurdities, when you are dealing with a man like Arsène Lupin. Holmlock Shears himself fell into the trap.'

'Arsène Lupin is dead.'

76

'No matter. His gang remains and the pupils of such a master are masters themselves.'

M. Filleul took Isidore by the arm and, leading him away:

'Words, young man, words. Here is something of more importance. Listen to me. Ganimard is otherwise engaged at this moment and will not be here for a few days. On the other hand, the Comte de Gesvres has telegraphed to Holmlock Shears, who has promised his assistance next week. Now don't you think, young man, that it would be a feather in our cap if we were able to say to those two celebrities, on the day of their arrival, 'Awfully sorry, gentlemen, but we couldn't wait. The business is done'?'

It was impossible for M. Filleul to confess helplessness with greater candour. Beautrelet suppressed a smile and, pretending not to see through the worthy magistrate, replied:

'I confess. Monsieur le Juge d'Instruction, that, if I was not present at your inquiry just now, it was because I hoped that you would consent to tell me the results. May I ask what you have learned?'

'Well, last night, at eleven o'clock, the three gendarmes whom Sergeant Quevillon had left on guard at the chateau received a note from the sergeant telling them to hasten with all speed to Ouville, where they are stationed.

They at once rode off, and when they arrived at Ouville — '

'They discovered that they had been tricked, that the order was a forgery and that there was nothing for them to do but return to Ambrumesy.'

'This they did, accompanied by Sergeant Quevillon. But they were away for an hour and a half and, during this time, the crime was committed.'

'In what circumstances?'

'Very simple circumstances, indeed. A ladder was removed from the farm buildings and placed against the second story of the chateau. A pane of glass was cut out and a window opened. Two men, carrying a dark lantern, entered Mlle. de Gesvres's room and gagged her before she could cry out. Then, after binding her with cords, they softly opened the door of the room in which Mlle. de Saint-Veran was sleeping. Mlle. de Gesvres heard a stifled moan, followed by the sound of a person struggling. A moment later, she saw two men carrying her cousin, who was also bound and gagged. They passed in front of her and went out through the window. Then Mlle. de Gesvres, terrified and exhausted, fainted.'

'But what about the dogs? I thought M. de Gesvres had bought two almost wild sheepdogs, which were let loose at night?'

'They were found dead, poisoned.'

'By whom? Nobody could get near them.'

'It's a mystery. The fact remains that the two men crossed the ruins without let or hindrance and went out by the little door which we have heard so much about. They passed through the copsewood, following the line of the disused quarries. It was not until they were nearly half a mile from the chateau, at the foot of the tree known as the Great Oak, that they stopped — and executed their purpose.'

'If they came with the intention of killing Mlle. de Saint-Veran, why didn't they murder her in her room?'

'I don't know. Perhaps the incident that settled their determination only occurred after they had left the house. Perhaps the girl succeeded in releasing herself from her bonds. In my opinion, the scarf which was picked up was used to fasten her wrists. In any case, the blow was struck at the foot of the Great Oak. I have collected indisputable proofs — '

'But the body?'

'The body has not been found, but there is nothing excessively surprising in that. As a matter of fact, the trail which I followed brought me to the church at Varengeville and the old cemetery perched on the top of the cliff. From there it is a sheer precipice, a fall of over three hundred feet to the rocks and the sea below. In a day or two, a stronger tide than usual will cast up the body on the beach.'

'Obviously. This is all very simple.'

'Yes, it is all very simple and doesn't trouble me in the least. Lupin is dead, his accomplices heard of it and, to revenge themselves, have killed Mlle. de Saint-Veran. These are facts which did not even require checking. But Lupin?'

'What about him?'

'What has become of him? In all probability, his confederates removed his corpse at the same time that they carried away the girl; but what proof have we? None at all. Any more than of his staying in the ruins, or of his death, or of his life. And that is the real mystery, M. Beautrelet. The murder of Mlle. Raymonde solves nothing. On the contrary, it only complicates matters. What has been happening during the past two months at the Chateau d'Ambrumesy? If we don't clear up the riddle, young man, others will give us the go-by.'

'On what day are those others coming?'

'Wednesday — Tuesday perhaps — '

Beautrelet seemed to be making an inward

calculation and then declared:

'Monsieur le Juge d'Instruction, this is Saturday. I have to be back at school on Monday evening. Well, if you will have the goodness to be here at ten o'clock exactly on Monday morning, I will try to give you the key to the riddle.'

'Really, M. Beautrelet — do you think so? Are you sure?'

'I hope so, at any rate.'

'And where are you going now?'

'I am going to see if the facts consent to fit in with the general theory which I am beginning to perceive.'

'And if they don't fit in?'

'Well, Monsieur le Juge d'Instruction,' said Beautrelet, with a laugh, 'then it will be their fault and I must look for others which, will prove more tractable. Till Monday, then?'

'Till Monday.'

A few minutes later, M. Filleul was driving toward Dieppe, while Isidore mounted a bicycle which he had borrowed from the Comte de Gesvres and rode off along the road to Yerville and Caudebec-en-Caux.

★ ★ ★

There was one point in particular on which the young man was anxious to form a clear opinion, because this just appeared to him to be the enemy's weakest point. Objects of the size of the four Rubens pictures cannot be juggled away. They were bound to be somewhere. Granting that it was impossible to find them for the moment, might one not discover the road by which they had disappeared?

What Beautrelet surmised was that the four pictures had undoubtedly been carried off in the motor car, but that, before reaching Caudebec, they were transferred to another car, which had crossed the Seine either above Caudebec or below it. Now the first horse-boat down the stream was at Quillebeuf, a greatly frequented ferry and, consequently, dangerous. Up stream, there was the ferry-boat at La Mailleraie, a large, but lonely market-town, lying well off the main road.

By midnight, Isidore had covered the thirty-five or forty miles to La Mailleraie and was knocking at the door of an inn by the water-side. He slept there and, in the morning, questioned the ferrymen.

They consulted the counterfoils in the traffic-book. No motor-car had crossed on Thursday the 23rd of April.

'A horse-drawn vehicle, then?' suggested Beautrelet. 'A cart? A van?'

'No, not either.'

Isidore continued his inquiries all through

the morning. He was on the point of leaving for Quillebeuf, when the waiter of the inn at which he had spent the night said:

'I came back from my thirteen days' training on the morning of which you are speaking and I saw a cart, but it did not go across.'

'Really?'

'No, they unloaded it onto a flat boat, a barge of sorts, which was moored to the wharf.'

'And where did the cart come from?'

'Oh, I knew it at once. It belonged to Master Vatinel, the carter.'

'And where does he live?'

'At Louvetot.'

Beautrelet consulted his military map. The hamlet of Louvetot lay where the highroad between Yvetot and Caudebec was crossed by a little winding road that ran through the woods to La Mailleraie.

Not until six o'clock in the evening did Isidore succeed in discovering Master Vatinel, in a pothouse. Master Vatinel was one of those artful old Normans who are always on their guard, who distrust strangers, but who are unable to resist the lure of a gold coin or the influence of a glass or two:

'Well, yes, sir, the men in the motor car that morning had told me to meet them at five o'clock at the crossroads. They gave me four great, big things, as high as that. One of them went with me and we carted the things to the barge.'

'You speak of them as if you knew them before.'

'I should think I did know them! It was the sixth time they were employing me.'

Isidore gave a start:

'The sixth time, you say? And since when?'

'Why every day before that one, to be sure! But it was other things then — great blocks of stone — or else smaller, longish ones, wrapped up in newspapers, which they carried as if they were worth I don't know what. Oh, I mustn't touch those on any account! — But what's the matter? You've turned quite white.'

'Nothing — the heat of the room — '

Beautrelet staggered out into the air. The joy, the surprise of the discovery made him feel giddy. He went back very quietly to Varengeville, slept in the village, spent an hour at the mayor's offices with the school-master and returned to the chateau. There he found a letter awaiting him 'care of M. le Comte de Gesvres.' It consisted of a single line:

'Second warning. Hold your tongue. If not — '

'Come,' he muttered. 'I shall have to make

84

up my mind and take a few precautions for my personal safety. If not, as they say — '

It was nine o'clock. He strolled about among the ruins and then lay down near the cloisters and closed his eyes.

'Well, young man, are you satisfied with the results of your campaign?'

It was M. Filleul.

'Delighted, Monsieur le Juge d'Instruction.'

'By which you mean to say — ?'

'By which I mean to say that I am prepared to keep my promise — in spite of this very uninviting letter.'

He showed the letter to M. Filleul.

'Pooh! Stuff and nonsense!' cried the magistrate. 'I hope you won't let that prevent you — '

'From telling you what I know? No, Monsieur le Juge d'Instruction. I have given my word and I shall keep it. In less than ten minutes, you shall know — a part of the truth.'

'A part?'

'Yes, in my opinion, Lupin's hiding-place does not constitute the whole of the problem. Far from it. But we shall see later on.'

'M. Beautrelet, nothing that you do could astonish me now. But how were you able to discover — ?'

'Oh, in a very natural way! In the letter

85

from old man Harlington to M. Etienne de Vaudreix, or rather to Lupin — '

'The intercepted letter?'

'Yes. There is a phrase which always puzzled me. After saying that the pictures are to be forwarded as arranged, he goes on to say, 'You may add *the rest*, if you are able to succeed, which I doubt.''

'Yes, I remember.'

'What was this 'rest'? A work of art, a curiosity? The chateau contains nothing of any value besides the Rubenses and the tapestries. Jewellery? There is very little and what there is of it is not worth much. In that case, what could it be? — On the other hand, was it conceivable that people so prodigiously clever as Lupin should not have succeeded in adding 'the rest,' which they themselves had evidently suggested? A difficult undertaking, very likely; exceptional, surprising, I dare say; but possible and therefore certain, since Lupin wished it.'

'And yet he failed: nothing has disappeared.'

'He did not fail: something has disappeared.'

'Yes, the Rubenses — but — '

'The Rubenses and something besides — something which has been replaced by a similar thing, as in the case of the Rubenses; something much more uncommon, much rarer, much more valuable than the Rubenses.'

'Well, what? You're killing me with this procrastination!'

While talking, the two men had crossed the ruins, turned toward the little door and were now walking beside the chapel. Beautrelet stopped:

'Do you really want to know, Monsieur le Juge d'Instruction?'

'Of course, I do.'

Beautrelet was carrying a walking-stick, a strong, knotted stick. Suddenly, with a back stroke of this stick, he smashed one of the little statues that adorned the front of the chapel.

'Why, you're mad!' shouted M. Filleul, beside himself, rushing at the broken pieces of the statue. 'You're mad! That old saint was an admirable bit of work — '

'An admirable bit of work!' echoed Isidore, giving a whirl which brought down the Virgin Mary.

M. Filleul took hold of him round the body:

'Young man, I won't allow you to commit — '

A wise man of the East came toppling to the ground, followed by a manger containing the Mother and Child . . .

'If you stir another limb, I fire!'

The Comte de Gesvres had appeared upon the scene and was cocking his revolver.

Beautrelet burst out laughing:

'That's right, Monsieur le Comte, blaze away! — Take a shot at them, as if you were at a fair! — Wait a bit — this chap carrying his head in his hands — '

St. John the Baptist fell, shattered to pieces.

'Oh!' shouted the count, pointing his revolver. 'You young vandal! — Those masterpieces!'

'Sham, Monsieur le Comte!'

'What? What's that?' roared M. Filleul, wresting the Comte de Gesvres's weapon from him.

'Sham!' repeated Beautrelet. 'Paper-pulp and plaster!'

'Oh, nonsense! It can't be true!'

'Hollow plaster, I tell you! Nothing at all!'

The count stooped and picked up a sliver of a statuette.

'Look at it, Monsieur le Comte, and see for yourself: it's plaster! Rusty, musty, mildewed plaster, made to look like old stone — but plaster for all that, plaster casts! — That's all that remains of your perfect masterpiece! — That's what they've done in just a few days! — That's what the Sieur Charpenais who copied the Rubenses, prepared a year ago.' He seized M. Filleul's arm in his turn. 'What do you think of it, Monsieur le Juge d'Instruction? Isn't it fine? Isn't it grand?

Isn't it gorgeous? The chapel has been removed! A whole Gothic chapel collected stone by stone! A whole population of statues captured and replaced by these chaps in stucco! One of the most magnificent specimens of an incomparable artistic period confiscated! The chapel, in short, stolen! Isn't it immense? Ah, Monsieur le Juge d'Instruction, what a genius the man is!'

'You're allowing yourself to be carried away, M. Beautrelet.'

'One can't be carried away too much, monsieur, when one has to do with people like that. Every-thing above the average deserves our admiration. And this man soars above everything. There is in his flight a wealth of imagination, a force and power, a skill and freedom that send a thrill through me!'

'Pity he's dead,' said M. Filleul, with a grin. 'He'd have ended by stealing the towers of Notre-Dame.'

Isidore shrugged his shoulders:

'Don't laugh, monsieur. He upsets you, dead though he may be.'

'I don't say not, I don't say not, M. Beautrelet, I confess that I feel a certain excitement now that I am about to set eyes on him — unless, indeed, his friends have taken away the body.'

'And always admitting,' observed the

Comte de Gesvres, 'that it was really he who was wounded by my poor niece.'

'It was he, beyond a doubt, Monsieur le Comte,' declared Beautrelet; 'it was he, believe me, who fell in the ruins under the shot fired by Mlle. de Saint-Veran; it was he whom she saw rise and who fell again and dragged himself toward the cloisters to rise again for the last time — this by a miracle which I will explain to you presently — to rise again for the last time and reach this stone shelter — which was to be his tomb.'

And Beautrelet struck the threshold of the chapel with his stick.

'Eh? What?' cried M. Filleul, taken aback. 'His tomb? — Do you think that that impenetrable hiding-place — '

'It was here — there,' he repeated.

'But we searched it.'

'Badly.'

'There is no hiding-place here,' protested M. de Gesvres. 'I know the chapel.'

'Yes, there is, Monsieur le Comte. Go to the mayor's office at Varengeville, where they have collected all the papers that used to be in the old parish of Ambrumesy, and you will learn from those papers, which belong to the eighteenth century, that there is a crypt below the chapel. This crypt doubtless dates back to the Roman chapel, upon the site of which the

90

present one was built.'

'But how can Lupin have known this detail?' asked M. Filleul.

'In a very simple manner: because of the works which he had to execute to take away the chapel.'

'Come, come, M. Beautrelet, you're exaggerating. He has not taken away the whole chapel. Look, not one of the stones of this top course has been touched.'

'Obviously, he cast and took away only what had a financial value: the wrought stones, the sculptures, the statuettes, the whole treasure of little columns and carved arches. He did not trouble about the groundwork of the building itself. The foundations remain.'

'Therefore, M. Beautrelet, Lupin was not able to make his way into the crypt.'

At that moment, M. de Gesvres, who had been to call a servant, returned with the key of the chapel. He opened the door. The three men entered. After a short examination Beautrelet said:

'The flag-stones on the ground have been respected, as one might expect. But it is easy to perceive that the high altar is nothing more than a cast. Now, generally, the staircase leading to the crypt opens in front of the high altar and passes under it.'

'What do you conclude?'

'I conclude that Lupin discovered the crypt when working at the altar.'

The count sent for a pickaxe and Beautrelet attacked the altar. The plaster flew to right and left. He pushed the pieces aside as he went on.

'By Jove!' muttered M. Filleul, 'I am eager to know — '

'So am I,' said Beautrelet, whose face was pale with anguish.

He hurried his blows. And, suddenly, his pickaxe, which, until then, had encountered no resistance, struck against a harder material and rebounded. There was a sound of something falling in; and all that remained of the altar went tumbling into the gap after the block of stone which had been struck by the pickaxe. Beautrelet bent forward. A puff of cold air rose to his face. He lit a match and moved it from side to side over the gap:

'The staircase begins farther forward than I expected, under the entrance-flags, almost. I can see the last steps, there, right at the bottom.'

'Is it deep?'

'Three or four yards. The steps are very high — and there are some missing.'

'It is hardly likely,' said M. Filleul, 'that the accomplices can have had time to remove the body from the cellar, when they were engaged in carrying off Mlle. de Saint-Veran — during the short absence of the gendarmes. Besides, why should they? — No, in my opinion, the body is here.'

A servant brought them a ladder. Beautrelet let it down through the opening and fixed it, after groping among the fallen fragments. Holding the two uprights firmly:

'Will you go down, M. Filleul?' he asked.

The magistrate, holding a candle in his hand, ventured down the ladder. The Comte de Gesvres followed him and Beautrelet, in his turn, placed his foot on the first rung.

Mechanically, he counted eighteen rungs, while his eyes examined the crypt, where the glimmer of the candle struggled against the heavy darkness. But, at the bottom, his nostrils were assailed by one of those foul and violent smells which linger m the memory for many a long day. And, suddenly, a trembling hand seized him by the shoulder.

'Well, what is it?'

'B-beautrelet,' stammered M. Filleul. 'B-beautrelet — '

He could not get a word out for terror.

'Come, Monsieur le Juge d'Instruction, compose yourself!'

'Beautrelet — he is there — '

'Eh?'

'Yes — there was something under the big

stone that broke off the altar — I pushed the stone — and I touched — I shall never — shall never forget. — '

'Where is it?'

'On this side. — Don't you notice the smell? — And then look — see.'

He took the candle and held it towards a motionless form stretched upon the ground.

'Oh!' exclaimed Beautrelet, in a horror-stricken tone.

The three men bent down quickly. The corpse lay half-naked, lean, frightful. The flesh, which had the greenish hue of soft wax, appeared in places through the torn clothes. But the most hideous thing, the thing that had drawn a cry of terror from the young man's lips, was the head, the head which had just been crushed by the block of stone, the shapeless head, a repulsive mass in which not one feature could be distinguished.

Beautrelet took four strides up the ladder and fled into the daylight and the open air.

M. Filleul found him again lying flat on the around, with his hands glued to his face:

'I congratulate you, Beautrelet,' he said. 'In addition to the discovery of the hiding-place, there are two points on which I have been able to verify the correctness of your assertions. First of all, the man on whom Mlle. de Saint-Veran fired was indeed Arsène

Lupin, as you said from the start. Also, he lived in Paris under the name of Etienne de Vaudreix. His linen is marked with the initials E. V. That ought to be sufficient proof, I think: don't you?'

Isidore did not stir.

'Monsieur le Comte has gone to have a horse put to. They're sending for Dr. Jouet, who will make the usual examination. In my opinion, death must have taken place a week ago, at least. The state of decomposition of the corpse — but you don't seem to be listening — '

'Yes, yes.'

'What I say is based upon absolute reasons. Thus, for instance — '

M. Filleul continued his demonstrations, with-out, however, obtaining any more manifest marks of attention. But M. de Gesvres's return interrupted his monologue. The comte brought two letters. One was to tell him that Holmlock Shears would arrive next morning.

'Capital!' cried M. Filleul, joyfully. 'Inspector Ganimard will be here too. It will be delightful.'

'The other letter is for you, Monsieur le Juge d'Instruction,' said the comte.

'Better and better,' said M. Filleul, after reading it. 'There will certainly not be much

95

for those two gentlemen to do. M. Beautrelet, I hear from Dieppe that the body of a young woman was found by some shrimpers, this morning, on the rocks.'

Beautrelet gave a start:

'What's that? The body — '

'Of a young woman. — The body is horribly mutilated, they say, and it would be impossible to establish the identity, but for a very narrow little gold curb-bracelet on the right arm which has become encrusted in the swollen skin. Now Mlle. de Saint-Veran used to wear a gold curb-bracelet on her right arm. Evidently, therefore, Monsieur le Comte, this is the body of your poor niece, which the sea must have washed to that distance. What do you think, Beautrelet?'

'Nothing — nothing — or, rather, yes — everything is connected, as you see — and there is no link missing in my argument. All the facts, one after the other, however contradictory, however disconcerting they may appear, end by supporting the supposition which I imagined from the first.'

'I don't understand.'

'You soon will. Remember, I promised you the whole truth.'

'But it seems to me — '

'A little patience, Monsieur le Juge d'Instruction. So far, you have had no cause to complain of me. It is a fine day. Go for a walk, lunch at the chateau, smoke your pipe. I shall be back by four o'clock. As for my school, well, I don't care: I shall take the night train.'

They had reached the out-houses at the back of the chateau. Beautrelet jumped on his bicycle and rode away.

At Dieppe, he stopped at the office of the local paper, the *Vigie*, and examined the file for the last fortnight. Then he went on to the market-town of Envermeu, six or seven miles farther. At Envermeu, he talked to the mayor, the rector and the local policeman. The church-clock struck three. His inquiry was finished.

He returned singing for joy. He pressed upon the two pedals turn by turn, with an equal and powerful rhythm; his chest opened wide to take in the keen air that blew from the sea. And, from time to time, he forgot himself to the extent of uttering shouts of triumph to the sky, when he thought of the aim which he was pursuing and of the success that was crowning his efforts.

Ambrumesy appeared in sight. He coasted at full speed down the slope leading to the chateau. The top rows of venerable trees that line the road seemed to run to meet him and to vanish behind him forthwith. And, all at once, he uttered a cry. In a sudden vision, he had seen a rope stretched from one tree to another, across the road.

His machine gave a jolt and stopped short. Beautrelet was flung three yards forward, with immense violence, and it seemed to him that only chance, a miraculous chance, caused him to escape a heap of pebbles on which, logically, he ought to have broken his head.

He lay for a few seconds stunned. Then, all covered with bruises, with the skin flayed from his knees, he examined the spot. On the right lay a small wood, by which his aggressor had no doubt fled. Beautrelet untied the rope. To the tree on the left around which it was fastened a small piece of paper was fixed with string. Beautrelet unfolded it and read:

'The third and last warning.'

He went on to the chateau, put a few questions to the servants and joined the examining magistrate in a room on the ground floor, at the end of the right wing, where M. Filleul used to sit in the course of his operations. M. Filleul was writing, with his clerk seated opposite to him. At a sign from him, the clerk left the room; and the magistrate exclaimed:

'Why, what have you been doing to yourself, M. Beautrelet? Your hands are covered with blood.'

'It's nothing, it's nothing,' said the young man. 'Just a fall occasioned by this rope, which was stretched in front of my bicycle. I will only ask you to observe that the rope comes from the chateau. Not longer than twenty minutes ago, it was being used to dry linen on, outside the laundry.'

'You don't mean to say so!'

'Monsieur le Juge d'Instruction, I am being watched here, by some one in the very heart of the place, who can see me, who can hear me and who, minute by minute, observes my actions and knows my intentions.'

'Do you think so?'

'I am sure of it. It is for you to discover him and you will have no difficulty in that. As for myself, I want to have finished and to give you the promised explanations. I have made faster progress than our adversaries expected and I am convinced that they mean to take vigorous measures on their side. The circle is closing around me. The danger is approaching. I feel it.'

'Nonsense, Beautrelet — '

'You wait and see! For the moment, let us lose no time. And, first, a question on a point which I want to have done with at once. Have you spoken to anybody of that document which Sergeant Quevillon picked up and handed you in my presence?'

'No, indeed; not to a soul. But do you attach any value — ?'

'The greatest value. It's an idea of mine, an idea, I confess, which does not rest upon a proof of any kind — for, up to the present, I have not succeeded in deciphering the document. And therefore I am mentioning it — so that we need not come back to it.'

Beautrelet pressed his hand on M. Filleul's and whispered:

'Don't speak — there's some one listening — outside — '

The gravel creaked. Beautrelet ran to the window and leaned out:

'There's no one there — but the border has been trodden down — we can easily identify the footprints — '

He closed the window and sat down again:

'You see, Monsieur le Juge d'Instruction, the enemy has even ceased to take the most ordinary precautions — he has not time left — he too feels that the hour is urgent. Let us be quick, there-fore, and speak, since they do not wish us to speak.'

He laid the document on the table and held it in position, unfolded:

'One observation, Monsieur le Juge d'Instruction, to begin with. The paper con-sists almost entirely of dots and figures. And in the first three lines and the fifth — the only ones with which we have to do at present, for the fourth seems to present an entirely different character — not one of those figures is higher than the figure 5. There is, therefore, a great chance that each of these figures represents one of the five vowels, taken in alphabetical order. Let us put down the result.'

He wrote on a separate piece of paper:

$$e\,.\,a\,.\,a\,.\,.\,e\,.\,.\,e\,.\,a\,.\,.\,a\,.\,.$$
$$a\,.\,.\,.\,e\,.\,e\,.\quad.\,e\,.\,oi\,.\,e\,.\,.\,e.$$
$$.\,ou\,.\,.\,e\,.\,o\,.\,.\,.\,e\,.\,.\,e\,.\,o\,.\,.\,e.$$
$$ai\,.\,ui\,.\,.\,e\qquad.\,.\,eu\,.\,e$$

Then he continued:

'As you see, this does not give us much to go upon. The key is, at the same time, very easy, because the inventor has contented himself with replacing the vowels by figures and the consonants by dots, and very difficult, if not impossible, because he has taken no further trouble to complicate the problem.'

'It is certainly pretty obscure.'

'Let us try to throw some light upon it. The second line is divided into two parts; and the second part appears in such a way that it probably forms one word. If we now seek to replace the intermediary dots by consonants, we arrive at the conclusion, after searching and casting about, that the only consonants which are logically able to support the vowels are also logically able to produce only one word, the word *demoiselles*.'

'That would refer to Mlle. de Gesvres and Mlle. de Saint-Veran.'

'Undoubtedly.'

'And do you see nothing more?'

'Yes. I also note an hiatus in the middle of the last line; and, if I apply a similar operation to the beginning of the line, I at once see that the only consonant able to take the place of the dot between the diphthongs *ai* and *ui* is the letter *g* and that, when I have thus formed the first five letters of the word, *aigui*, it is natural and inevitable that, with the two next dots and the final *e*, I should arrive at the word *aiguille*.'

'Yes, the word *aiguille* forces itself upon us.'

'Finally, for the last word, I have three vowels and three consonants. I cast about again, I try all the letters, one after the other, and, starting with the principle that the two first letters are necessary consonants, I find that three words apply: *fleuve, preuve* and *creuse*. I eliminate the words *fleuve* and *preuve*, as possessing no possible relation to a needle, and I keep the word *creuse*.'

'Making 'hollow needle'! By jove! I admit that your solution is correct, because it needs must be; but how does it help us?'

'Not at all,' said Beautrelet, in a thoughtful tone. 'Not at all, for the moment. — Later on, we shall see. — I have an idea that a number of things are included in the puzzling conjunction of those two words, *aiguille creuse*. What is troubling me at present is rather the material on which the document is written, the paper employed. — Do they still manufacture this sort of rather coarse-grained parchment? And then this ivory colour. — And those folds — the wear of those folds — and, lastly, look, those marks of red sealing-wax, on the back — '

At that moment Beautrelet, was interrupted by Bredoux, the magistrate's clerk, who opened the door and announced the unexpected arrival of the chief public prosecutor. M. Filleul rose:

'Anything new? Is Monsieur le Procureur General downstairs?'

'No, Monsieur le Juge d'Instruction. Monsieur le Procureur General has not left his carriage. He is only passing through Ambrumesy and begs you to be good enough to go down to him at the gate. He only has a word to say to you.'

'That's curious,' muttered M. Filleul. 'How-ever — we shall see. Excuse me, Beautrelet, I shan't be long.'

He went away. His footsteps sounded outside. Then the clerk closed the door, turned the key and put it in his pocket.

'Hullo!' exclaimed Beautrelet, greatly surprised. 'What are you locking us in for?'

'We shall be able to talk so much better,' retorted Bredoux.

Beautrelet rushed toward another door, which led to the next room. He had understood: the accomplice was Bredoux, the clerk of the examining magistrate himself. Bredoux grinned:

'Don't hurt your fingers, my young friend. I have the key of that door, too.'

'There's the window!' cried Beautrelet.

'Too late,' said Bredoux, planting himself in front of the casement, revolver in hand.

Every chance of retreat was cut off. There was nothing more for Isidore to do, nothing except to defend himself against the enemy who was revealing himself with such brutal daring. He crossed his arms.

'Good,' mumbled the clerk. 'And now let us waste no time.' He took out his watch. 'Our worthy M. Filleul will walk down to the gate. At the gate, he will find nobody, of course: no more public prosecutor than my eye. Then he will come back. That gives us about four minutes. It will take me one minute to escape by this window, clear through the little door by the ruins and jump on the motor cycle waiting for me. That leaves three minutes, which is just enough.'

Bredoux was a queer sort of misshapen creature, who balanced on a pair of very long spindle-legs a huge trunk, as round as the body of a spider and furnished with immense arms. A bony face and a low, small stubborn forehead pointed to the man's narrow obstinacy.

Beautrelet felt a weakness in the legs and staggered. He had to sit down:

'Speak,' he said. 'What do you want?'

'The paper. I've been looking for it for three days.'

'I haven't got it.'

'You're lying. I saw you put it back in your pocket-book when I came in.'

'Next?'

'Next, you must undertake to keep quite quiet. You're annoying us. Leave us alone and mind your own business. Our patience is at an end.'

He had come nearer, with the revolver still aimed at the young man's head, and spoke in a hollow voice, with a powerful stress on each syllable that he uttered. His eyes were hard, his smile cruel.

Beautrelet gave a shudder. It was the first time that he was experiencing the sense of danger. And such danger! He felt himself in the presence of an implacable enemy, endowed with blind and irresistible strength.

'And next?' he asked, with less assurance in his voice.

'Next? Nothing. — You will be free. — We will forget — '

There was a pause. Then Bredoux resumed:

'There is only a minute left. You must make up your mind. Come, old chap, don't be a fool. — We are the stronger, you know, always and everywhere. — Quick, the paper — '

Isidore did not flinch. With a livid and terrified face, he remained master of himself, nevertheless, and his brain remained clear amid the breakdown of his nerves. The little black hole of the revolver was pointing at six inches from his eyes. The finger was bent and obviously pressing on the trigger. It only wanted a moment —

'The paper,' repeated Bredoux. 'If not — '

'Here it is,' said Beautrelet.

He took out his pocket-book and handed it to the clerk, who seized it eagerly.

'Capital! We've come to our senses. I've no doubt there's something to be done with you. — You're troublesome, but full of common sense. I'll talk about it to my pals. And now I'm off. Good-bye!'

He pocketed his revolver and turned back the fastening of the window. There was a noise in the passage.

'Good-bye,' he said again. 'I'm only just in time.'

But the idea stopped him. With a quick movement, he examined the pocket-book:

'Damn and blast it!' He grated through his teeth. 'The paper's not there. — You've done me — '

He leaped into the room. Two shots rang out. Isidore, in his turn, had seized his pistol and fired.

'Missed, old chap!' shouted Bredoux. 'Your hand's shaking. — You're afraid — '

They caught each other round the body and came down to the floor together. There was a violent and incessant knocking at the door. Isidore's strength gave way and he was at once over come by his adversary. It was the end. A hand was lifted over him, armed with a knife, and fell. A fierce pain burst into his shoulder. He let go.

He had an impression of some one fumbling in the inside pocket of his jacket and taking the paper from it. Then, through the lowered veil of his eyelids, he half saw the man stepping over the window-sill.

* * *

The same newspapers which, on the following morning, related the last episodes that had occurred at the Chateau d'Ambrumesy — the trickery at the chapel, the discovery of Arsène Lupin's body and of Raymonde's body and, lastly, the murderous attempt made upon Beautrelet by the clerk to the examining magistrate — also announced two further pieces of news: the disappearance of Ganimard, and the kidnapping of Holmlock Shears, in broad daylight, in the heart of London, at the moment when he was about to take the train for Dover.

Lupin's gang, therefore, which had been disorganized for a moment by the extraordinary ingenuity of a seventeen-year-old schoolboy, was now resuming the offensive and was winning all along the line from the first. Lupin's two great adversaries, Shears and Ganimard, were put away. Isidore Beautrelet was disabled. The police were powerless. For the moment there was no one left capable of struggling against such enemies.

4

Face to Face

One evening, five weeks later, I had given my man leave to go out. It was the day before the 14th of July. The night was hot, a storm threatened and I felt no inclination to leave the flat. I opened wide the glass doors leading to my balcony, lit my reading lamp and sat down in an easy-chair to look through the papers, which I had not yet seen.

It goes without saying that there was something about Arsène Lupin in all of them. Since the attempt at murder of which poor Isidore Beautrelet had been the victim, not a day had passed without some mention of the Ambrumésy mystery. It had a permanent headline devoted to it. Never had public opinion been excited to that extent, thanks to the extraordinary series of hurried events, of unexpected and disconcerting surprises. M. Filleul, who was certainly accepting the secondary part allotted to him with a good faith worthy of all praise, had let the interviewers into the secret of his young advisor's exploits during the memorable three days, so that the public was able to indulge in the rashest suppositions. And the public gave itself free scope. Specialists and experts in crime, novelists and playwrights, retired magistrates and chief-detectives, erstwhile Lecocqs and budding Holmlock Shearses, each had his theory and expounded it in lengthy contributions to the press. Everybody corrected and supplemented the inquiry of the examining magistrate; and all on the word of a child, on the word of Isidore Beautrelet, a sixth-form schoolboy at the Lycee Janson-de-Sailly!

For really, it had to be admitted, the complete elements of the truth were now in everybody's possession. What did the mystery consist of? They knew the hiding-place where Arsène Lupin had taken refuge and lain a-dying; there was no doubt about it: Dr. Delattre, who continued to plead professional secrecy and refused to give evidence, nevertheless confessed to his intimate friends — who lost no time in blabbing — that he really had been taken to a crypt to attend a wounded man whom his confederates introduced to him by the name of Arsène Lupin. And, as the corpse of Etienne de Vaudreix was found in that same crypt and as the said Etienne de Vaudreix was none other than Arsène Lupin — as the official examination went to show — all this provided an additional proof, if one were needed, of the identity of Arsène Lupin and the wounded man. Therefore, with Lupin dead and Mlle. de Saint-Veran's body recognized by the curb-bracelet on her wrist, the tragedy was finished.

It was not. Nobody thought that it was, because Beautrelet had said the contrary. Nobody knew in what respect it was not finished, but, on the word of the young man, the mystery remained complete. The evidence of the senses did not prevail against the statement of a Beautrelet. There was something which people did not know, and of that something they were convinced that he was in position to supply a triumphant explanation.

It is easy, therefore, to imagine the anxiety with which, at first, people awaited the bulletins issued by the two Dieppe doctors to whose care the Comte de Gesvres entrusted his patient; the distress that prevailed during the first few days, when his life was thought to be in danger; and the enthusiasm of the morning when the newspapers announced that there was no further cause for fear. The least details excited the crowd. People wept at the thought of Beautrelet nursed by his old father, who had been hurriedly summoned by telegram, and they also admired the devotion of Mlle. Suzanne de Gesvres, who spent night after night by the wounded lad's bedside.

Next came a swift and glad convalescence. At last, the public were about to know! They would know what Beautrelet had promised to reveal to M. Filleul and the decisive words which the knife of the would-be assassin had prevented him from uttering! And they would also know everything, outside the tragedy itself, that remained impenetrable or inaccessible to the efforts of the police.

With Beautrelet free and cured of his wound, one could hope for some certainty regarding Harlington, Arsène Lupin's mysterious accomplice, who was still detained at the Sante prison. One would learn what had become, after the crime, of Bredoux the clerk, that other accomplice, whose daring was really terrifying.

With Beautrelet free, one could also form a precise idea concerning the disappearance of Ganimard and the kidnapping of Shears. How was it possible for two attempts of this kind to take place? Neither the English detectives nor their French colleagues possessed the slightest clue on the subject. On Whit-Sunday, Ganimard did not come home, nor on the Monday either, nor during the five weeks that followed. In London, on Whit-Monday, Holmlock Shears took a cab at eight o'clock in the evening to drive to the station. He had hardly stepped in, when he tried to alight, probably feeling a presentiment of danger. But two men jumped into the hansom, one on either side, flung him back on the seat and kept him there between them, or rather under them. All this happened in sight of nine or ten witnesses, who had no time to interfere. The cab drove off at a gallop. And, after that, nothing. Nobody knew anything.

Perhaps, also, Beautrelet would be able to give the complete explanation of the document, the mysterious paper to which. Bredoux, the magistrate's clerk, attached enough importance to recover it, with blows of the knife, from the person in whose possession it was. The problem of the Hollow Needle it was called, by the countless solvers of riddles who, with their eyes bent upon the figures and dots, strove to read a meaning into them. The Hollow Needle! What a bewildering conjunction of two simple words! What an incomprehensible question was set by that scrap of paper, whose very origin and manufacture were unknown! The Hollow Needle! Was it a meaningless expression, the puzzle of a schoolboy scribbling with pen and ink on the corner of a page? Or were they two magic words which could compel the whole great adventure of Lupin the great adventurer to assume its true significance? Nobody knew.

But the public soon would know. For some days, the papers had been announcing the approaching arrival of Beautrelet. The struggle was on the point of recommencing; and, this time, it would be implacable on the part of the young man, who was burning to take his revenge. And, as it happened, my attention, just then, was drawn to his name, printed in capitals. The *Grand Journal* headed its front page with the following paragraph:

We have persuaded

M. ISIDORE BEAUTRELET

to give us the first right of printing his revelations. To-morrow, Tuesday, before the police themselves are informed, the Grand Journal *will publish the whole truth of the Ambrumesy mystery.*

'That's interesting, eh? What do you think of it, my dear chap?'

I started from my chair. There was some one sitting beside me, some one I did not know. I cast my eyes round for a weapon. But, as my visitor's attitude appeared quite inoffensive, I restrained myself and went up to him.

He was a young man with strongly-marked features, long, fair hair and a short, tawny beard, divided into two points. His dress suggested the dark clothes of an English clergyman; and his whole person, for that matter, wore an air of austerity and gravity that inspired respect.

'Who are you?' I asked. And, as he did not reply, I repeated, 'Who are you? How did you get in? What are you here for?'

He looked at me and said:

'Don't you know me?'

'No — no!'

'Oh, that's really curious! Just search your memory — one of your friends — a friend of a rather special kind — however — '

I caught him smartly by the arm:

'You lie! You lie! No, you're not the man you say you are — it's not true.'

'Then why are you thinking of that man rather than another?' he asked, with a laugh.

Oh, that laugh! That bright and clear young laugh, whose amusing irony had so often contributed to my diversion! I shivered. Could it be?

'No, no,' I protested, with a sort of terror. 'It cannot be.'

'It can't be I, because I'm dead, eh?' he retorted. 'And because you don't believe in ghosts.' He laughed again. 'Am I the sort of man who dies? Do you think I would die like that, shot in the back by a girl? Really, you misjudge me! As though I would ever consent to such a death as that!'

'So it is you!' I stammered, still incredulous and yet greatly excited. 'So it is you! I can't manage to recognize you.'

'In that case,' he said, gaily, 'I am quite easy. If the only man to whom I have shown myself in my real aspect fails to know me to-day, then everybody who will see me henceforth as I am to-day is bound not to know me either, when he sees me in my real aspect — if, indeed, I have a real aspect — '

I recognized his voice, now that he was no longer changing its tone, and I recognized his eyes also and the expression of his face and his whole attitude and his very being, through the counterfeit appearance in which he had shrouded it:

'Arsène Lupin!' I muttered.

'Yes, Arsène Lupin!' he cried, rising from his chair. 'The one and only Arsène Lupin, returned from the realms of darkness, since it appears that I expired and passed away in a crypt! Arsène Lupin, alive and kicking, in the full exercise of his will, happy and free and more than ever resolved to enjoy that happy freedom in a world where hitherto he has received nothing but favours and privileges!'

It was my turn to laugh:

'Well, it's certainly you, and livelier this time than on the day when I had the pleasure of seeing you, last year — I congratulate you.'

I was alluding to his last visit, the visit following on the famous adventure of the diadem, his interrupted marriage, his flight with Sonia Kirchnoff and the Russian girl's horrible death. On that day, I had seen an Arsène Lupin whom I did not know, weak, down-hearted, with eyes tired with weeping, seeking for a little sympathy and affection.

'Be quiet,' he said. 'The past is far away.'

'It was a year ago,' I observed.

'It was ten years ago,' he declared. 'Arsène Lupin's years count for ten times as much as another man's.'

I did not insist and, changing the conversation:

'How did you get in?'

'Why, how do you think? Through the door, of course. Then, as I saw nobody, I walked across the drawing room and out by the balcony, and here I am.'

'Yes, but the key of the door — ?'

'There are no doors for me, as you know. I wanted your flat and I came in.'

'It is at your disposal. Am I to leave you?'

'Oh, not at all! You won't be in the way. In fact, I can promise you an interesting evening.'

'Are you expecting some one?'

'Yes. I have given him an appointment here at ten o'clock.' He took out his watch. 'It is ten now. If the telegram reached him, he ought to be here soon.'

The front-door bell rang.

'What did I tell you? No, don't trouble to get up: I'll go.'

With whom on earth could he have made an appointment? And what sort of scene was I about to assist at: dramatic or comic? For Lupin himself to consider it worthy of interest, the situation must be somewhat exceptional.

He returned in a moment and stood back to make way for a young man, tall and thin and very pale in the face.

Without a word and with a certain solemnity about his movements that made me feel ill at ease. Lupin switched on all the electric lamps, one after the other, till the room was flooded with light. Then the two men looked at each other, exchanged profound and penetrating glances, as if, with all the effort of their gleaming eyes, they were trying to pierce into each other's souls.

It was an impressive sight to see them thus, grave and silent. But who could the newcomer be?

I was on the point of guessing the truth, through his resemblance to a photograph which had recently appeared in the papers, when Lupin turned to me:

'My dear chap, let me introduce M. Isidore Beautrelet.' And, addressing the young man, he continued, 'I have to thank you, M. Beautrelet, first, for being good enough, on receipt of a letter from me, to postpone your revelations until after this interview and, secondly, for granting me this interview with so good a grace.'

Beautrelet smiled:

'Allow me to remark that my good grace consists, above all, in obeying your orders. The threat which you made to me in the letter in question was the more peremptory in being aimed not at me, but at my father.'

'My word,' said Lupin laughing, 'we must do the best we can and make use of the means of action vouchsafed to us. I knew by experience that your own safety was indifferent to you, seeing that you resisted the arguments of Master Bredoux. There remained your father — your father for whom you have a great affection — I played on that string.'

'And here I am,' said Beautrelet, approvingly.

I motioned them to be seated. They consented and Lupin resumed, in that tone of imperceptible banter which is all his own:

'In any case, M. Beautrelet, if you will not

accept my thanks, you will at least not refuse my apologies.'

'Apologies! Bless my soul, what for?'

'For the brutality which Master Bredoux showed you.'

'I confess that the act surprised me. It was not Lupin's usual way of behaving. A stab — '

'I assure you I had no hand in it. Bredoux is a new recruit. My friends, during the time that they had the management of our affairs, thought that it might be useful to win over to our cause the clerk of the magistrate himself who was conducting the inquiry.'

'Your friends were right.'

'Bredoux, who was specially attached to your person, was, in fact, most valuable to us. But, with the ardour peculiar to any neophyte who wishes to distinguish himself, he pushed his zeal too far and thwarted my plans by permitting himself, on his own initiative, to strike you a blow.'

'Oh, it was a little accident!'

'Not at all, not at all! And I have reprimanded him severely! I am bound, however, to say in his favour that he was taken unawares by the really unexpected rapidity of your investigation. If you had only left us a few hours longer, you would have escaped that unpardonable attempt.'

'And I should doubtless have enjoyed the enormous advantage of undergoing the same fate as M. Ganimard and Mr. Holmlock Shears?'

'Exactly,' said Lupin, laughing heartily. 'And I should not have known the cruel terrors which your wound caused me. I have had an atrocious time because of it, believe me, and, at this moment, your pallor fills me with all the stings of remorse. Can you ever forgive me?'

'The proof of confidence which you have shown me in delivering yourself unconditionally into my hands — it would have been so easy for me to bring a few of Ganimard's friends with me — that proof of confidence wipes out everything.'

Was he speaking seriously? I confess frankly that I was greatly perplexed. The struggle between the two men was beginning in a manner which I was simply unable to understand. I had been present at the first meeting between Lupin and Holmlock Shears, in the café near the Gare Montparnesse, and I could not help recalling the haughty carriage of the two combatants, the terrific clash of their pride under the politeness of their manners, the hard blows which they dealt each other, their feints, their arrogance.

Here, it was quite different. Lupin, it is true, had not changed; he exhibited the same tactics, the same crafty affability. But what a strange adversary he had come upon! Was it even an adversary? Really, he had neither the tone of one nor the appearance. Very calm, but with a real calmness, not one assumed to cloak the passion of a man endeavouring to restrain himself; very polite, but without exaggeration; smiling, but without chaff, he presented the most perfect contrast to Arsène Lupin, a contrast so perfect even that, to my mind, Lupin appeared as much perplexed as myself.

No, there was no doubt about it: in the presence of that frail stripling, with cheeks smooth as a girl's and candid and charming eyes, Lupin was losing his ordinary self-assurance. Several times over, I observed traces of embarrassment in him. He hesitated, did not attack frankly, wasted time in mawkish and affected phrases.

It also looked as though he wanted something. He seemed to be seeking, waiting. What for? Some aid?

There was a fresh ring of the bell. He himself ran and opened the door. He returned with a letter:

'Will you allow me, gentlemen?' he asked.

He opened the letter. It contained a

telegram. He read it — and became as though transformed. His face lit up, his figure righted itself and I saw the veins on his forehead swell. It was the athlete who once more stood before me, the ruler, sure of himself, master of events and master of persons. He spread the telegram on the table and, striking it with his fist, exclaimed:

'Now, M. Beautrelet, it's you and I!'

Beautrelet adopted a listening attitude and Lupin began, in measured, but harsh and masterful tones:

'Let us throw off the mask — what say you? — and have done with hypocritical compliments. We are two enemies, who know exactly what to think of each other; we act toward each other as enemies; and therefore we ought to treat with each other as enemies.'

'To treat?' echoed Beautrelet, in a voice of surprise.

'Yes, to treat. I did not use that word at random and I repeat it, in spite of the effort, the great effort, which it costs me. This is the first time I have employed it to an adversary. But also, I may as well tell you at once, it is the last. Make the most of it. I shall not leave this flat without a promise from you. If I do, it means war.'

Beautrelet seemed more and more surprised. He said very prettily:

'I was not prepared for this — you speak so funnily! It's so different from what I expected! Yes, I thought you were not a bit like that! Why this display of anger? Why use threats? Are we enemies because circumstances bring us into opposition? Enemies? Why?'

Lupin appeared a little out of countenance, but he snarled and, leaning over the boy:

'Listen to me, youngster,' he said. 'It's not a question of picking one's words. It's a question of a fact, a positive, indisputable fact; and that fact is this: in all the past ten years, I have not yet knocked up against an adversary of your capacity. With Ganimard and Holmlock Shears I played as if they were children. With you, I am obliged to defend myself, I will say more, to retreat. Yes, at this moment, you and I well know that I must look upon myself as worsted in the fight. Isidore Beautrelet has got the better of Arsène Lupin. My plans are upset. What I tried to leave in the dark you have brought into the full light of day. You annoy me, you stand in my way. Well, I've had enough of it — Bredoux told you so to no purpose. I now tell you so again; and I insist upon it, so that you may take it to heart: I've had enough of it!'

Beautrelet nodded his head:

'Yes. but what do you want?'

'Peace! Each of us minding his own business, keeping to his own side!'

'That is to say, you free to continue your burglaries undisturbed, I free to return to my studies.'

'Your studies — anything you please — I don't care. But you must leave me in peace — I want peace.'

'How can I trouble it now?'

Lupin seized his hand violently:

'You know quite well! Don't pretend not to know. You are at this moment in possession of a secret to which I attach the highest importance. This secret you were free to guess, but you have no right to give it to the public.'

'Are you sure that I know it?'

'You know it, I am certain: day by day, hour by hour, I have followed your train of thought and the progress of your investigations. At the very moment when Bredoux struck you, you were about to tell all. Subsequently, you delayed your revelations, out of solicitude for your father. But they are now promised to this paper here. The article is written. It will be set up in an hour. It will appear to-morrow.'

'Quite right.'

Lupin rose, and slashing the air with his hand, 'It shall not appear!' he cried.

'It shall appear!' said Beautrelet, starting up in his turn.

At last, the two men were standing up to each other. I received the impression of a shock, as if they had seized each other round the body. Beautrelet seemed to burn with a sudden energy. It was as though a spark had kindled within him a group of new emotions: pluck, self-respect, the passion of fighting, the intoxication of danger. As for Lupin, I read in the radiance of his glance the joy of the duellist who at length encounters the sword of his hated rival.

'Is the article in the printer's hands?'

'Not yet.'

'Have you it there — on you?'

'No fear! I shouldn't have it by now, in that case!'

'Then — '

'One of the assistant editors has it, in a sealed envelope. If I am not at the office by midnight, he will have set it up.'

'Oh, the scoundrel!' muttered Lupin. 'He has provided for everything!'

His anger was increasing, visibly and frightfully. Beautrelet chuckled, jeering in his turn, carried away by his success.

'Stop that, you brat!' roared Lupin. 'You're forgetting who I am — and that, if I wished — upon my word, he's daring to laugh!'

A great silence fell between them. Then Lupin stepped forward and, in muttered tones, with his eyes on Beautrelet's:

'You shall go straight to the Grand Journal.'

'No.'

'Tear up your article.'

'No.'

'See the editor.'

'No.'

'Tell him you made a mistake.'

'No.'

'And write him another article, in which you will give the official version of the Ambrumesy mystery, the one which every one has accepted.'

'No.'

Lupin took up a steel ruler that lay on my desk and broke it in two without an effort. His pallor was terrible to see. He wiped away the beads of perspiration that stood on his forehead. He, who had never known his wishes resisted, was being maddened by the obstinacy of this child. He pressed his two hands on Beautrelet's shoulder and, emphasizing every syllable, continued:

'You shall do as I tell you, Beautrelet. You shall say that your latest discoveries have convinced you of my death, that there is not the least doubt about it. You shall say so because I wish it, because it has to be

127

believed that I am dead. You shall say so, above all, because, if you do not say so — '

'Because, if I do not say so — ?'

'Your father will be kidnapped to-night, as Ganimard and Holmlock Shears were.'

Beautrelet gave a smile.

'Don't laugh — answer!'

'My answer is that I am very sorry to disappoint you, but I have promised to speak and I shall speak.'

'Speak in the sense which I have told you.'

'I shall speak the truth,' cried Beautrelet, eagerly. 'It is something which you can't understand, the pleasure, the need, rather, of saying the thing that is and saying it aloud. The truth is here, in this brain which has guessed it and discovered it; and it will come out, all naked and quivering. The article, therefore, will be printed as I wrote it. The world shall know that Lupin is alive and shall know the reason why he wished to be considered dead. The world shall know all.' And he added, calmly, 'And my father shall not be kidnapped.'

Once again, they were both silent, with their eyes still fixed upon each other. They watched each other. Their swords were engaged up to the hilt. And it was like the heavy silence that goes before the mortal blow. Which of the two was to strike it?

Lupin said, between his teeth:

'Failing my instructions to the contrary, two of my friends have orders to enter your father's room to-night, at three o'clock in the morning, to seize him and carry him off to join Ganimard and Holmlock Shears.'

A burst of shrill laughter interrupted him:

'Why, you highwayman, don't you understand,' cried Beautrelet, 'that I have taken my precautions? So you think that I am innocent enough, ass enough, to have sent my father home to his lonely little house in the open country!' Oh, the gay, bantering laughter that lit up the boy's face! It was a new sort of laugh on his lips, a laugh that showed the influence of Lupin himself. And the familiar form of address which he adopted placed him at once on his adversary's level. He continued:

'You see, Lupin, your great fault is to believe your schemes infallible. You proclaim yourself beaten, do you? What humbug! You are convinced that you will always win the day in the end — and you forget that others can have their little schemes, too. Mine is a very simple one, my friend.'

It was delightful to hear him talk. He walked up and down, with his hands in his pockets and with the easy swagger of a boy teasing a caged beast. Really, at this moment, he was revenging, with the most terrible revenges, all the victims of the great adventurer. And he concluded:

'Lupin, my father is not in Savoy. He is at the other end of France, in the centre of a big town, guarded by twenty of our friends, who have orders not to lose sight of him until our battle is over. Would you like details? He is at Cherbourg, in the house of one of the keepers of the arsenal. And remember that the arsenal is closed at night and that no one is allowed to enter it by day, unless he carries an authorization and is accompanied by a guide.'

He stopped in front of Lupin and defied him, like a child making faces at his playmate:

'What do you say to that, master?'

For some minutes, Lupin had stood motionless. Not a muscle of his face had moved. What were his thoughts? Upon what action was he resolving? To any one knowing the fierce violence of his pride the only possible solution was the total, immediate, final collapse of his adversary. His fingers twitched. For a second, I had a feeling that he was about to throw himself upon the boy and wring his neck.

'What do you say to that, master?' Beautrelet repeated.

Lupin took up the telegram that lay on the table, held it out and said, very calmly:

'Here, baby, read that.'

Beautrelet became serious, suddenly, impressed by the gentleness of the movement. He unfolded the paper and, at once, raising his eyes, murmured:

'What does it mean? I don't understand.'

'At any rate, you understand the first word,' said Lupin, 'the first word of the telegram — that is to say, the name of the place from which it was sent — look — 'Cherbourg.''

'Yes — yes,' stammered Beautrelet. 'Yes — I understand — 'Cherbourg' — and then?'

'And then? — I should think the rest is quite plain: 'Removal of luggage finished. Friends left with it and will wait instructions till eight morning. All well.' Is there anything there that seems obscure? The word 'luggage'? Pooh, you wouldn't have them write 'M. Beautrelet, senior'! What then? The way in which the operation was performed? The miracle by which your father was taken out of Cherbourg Arsenal, in spite of his twenty bodyguards? Pooh, it's as easy as A B C! And the fact remains that the luggage has been dispatched. What do you say to that, baby?'

With all his tense being, with all his exasperated energy, Isidore tried to preserve a good countenance. But I saw his lips quiver, his jaw shrink, his eyes vainly strive to fix upon a point. He lisped a few words, then was silent and, suddenly, gave way and, with his hands before his face, burst into loud sobs:

'Oh, father! Father!'

An unexpected result, which was certainly the collapse which Lupin's pride demanded, but also something more, something infinitely touching and infinitely artless. Lupin gave a movement of annoyance and took up his hat, as though this unaccustomed display of sentiment were too much for him. But, on reaching the door, he stopped, hesitated and then returned, slowly, step by step.

The soft sound of the sobs rose like the sad wailing of a little child overcome with grief. The lad's shoulders marked the heart-rending rhythm. Tears appeared through the crossed fingers. Lupin leaned forward and, without touching Beautrelet, said, in a voice that had not the least tone of pleasantry, nor even of the offensive pity of the victor:

'Don't cry, youngster. This is one of those blows which a man must expect when he rushes headlong into the fray, as you did. The worst disasters lie in wait for him. The destiny of fighters will have it so. We must suffer it as bravely as we can.' Then, with a sort of gentleness, he continued, 'You were right, you see: we are not enemies. I have known it for long. From the very first, I felt for you, for the intelligent creature that you are, an involuntary sympathy — and admiration. And that is why I wanted to say this to you — don't be offended, whatever you do: I should be extremely sorry to offend you — but I must say it: well, give up struggling against me. I am not saying this out of vanity — nor because I despise you — but, you see, the struggle is too unequal. You do not know — nobody knows all the resources which I have at my command. Look here, this secret of the Hollow Needle which you are trying so vainly to unravel: suppose, for a moment, that it is a formidable, inexhaustible treasure — or else an invisible, prodigious, fantastic refuge — or both perhaps. Think of the superhuman power which I must derive from it! And you do not know, either, all the resources which I have within myself — all that my will and my imagination enable me to undertake and to undertake successfully. Only think that my whole life — ever since I was born, I might almost say — has tended toward the same aim, that I worked like a convict before becoming what I am and to realize, in its perfection, the type which I wished to create — which I have succeeded in creating. That being so — what can you do? At that very moment when you think that victory lies within your grasp, it will escape you — there will be something of which you have not thought — a trifle — a grain of sand which I shall have put in the right place, unknown to you. I entreat vou, give up — I should be obliged to hurt you; and the thought distresses me.' And, placing his hand on the boy's forehead, he repeated, 'Once more, youngster, give up. I should only hurt you. Who knows if the trap into which you will inevitably fall has not already opened under your footsteps?'

Beautrelet uncovered his face. He was no longer crying. Had he heard Lupin's words? One might have doubted it, judging by his inattentive air.

For two or three minutes, he was silent. He seemed to weigh the decision which he was about to take, to examine the reasons for and against, to count up the favourable and unfavourable chances. At last, he said to Lupin:

'If I change the sense of the article, if I confirm the version of your death and if I undertake never to contradict the false version which I shall have sanctioned, do you swear that my father will be free?'

'I swear it. My friends have taken your father by motor car to another provincial town. At seven o'clock to-morrow morning, if the article in the Grand Journal is what I want it to be, I shall telephone to them and they will restore your father to liberty.'

'Very well,' said Beautrelet. 'I submit to your conditions.'

Quickly, as though he saw no object in prolonging the conversation after accepting his defeat, he rose, took his hat, bowed to me, bowed to Lupin and went out. Lupin watched him go, listened to the sound of the door closing and muttered:

'Poor little beggar!'

*   *   *

At eight o'clock the next morning, I sent my man out to buy the Grand Journal. It was twenty minutes before he brought me a copy, most of the kiosks being already sold out.

I unfolded the paper with feverish hands. Beautrelet's article appeared on the front page. I give it as it stood and as it was quoted in the press of the whole world:

THE AMBRUMESY MYSTERY

I do not intend in these few sentences to set out in detail the mental processes and the investigations that have enabled me to reconstruct the tragedy — I should say the twofold tragedy — of Ambrumesy. In my opinion, this sort of work and the judgments which it entails, deductions, inductions, analyses and so on, are only interesting in a minor degree and, in any case, are highly commonplace. No, I shall content myself with setting forth the two leading ideas which I followed; and, if I do that, it will be seen that, in so setting them forth and in solving the two problems which they raise, I shall have told the story just as it happened, in the exact order of the different incidents.

It may be said that some of these incidents are not proved and that I leave too large a field to conjecture. That is quite true. But, in my view, my theory is founded upon a sufficiently large number of proved facts to be able to say that even those facts which are not proved must follow from the strict logic of events. The stream is so often lost under the pebbly bed: it is nevertheless the same stream that reappears at intervals and mirrors back the blue sky.

The first riddle that confronted me, a riddle not in detail, but as a whole, was how came it that Lupin, mortally wounded, one might say, managed to live for five or six weeks without nursing, medicine or food, at the bottom of a dark hole?

Let us start at the beginning. On Thursday the sixteenth of April, at four o'clock in the morning, Arsène Lupin, surprised in the middle of one of his most daring burglaries, runs away by the path leading to the ruins and drops down shot. He drags himself painfully along, falls again and picks himself up in the desperate hope of reaching the chapel. The chapel contains a crypt, the existence of which he has discovered by accident. If he can burrow there, he may be saved. By dint of an effort, he approaches it, he is but a few yards away, when a sound of footsteps approaches. Harassed and lost, he lets himself go. The enemy arrives. It is Mlle. Raymonde de Saint-Veran.

This is the prologue or rather the first scene of the drama.

What happened between them? This is the easier to guess inasmuch as the sequel of the adventure gives us all the necessary clues. At the girl's feet lies a wounded man, exhausted by suffering, who will be captured in two minutes. *This man has been wounded by herself.* Will she also give him up?

If he is Jean Daval's murderer, yes, she will let destiny take its course. But, in quick sentences, he tells her the truth about this awful murder committed by her uncle, M. de Gesvres. She believes him. What will she do?

Nobody can see them. The footman Victor is watching the little door. The other, Albert, posted at the drawing-room window, has lost sight of both of them. *Will she give up the man she has wounded?*

The girl is carried away by a movement of irresistible pity, which any woman will understand. Instructed by Lupin, with a few movements she binds up the wound with his handkerchief, to avoid the marks which the blood would leave. Then, with the aid of the key which he gives her, she opens the door of the chapel. He enters, supported by the girl. She locks the door again and walks away. Albert arrives.

If the chapel had been visited at that moment or at least during the next few minutes, before Lupin had had time to recover his strength, to raise the flagstone and disappear by the stairs leading to the crypt, he would have been taken. But this visit did not take place until six hours later and then only in the most superficial way. As it is, Lupin is saved; and saved by whom? By the girl who very nearly killed him.

Thenceforth, whether she wishes it or no, Mlle. de Saint-Veran is his accomplice. Not only is she no longer able to give him up, but she is obliged to continue her work, else the wounded man will perish in the shelter in which she has helped to conceal him. Therefore she continues.

For that matter, if her feminine instinct makes the task a compulsory one, it also makes it easy. She is full of artifice, she foresees and forestalls everything. It is she who gives the examining magistrate a false description of Arsène Lupin (the reader will remember the difference of opinion on this subject between the cousins). It is she, obviously, who, thanks to certain signs which I do not know of, suspects an accomplice of Lupin's in the driver of the fly. She warns him. She informs him of the urgent need of an operation. It is she, no doubt, who substitutes one cap for the other. It is she who causes the famous letter to be written in which she is personally threatened. How, after that, is it possible to suspect her?

It is she, who at that moment when I was about to confide my first impressions to the examining magistrate, pretends to have seen me, the day before, in the copsewood, alarms M. Filleul on my score and reduces me to silence: a dangerous move, no doubt, because it arouses my attention and directs it against the person who assails me with an accusation which I know to be false; but an efficacious move, because the most important thing of all is to gain time and close my lips.

Lastly, it is she who, during forty days, feeds Lupin, brings him his medicine (the chemist at Ouville will produce the prescriptions which he made up for Mile, de Saint-Veran), nurses him, dresses his wound, watches over him *and cures him.*

Here we have the first of our two problems solved, at the same time that the Ambrumesy mystery is set forth. Arsène Lupin found, close at hand, in the chateau itself, the assistance which was indispensable to him in order, first, not to be discovered and, secondly, to live.

He now lives. And we come to the second problem, corresponding with the second Ambrumesy mystery, the study of which served me as a conducting medium. Why does Lupin, alive, free, at the head of his gang, omnipotent as before, why does Lupin make desperate efforts, efforts with which I am constantly coming into collision, to force the idea of his death upon the police and the public?

We must remember that Mlle. de Saint-Veran was a very pretty girl. The photographs reproduced in the papers after her disappearance give but an imperfect notion of her beauty. That follows which was bound to follow. Lupin, seeing this lovely girl daily for five or six weeks, longing for her presence when she is not there, subjected to her charm and grace when she is there, inhaling the cool perfume of her breath when she bends over him, Lupin becomes enamoured of his nurse. Gratitude turns to love, admiration to passion. She is his salvation, but she is also the joy of his eyes, the dream of his lonely hours, his light, his hope, his very life.

He respects her sufficiently not to take advantage of the girl's devotion and not to make use of her to direct his confederates. There is, in fact, a certain lack of decision apparent in the acts of the gang. But he loves her also, his scruples weaken and, as Mlle. de Saint-Veran refuses to be touched by a love that offends her, as she relaxes her visits when they become less necessary, as she ceases them entirely on the day when he is cured — desperate, maddened by grief, he takes a terrible resolve. He leaves his lair, prepares his stroke and, on Saturday the sixth of June, assisted by his accomplices, he carries off the girl.

This is not all. The abduction must not be known. All search, all surmises, all hope, even, must be cut short. Mlle. de Saint-Veran must pass for dead. There is a mock murder: proofs are supplied for the police inquiries. There is doubt about the crime, a crime, for that matter, not unexpected, a crime foretold by the accomplices, a crime perpetrated to revenge the chief's death. And, through this very fact — observe the marvellous ingenuity of the conception — through this very fact, the belief in this death is, so to speak, stimulated.

It is not enough to suggest a belief; it is necessary to compel a certainty. Lupin foresees my interference. I am sure to guess the trickery of the chapel. I am sure to discover the crypt. And, as the crypt will be empty, the whole scaffolding will come to the ground.

The crypt shall not be empty.

In the same way, the death of Mlle. de Saint-Veran will not be definite, unless the sea gives up her corpse.

The sea shall give up the corpse of Mlle. de Saint-Veran.

The difficulty is tremendous. The double obstacle seems insurmountable. Yes, to any one but Lupin, but not to Lupin.

As he had foreseen, I guess the trickery of the chapel, I discover the crypt and I go down into the lair where Lupin has taken refuge. His corpse is there!

Any person who had admitted the death of Lupin as possible would have been baffled. But I had not admitted this eventuality for an instant (first, by intuition and, secondly, by reasoning). Pretence thereupon became useless and every scheme vain. I said to myself at once that the block of stone disturbed by the pickaxe had been placed there with a very curious exactness, that the least knock was bound to make it fall and that, in falling, it must inevitably reduce the head of the false Arsène Lupin to pulp, in such a way as to make it utterly irrecognisable.

Another discovery: half an hour later, I hear that the body of Mlle. de Saint-Veran has been found on the rocks at

Dieppe — or rather a body which is considered to be Mlle. de Saint-Veran's, for the reason that the arm has a bracelet similar to one of that young lady's bracelets. This, however, is the only mark of identity, for the corpse is irrecognisable.

Thereupon I remember and I understand. A few days earlier, I happened to read in a number of the *Vigie de Dieppe* that a young American couple staying at Envermeu had committed suicide by taking poison and that their bodies had disappeared on the very night of the death. I hasten to Envermeu. The story is true, I am told, except in so far as concerns the disappearance, because the brothers of the victims came to claim the corpses and took them away after the usual formalities. The name of these brothers, no doubt, was Arsène Lupin & Co.

Consequently, the thing is proved. We know why Lupin shammed the murder of the girl and spread the rumour of his own death. He is in love and does not wish it known. And, to reach his ends, he shrinks from nothing, he even undertakes that incredible theft of the two corpses which he needs in order to impersonate himself and Mlle. de Saint-Veran. In this way, he will be at ease. No one can disturb him. No one will ever suspect the truth which he wishes to suppress.

No one? Yes — three adversaries, at the most, might conceive doubts: Ganimard, whose arrival is hourly expected; Holmlock Shears, who is about to cross the Channel; and I, who am on the spot. This constitutes a threefold danger. He removes it. He kidnaps Ganimard. He kidnaps Holmlock Shears. He has me stabbed by Bredoux.

One point alone remains obscure. Why was Lupin so fiercely bent upon snatching the document about the Hollow Needle from me? He surely did not imagine that, by taking it away, he could wipe out from my memory the text of the five lines of which it consists! Then why? Did he fear that the character of the paper itself, or some other clue, could give me a hint?

Be that as it may, this is the truth of the Ambrumesy mystery. I repeat that conjecture plays a certain part in the explanation which I offer, even as it played a great part in my personal investigation. But, if one waited for proofs and facts to fight Lupin, one would run a great risk either of waiting forever or else of discovering proofs and facts carefully prepared by Lupin, which would lead in a direction immediately opposite to the object in view. I feel confident that the facts, when they are known, will confirm my surmise in every respect.

So Isidore Beautrelet, mastered for a moment by Arsène Lupin, distressed by the abduction of his father and resigned to defeat, Isidore Beautrelet, in the end, was unable to persuade himself to keep silence. The truth was too beautiful and too curious, the proofs which he was able to produce were too logical and too conclusive for him to consent to misrepresent it. The whole world was waiting for his revelations. He spoke.

★　★　★

On the evening of the day on which his article appeared, the newspapers announced the kidnapping of M. Beautrelet, senior. Isidore was informed of it by a telegram from Cherbourg, which reached him at three o'clock.

5

On the Track

Young Beautrelet was stunned by the violence of the blow. As a matter of fact, although, in publishing his article, he had obeyed one of those irresistible impulses which make a man despise every consideration of prudence, he had never really believed in the possibility of an abduction. His precautions had been too thorough. The friends at Cherbourg not only had instructions to guard and protect Beautrelet the elder: they were also to watch his comings and goings, never to let him walk out alone and not even to hand him a single letter without first opening it. No, there was no danger. Lupin, wishing to gain time, was trying to intimidate his adversary.

The blow, therefore, was almost unexpected; and Isidore, because he was powerless to act, felt the pain of the shock during the whole of the remainder of the day. One idea alone supported him: that of leaving Paris, going down there, seeing for himself what had happened and resuming the offensive.

He telegraphed to Cherbourg. He was at

Saint-Lazare a little before nine. A few minutes after, he was steaming out of the station in the Normandy express.

It was not until an hour later, when he mechanically unfolded a newspaper which he had bought on the platform, that he became aware of the letter by which Lupin indirectly replied to his article of that morning:

To the Editor of the Grand Journal.

SIR: I cannot pretend but that my modest personality, which would certainly have passed unnoticed in more heroic times, has acquired a certain prominence in the dull and feeble period in which we live. But there is a limit beyond which the morbid curiosity of the crowd cannot go without becoming indecently indiscreet. If the walls that surround our private lives be not respected, what is to safeguard the rights of the citizen?

Will those who differ plead the higher interest of truth? An empty pretext in so far as I am concerned, because the truth is known and I raise no difficulty about making an official confession of the truth in writing. Yes, Mlle. de Saint-Veran is alive. Yes, I love her. Yes, I have the

148

mortification not to be loved by her. Yes, the results of the boy Beautrelet's inquiry are wonderful in their precision and accuracy. Yes, we agree on every point. There is no riddle left. There is no mystery. Well, then, what?

Injured to the very depths of my soul, bleeding still from cruel wounds, I ask that my more intimate feelings and secret hopes may no longer be delivered to the malevolence of the public. I ask for peace, the peace which I need to conquer the affection of Mlle. de Saint-Veran and to wipe out from her memory the thousand little injuries which she has had to suffer at the hands of her uncle and cousin — this has not been told — because of her position as a poor relation. Mlle. de Saint-Veran will forget this hateful past. All that she can desire, were it the fairest jewel in the world, were it the most unattainable treasure, I shall lay at her feet. She will be happy. She will love me.

But, if I am to succeed, once more, I require peace. That is why I lay down my arms and hold out the olive-branch to my enemies — while warning them, with every magnanimity on my part, that a refusal on theirs might bring down upon them the gravest consequences.

One word more on the subject of Mr. Harlington. This name conceals the identity of an excellent fellow, who is secretary to Cooley, the American millionaire, and instructed by him to lay hands upon every object of ancient art in Europe which it is possible to discover. His evil star brought him into touch with my friend Etienne de Vaudreix, ALIAS Arsène Lupin, ALIAS myself. He learnt, in this way, that a certain M. de Gesvres was willing to part with four pictures by Rubens, ostensibly on the condition that they were replaced by copies and that the bargain to which he was consenting remained unknown. My friend Vaudreix also undertook to persuade M. de Gesvres to sell his chapel. The negotiations were conducted with entire good faith on the side of my friend Vaudreix and with charming ingenuousness on the side of Mr. Harlington, until the day when the Rubenses and the carvings from the chapel were in a safe place and Mr. Harlington in prison. There remains nothing, therefore, to be done but to release the unfortunate American, because he was content to play the modest part of a dupe; to brand the millionaire Cooley,

because, for fear of possible unpleasant-
ness, he did not protest against his
secretary's arrest; and to congratulate my
friend Etienne de Vaudreix, because he is
revenging the outraged morality of the
public by keeping the hundred thousand
francs which he was paid on account by
that singularly unattractive person, Cooley.

Pray, pardon the length of this letter
and permit me to be, Sir,

Your obedient servant,
ARSÈNE LUPIN.

Isidore weighed the words of this communication as minutely, perhaps, as he had studied
the document concerning the Hollow Needle.
He went on the principle, the correctness of
which was easily proved, that Lupin had
never taken the trouble to send one of his
amusing letters to the press without absolute
necessity, without some motive which events
were sure, sooner or later, to bring to light.

What was the motive for this particular
letter? For what hidden reason was Lupin
confessing his love and the failure of that
love? Was it there that Beautrelet had to seek,
or in the explanations regarding Mr. Harlington, or further still, between the lines, behind
all those words whose apparent meaning had

perhaps no other object than to suggest some wicked, perfidious, misleading little idea?

For hours, the young man, confined to his compartment, remained pensive and anxious. The letter filled him with mistrust, as though it had been written for his benefit and were destined to lead him, personally, into error. For the first time and because he found himself confronted not with a direct attack, but with an ambiguous, indefinable method of fighting, he underwent a distinct sensation of fear. And, when he thought of his good old, easy-going father, kidnapped through his fault, he asked himself, with a pang, whether he was not mad to continue so unequal a contest. Was the result not certain? Had Lupin not won the game in advance?

It was but a short moment of weakness. When he alighted from his compartment, at six o'clock in the morning, refreshed by a few hours' sleep, he had recovered all his confidence.

On the platform, Froberval, the dockyard clerk who had given hospitality to M. Beautrelet, senior, was waiting for him, accompanied by his daughter Charlotte, an imp of twelve or thirteen.

'Well?' cried Isidore.

The worthy man beginning to moan and groan, he interrupted him, dragged him to a neighbouring tavern, ordered coffee and began to put plain questions, without permitting the other the slightest digression:

'My father has not been carried off, has he? It was impossible.'

'Impossible. Still, he has disappeared.'

'Since when?'

'We don't know.'

'What!'

'No. Yesterday morning, at six o'clock, as I had not seen him come down as usual, I opened his door. He was gone.'

'But was he there on the day before, two days ago?'

'Yes. On the day before yesterday, he did not leave his room. He was a little tired; and Charlotte took his lunch up to him at twelve and his dinner at seven in the evening.'

'So it was between seven o'clock in the evening, on the day before yesterday, and six o'clock on yesterday morning that he disappeared?'

'Yes, during the night before last. Only — '

'Only what?'

'Well, it's like this: you can't leave the arsenal at night.'

'Do you mean that he has not left it?'

'That's impossible! My friends and I have searched the whole naval harbour.'

'Then he has left it!'

'Impossible, every outlet is guarded!'

Beautrelet reflected and then said:

'What next?'

'Next, I hurried to the commandant's and informed the officer in charge.'

'Did he come to your house?'

'Yes; and a gentleman from the public prosecutor's also. They searched all through the morning; and, when I saw that they were making no progress and that there was no hope left, I telegraphed to you.'

'Was the bed disarranged in his room?'

'No.'

'Nor the room disturbed in any way?'

'No. I found his pipe in its usual place, with his tobacco and the book which he was reading. There was even this little photograph of yourself in the middle of the book, marking the page.'

'Let me see it.'

Froberval passed him the photograph. Beautrelet gave a start of surprise. He had recognized himself in the snapshot, standing, with his two hands in his pockets, on a lawn from which rose trees and ruins.

Froberval added:

'It must be the last portrait of yourself which you sent him. Look, on the back, you will see the date, 3 April, the name of the photographer, R. de Val, and the name of the

154

town, Lion — Lion-sur-Mer, perhaps.'

Isidore turned the photograph over and read this little note, in his own handwriting:

'R. de Val. — 3.4 — Lion.'

He was silent for a few minutes and resumed:

'My father hadn't shown you that snapshot yet?'

'No — and that's just what astonished me when I saw it yesterday — for your father used so often to talk to us about you.'

There was a fresh pause, greatly prolonged. Froberval muttered:

'I have business at the workshop. We might as well go in — '

He was silent. Isidore had not taken his eyes from the photograph, was examining it from every point of view. At last, the boy asked:

'Is there such a thing as an inn called the Lion d'Or at a short league outside the town?'

'Yes, about a league from here.'

'On the Route de Valognes, is it?'

'Yes, on the Route de Valognes.'

'Well, I have every reason to believe that this inn was the head-quarters of Lupin's friends. It was from there that they entered into communication with my father.'

'What an idea! Your father spoke to

nobody. He saw nobody.'

'He saw nobody, but they made use of an intermediary.'

'What proof have you?'

'This photograph.'

'But it's your photograph!'

'It's my photograph, but it was not sent by me. I was not even aware of its existence. It was taken, without my knowledge, in the ruins of Ambrumesy, doubtless by the examining-magistrate's clerk, who, as you know, was an accomplice of Arsène Lupin's.'

'And then?'

'Then this photograph became the passport, the talisman, by means of which they obtained my father's confidence.'

'But who? Who was able to get into my house?'

'I don't know, but my father fell into the trap. They told him and he believed that I was in the neighbourhood, that I was asking to see him and that I was giving him an appointment at the Golden Lion.'

'But all this is nonsense! How can you assert — ?'

'Very simply. They imitated my writing on the back of the photograph and specified the meeting-place: Valognes Road, 3 kilometres 400, Lion Inn. My father came and they seized him, that's all.'

'Very well,' muttered Froberval, dumbfounded, 'very well. I admit it — things happened as you say — but that does not explain how he was able to leave during the night.'

'He left in broad daylight, though he waited until dark to go to the meeting-place.'

'But, confound it, he didn't leave his room the whole of the day before yesterday!'

'There is one way of making sure: run down to the dockyard, Froberval, and look for one of the men who were on guard in the afternoon, two days ago. — Only, be quick, if you wish to find me here.'

'Are you going?'

'Yes, I shall take the next train back.'

'What! — Why, you don't know — your inquiry — '

'My inquiry is finished. I know pretty well all that I wanted to know. I shall have left Cherbourg in an hour.'

Froberval rose to go. He looked at Beautrelet with an air of absolute bewilderment, hesitated a moment and then took his cap:

'Are you coming, Charlotte?'

'No,' said Beautrelet, 'I shall want a few more particulars. Leave her with me. Besides, I want to talk to her. I knew her when she was quite small.'

Froberval went away. Beautrelet and the little girl remained alone in the tavern smoking room. A few minutes passed, a waiter entered, cleared away some cups and left the room again. The eyes of the young man and the child met; and Beautrelet placed his hand very gently on the little girl's hand. She looked at him for two or three seconds, distractedly, as though about to choke. Then, suddenly hiding her head between her folded arms, she burst into sobs.

He let her cry and, after a while, said:

'It was you, wasn't it, who did all the mischief, who acted as go-between? It was you who took him the photograph? You admit it, don't you? And, when you said that my father was in his room, two days ago, you knew that it was not true, did you not, because you yourself had helped him to leave it — ?'

She made no reply. He asked:

'Why did you do it? They offered you money, I suppose — to buy ribbons with a frock — ?'

He uncrossed Charlotte's arms and lifted up her head. He saw a poor little face all streaked with tears, the attractive, disquieting, mobile face of one of those little girls who seem marked out for temptation and weakness.

'Come,' said Beautrelet, 'it's over, we'll say no more about it. I will not even ask you how it happened. Only you must tell me everything that can be of use to me. — Did you catch anything — any remark made by those men? How did they carry him off?'

She replied at once:

'By motor car. I heard them talking about it — '

'And what road did they take?'

'Ah, I don't know that!'

'Didn't they say anything before you — something that might help us?'

'No — wait, though: there was one who said, 'We shall have no time to lose — the governor is to telephone to us at eight o'clock in the morning — ''

'Whereto?'

'I can't say. — I've forgotten — '

'Try — try and remember. It was the name of a town, wasn't it?'

'Yes — a name — like Chateau — '

'Chateaubriant? — Chateau-Thierry? — '

'No-no — '

'Chateauroux?'

'Yes, that was it — Chateauroux — '

Beautrelet did not wait for her to complete her sentence. Already he was on his feet and, without giving a thought to Froberval, without even troubling about the child, who stood gazing at him in stupefaction, he opened the door and ran to the station:

'Chateauroux, madame — a ticket for Chateauroux — '

'Over Mans and Tours?' asked the booking-clerk.

'Of course — the shortest way. Shall I be there for lunch?'

'Oh, no!'

'For dinner? Bedtime — ?'

'Oh, no! For that, you would have to go over Paris. The Paris express leaves at nine o'clock. You're too late — '

It was not too late. Beautrelet was just able to catch the train.

'Well,' said Beautrelet, rubbing his hands, 'I have spent only two hours or so at Cherbourg, but they were well employed.'

He did not for a moment think of accusing Charlotte of lying. Weak, unstable, capable of the worst treacheries, those petty natures also obey impulses of sincerity; and Beautrelet had read in her affrighted eyes her shame for the harm which she had done and her delight at repairing it in part. He had no doubt, therefore, that Chateauroux was the other town to which Lupin had referred and where his confederates were to telephone to him.

On his arrival in Paris, Beautrelet took every necessary precaution to avoid being followed. He felt that it was a serious moment. He was on the right road that was leading him to his father: one act of imprudence might ruin all.

He went to the flat of one of his schoolfellows and came out, an hour later, irrecognisable, rigged out as an Englishman of thirty, in a brown check suit, with knickerbockers, woollen stockings and a cap, a high-coloured complexion and a red wig. He jumped on a bicycle laden with a complete painter's outfit and rode off to the Gare d'Austerlitz.

He slept that night at Issoudun. The next morning, he mounted his machine at break of day. At seven o'clock, he walked into the Chateauroux post-office and asked to be put on to Paris. As he had to wait, he entered into conversation with the clerk and learnt that, two days before, at the same hour, a man dressed for motoring had also asked for Paris.

The proof was established. He waited no longer.

By the afternoon, he had ascertained, from undeniable evidence, that a limousine car, following the Tours road, had passed through the village of Buzancais and the town of Chateauroux and had stopped beyond the town, on the verge of the forest. At ten o'clock, a hired gig, driven by a man unknown, had stopped beside the car and then gone off south, through the valley of the Bouzanne. There was then another person seated beside the driver. As for the car, it had turned in the opposite direction and gone north, toward Issoudun.

Beautrelet easily discovered the owner of the gig, who, however, had no information to supply. He had hired out his horse and trap to a man who brought them back himself next day.

Lastly, that same evening, Isidore found out that the motor car had only passed through Issoudun, continuing its road toward Orleans, that is to say, toward Paris.

From all this, it resulted, in the most absolute fashion, that M. Beautrelet was somewhere in the neighbourhood. If not, how was it conceivable that people should travel nearly three hundred miles across France in order to telephone from Chateauroux and next to return, at an acute angle, by the Paris road?

This immense circuit had a more definite object: to move M. Beautrelet to the place assigned to him.

'And this place is within reach of my hand,' said Isidore to himself, quivering with hope and expectation. 'My father is waiting for me to rescue him at ten or fifteen leagues from here. He is close by. He is breathing the same air as I.'

He set to work at once. Taking a war-office map, he divided it into small squares, which he visited one after the other, entering the farmhouses making the peasants talk, calling on the schoolmasters, the mayors, the parish priests, chatting to the women. It seemed to him that he must attain his end without delay and his dreams grew until it was no longer his father alone whom he hoped to deliver, but all those whom Lupin was holding captive: Raymonde de Saint-Veran, Ganimard, Holmlock Shears, perhaps, and others, many others; and, in reaching them, he would, at the same time, reach Lupin's stronghold, his lair, the impenetrable retreat where he was piling up the treasures of which he had robbed the wide world.

But, after a fortnight's useless searching, his enthusiasm ended by slackening and he very soon lost confidence. Because success was slow in appearing, from one day to the next, almost, he ceased to believe in it; and, though he continued to pursue his plan of investigations, he would have felt a real surprise if his efforts had led to the smallest discovery.

More days still passed by, monotonous days of discouragement. He read in the newspapers that the Comte de Gesvres and his daughter had left Ambrumesy and gone to stay near Nice. He also learnt that Harlington had been released, that gentleman's innocence having become self-obvious, in accordance with the indications supplied by Arsène Lupin.

Isidore changed his head-quarters, established himself for two days at the Chatre, for two days at Argenton. The result was the same. Just then, he was nearly throwing up the game. Evidently, the gig in which his father had been carried off could only have furnished a stage, which had been followed by another stage, furnished by some other conveyance. And his father was far away.

He was thinking of leaving, when, one Monday morning, he saw, on the envelope of an unstamped letter, sent on to him from Paris, a handwriting that set him trembling with emotion. So great was his excitement that, for some minutes, he dared not open the letter, for fear of a disappointment. His hand shook. Was it possible? Was this not a trap laid for him by his infernal enemy?

He tore open the envelope. It was indeed a letter from his father, written by his father himself. The handwriting presented all the peculiarities, all the oddities of the hand which he knew so well.

He read:

Will these lines ever reach you, my dear son? I dare not believe it.

During the whole night of my abduction, we travelled by motor car; then, in the morning, by carriage. I could see nothing. My eyes were bandaged. The castle in which I am confined should be somewhere in the midlands, to judge by its construction and the vegetation in the park. The room which I occupy is on the second floor: it is a room with two windows, one of which is almost blocked by a screen of climbing glycines. In the afternoon, I am allowed to walk about the park, at certain hours, but I am kept under unrelaxing observation.

I am writing this letter, on the mere chance of its reaching you, and fastening it to a stone. Perhaps, one day, I shall be able to throw it over the wall and some peasant will pick it up.

But do not be distressed about me. I am treated with every consideration.

Your old father, who is very fond of you and very sad to think of the trouble he is giving you,
BEAUTRELET.

Isidore at once looked at the postmarks. They read, 'Cuzion, Indre.'

The Indre! The department which he had been stubbornly searching for weeks!

He consulted a little pocket-guide which he always carried. Cuzion, in the canton of Eguzon — he had been there too.

For prudence's sake, he discarded his personality as an Englishman, which was becoming too well known in the district, disguised himself as a workman and made for Cuzion. It was an unimportant village. He would easily discover the sender of the letter.

For that matter, chance served him without delay:

'A letter posted on Wednesday last?' exclaimed the mayor, a respectable tradesman in whom he confided and who placed himself at his disposal. 'Listen, I think I can give you a valuable clue: on Saturday morning, Gaffer Charel, an old knife-grinder who visits all the fairs in the department, met me at the end of the village and asked, 'Monsieur le maire, does a letter without a stamp on it go all the same?' 'Of course,' said I. 'And does it get there?' 'Certainly. Only there's double post-age to pay on it, that's all the difference.'

'And where does he live?'

'He lives over there, all alone — on the slope — the hovel that comes next after the churchyard. — Shall I go with you?'

It was a hovel standing by itself, in the middle of an orchard surrounded by tall trees. As they entered the orchard, three magpies flew away with a great splutter and they saw that the birds were flying out of the very hole in which the watch-dog was fastened. And the dog neither barked nor stirred as they approached.

Beautrelet went up in great surprise. The brute was lying on its side, with stiff paws, dead.

They ran quickly to the cottage. The door stood open. They entered. At the back of a low, damp room, on a wretched straw mattress, flung on the floor itself, lay a man fully dressed.

'Gaffer Charel!' cried the mayor. 'Is he dead, too?'

The old man's hands were cold, his face terribly pale, but his heart was still beating, with a faint, slow throb, and he seemed not to be wounded in any way.

They tried to resuscitate him and, as they failed in their efforts, Beautrelet went to fetch a doctor. The doctor succeeded no better than they had done. The old man did not seem to be suffering. He looked as if he were just asleep, but with an artificial slumber, as though he had been put to sleep by hypnotism or with the aid of a narcotic.

In the middle of the night that followed, however, Isidore, who was watching by his side, observed that the breathing became stronger and that his whole being appeared to be throwing off the invisible bonds that paralyzed it.

At daybreak, he woke up and resumed his normal functions: ate, drank and moved about. But, the whole day long, he was unable to reply to the young man's questions and his brain seemed as though still numbed by an inexplicable torpor.

The next day, he asked Beautrelet:

'What are you doing here, eh?'

It was the first time that he had shown surprise at the presence of a stranger beside him.

Gradually, in this way, he recovered all his faculties. He talked. He made plans. But, when Beautrelet asked him about the events immediately preceding his sleep, he seemed not to understand.

And Beautrelet felt that he really did not understand. He had lost the recollection of all that had happened since the Friday before. It was like a sudden gap in the ordinary flow of his life. He described his morning and afternoon on the Friday, the purchases he had made at the fair, the meals he had taken at the inn. Then — nothing — nothing more. He believed himself to be waking on the morrow of that day.

It was horrible for Beautrelet. The truth lay there, in those eyes which had seen the walls of the park behind which his father was waiting for him, in those hands which had picked up the letter, in that muddled brain which had recorded the whereabouts of that scene, the setting, the little corner of the world in which the play had been enacted. And from those hands, from that brain he was unable to extract the faintest echo of the truth so near at hand!

Oh, that impalpable and formidable obstacle, against which all his efforts hurled themselves in vain, that obstacle built up of silence and oblivion! How clearly it bore the mark of Arsène Lupin! He alone, informed, no doubt, that M. Beautrelet had attempted to give a signal, he alone could have struck with partial death the one man whose evidence could injure him. It was not that Beautrelet felt himself to be discovered or thought that Lupin, hearing of his stealthy attack and knowing that a letter had reached him, was defending himself against him personally. But what an amount of foresight and real intelligence it displayed to suppress any possible accusation on the part of that chance wayfarer! Nobody now knew that within the walls of a park there lay a prisoner asking for help.

Nobody? Yes, Beautrelet. Gaffer Charel was unable to speak. Very well. But, at least, one could find out which fair the old man had visited and which was the logical road that he had taken to return by. And, along this road, perhaps it would at last be possible to find —

Isidore, as it was, had been careful not to visit Gaffer Charel's hovel except with the greatest precautions and in such a way as not to give an alarm. He now decided not to go back to it. He made inquiries and learnt that Friday was market-day at Fresselines, a fair-sized town situated a few leagues off, which could be reached either by the rather winding highroad or by a series of short cuts.

On the Friday, he chose the road and saw nothing that attracted his attention, no high walled enclosure, no semblance of an old castle.

He lunched at an inn at Fresselines and was on the point of leaving when he saw Gaffer Charel arrive and cross the square, wheeling his little knife-grinding barrow before him. He at once followed him at a good distance.

The old man made two interminable waits, during which he ground dozens of knives. Then, at last, he went away by a quite different road, which ran in the direction of Crozant and the market-town of Eguzon.

Beautrelet followed him along this road. But he had not walked five minutes before he received the impression that he was not alone in shadowing the old fellow. A man was walking along between them, stopping at the same time as Charel and starting off again when he did, without, for that matter, taking any great precautions against being seen.

'He is being watched,' thought Beautrelet. 'Perhaps they want to know if he stops in front of the walls — '

His heart beat violently. The event was at hand.

The three of them, one behind the other, climbed up and down the steep slopes of the country and arrived at Crozant, famed for the colossal ruins of its castle. There Charel made a halt of an hour's duration. Next he went down to the riverside and crossed the bridge.

But then a thing happened that took Beautrelet by surprise. The other man did not cross the river. He watched the old fellow move away and, when he had lost sight of him, turned down a path that took him right across the fields.

Beautrelet hesitated for a few seconds as to what course to take, and then quietly decided. He set off in pursuit of the man.

'He has made sure,' he thought, 'that Gaffer Charel has gone straight ahead. That is all he wanted to know and so he is going — where? To the castle?'

He was within touch of the goal. He felt it by a sort of agonizing gladness that uplifted his whole being.

The man plunged into a dark wood overhanging the river and then appeared once more in the full light, where the path met the horizon.

When Beautrelet, in his turn, emerged from the wood, he was greatly surprised no longer to see the man. He was seeking him with his eyes when, suddenly, he gave a stifled cry and, with a backward spring, made for the line of trees which he had just left. On his right, he had seen a rampart of high walls, flanked, at regular distances, by massive buttresses.

It was there! It was there! Those walls held his father captive! He had found the secret place where Lupin confined his victim.

He dared not quit the shelter which the thick foliage of the wood afforded him. Slowly, almost on all fours, he bore to the right and in this way reached the top of a hillock that rose to the level of the neighbouring trees. The walls were taller still. Nevertheless, he perceived the roof of the castle which they surrounded, an old Louis XIII. roof, surmounted by very slender bell-turrets arranged corbel-wise around a higher steeple which ran to a point.

Beautrelet did no more that day. He felt the need to reflect and to prepare his plan of attack without leaving anything to chance. He held Lupin safe; and it was for Beautrelet now to select the hour and the manner of the combat.

He walked away.

Near the bridge, he met two country-girls carrying pails of milk. He asked:

'What is the name of the castle over there, behind the trees?'

'That's the Chateau de l'Aiguille, sir.'

He had put his question without attaching any importance to it. The answer took away his breath:

'The Chateau de l'Aiguille? — Oh! — But in what department are we? The Indre?'

'Certainly not. The Indre is on the other side of the river. This side, it's the Creuse.'

Isidore saw it all in a flash. The Chateau de l'Aiguille! The department of the Creuse! *L'Aiguille Creuse*! The Hollow Needle! The very key to the document! Certain, decisive, absolute victory!

Without another word, he turned his back on the two girls and went his way, tottering like a drunken man.

6

An Historic Secret

Beautrelet's resolve was soon taken: he would act alone. To inform the police was too dangerous. Apart from the fact that he could only offer presumptions, he dreaded the slowness of the police, their inevitable indiscretions, the whole preliminary inquiry, during which Lupin, who was sure to be warned, would have time to effect a retreat in good order.

At eight o'clock the next morning, with his bundle under his arm, he left the inn in which he was staying near Cuzion, made for the nearest thicket, took off his workman's clothes, became once more the young English painter that he had been and went to call on the notary at Eguzon, the largest place in the immediate neighbourhood.

He said that he liked the country and that he was thinking of taking up his residence there, with his relations, if he could find a suitable house.

The notary mentioned a number of properties. Beautrelet took note of them and let fall that some one had spoken to him of the Chateau de l'Aiguille, on the bank of the Creuse.

'Oh, yes, but the Chateau de l'Aiguille, which has belonged to one of my clients for the last five years, is not for sale.'

'He lives in it, then?'

'He used to live in it, or rather his mother did. But she did not care for it; found the castle rather gloomy. So they left it last year.'

'And is no one living there at present?'

'Yes, an Italian, to whom my client let it for the summer season: Baron Anfredi.'

'Oh, Baron Anfredi! A man still young, rather grave and solemn-looking — ?'

'I'm sure I can't say. — My client dealt with him direct. There was no regular agreement, just a letter — '

'But you know the baron?'

'No, he never leaves the castle. — Sometimes, in his motor, at night, so they say. The marketing is done by an old cook, who talks to nobody. They are queer people — '

'Do you think your client would consent to sell his castle?'

'I don't think so. It's an historic castle, built in the purest Louis XIII. style. My client was very fond of it; and, unless he has changed his mind — '

'Can you give me his name and address?'

175

'Louis Valmeras, 34, Rue du Mont-Thabor.'

Beautrelet took the train for Paris at the nearest station. On the next day but one, after three fruitless calls, he at last found Louis Valmeras at home. He was a man of about thirty, with a frank and pleasing face. Beautrelet saw no need to beat about the bush, stated who he was and described his efforts and the object of the step which he was now taking:

'I have good reason to believe,' he concluded, 'that my father is imprisoned in the Chateau de l'Aiguille, doubtless in the company of other victims. And I have come to ask you what you know of your tenant, Baron Anfredi.'

'Not much. I met Baron Anfredi last winter at Monte Carlo. He had heard by accident that I was the owner of the Chateau de l'Aiguille and, as he wished to spend the summer in France, he made me an offer for it.'

'He is still a young man — '

'Yes, with very expressive eyes, fair hair — '

'And a beard?'

'Yes, ending in two points, which fall over a collar fastened at the back, like a clergyman's. In fact, he looks a little like an English parson.'

'It's he,' murmured Beautrelet, 'it's he, as I have seen him: it's his exact description.'

'What! Do you think — ?'

'I think, I am sure that your tenant is none other than Arsène Lupin.'

The story amused Louis Valmeras. He knew all the adventures of Arsène Lupin and the varying fortunes of his struggle with Beautrelet. He rubbed his hands:

'Ha, the Chateau de l'Aiguille will become famous! — I'm sure I don't mind, for, as a matter of fact, now that my mother no longer lives in it, I have always thought that I would get rid of it at the first opportunity. After this, I shall soon find a purchaser. Only — '

'Only what?'

'I will ask you to act with the most extreme prudence and not to inform the police until you are quite sure. Can you picture the situation, supposing my tenant were not Arsène Lupin?'

Beautrelet set forth his plan. He would go alone at night; he would climb the walls; he would sleep in the park —

Louis Valmeras stopped him at once:

'You will not climb walls of that height so easily. If you do, you will be received by two huge sheep-dogs which belonged to my mother and which I left behind at the castle.'

'Pooh! A dose of poison — '

'Much obliged. But suppose you escaped them. What then? How would you get into the castle? The doors are massive, the windows barred. And, even then, once you were inside, who would guide you? There are eighty rooms.'

'Yes, but that room with two windows, on the second story — '

'I know it, we call it the glycine room. But how will you find it? There are three staircases and a labyrinth of passages. I can give you the clue and explain the way to you, but you would get lost just the same.'

'Come with me,' said Beautrelet, laughing.

'I can't. I have promised to go to my mother in the South.'

Beautrelet returned to the friend with whom he was staying and began to make his preparations. But, late in the day, as he was getting ready to go, he received a visit from Valmeras.

'Do you still want me?'

'Rather!'

'Well, I'm coming with you. Yes, the expedition fascinates me. I think it will be very amusing and I like being mixed up in this sort of thing. — Besides, my help will be of use to you. Look, here's something to start with.'

He held up a big key, all covered with rust

and looking very old.

'What does the key open?' asked Beautrelet.

'A little postern hidden between two buttresses and left unused since centuries ago. I did not even think of pointing it out to my tenant. It opens straight on the country, just at the verge of the wood.'

Beautrelet interrupted him quickly:

'They know all about that outlet. It was obviously by this way that the man whom I followed entered the park. Come, it's fine game and we shall win it. But, by Jupiter, we must play our cards carefully!'

★   ★   ★

Two days later, a half-famished horse dragged a gipsy caravan into Crozant. Its driver obtained leave to stable it at the end of the village, in an old deserted cart-shed. In addition to the driver, who was none other than Valmeras, there were three young men, who occupied themselves in the manufacture of wicker-work chairs: Beautrelet and two of his Janson friends.

They stayed there for three days, waiting for a propitious, moonless night and roaming singly round the outskirts of the park. Once Beautrelet saw the postern. Contrived between two buttresses placed very close together, it was almost merged, behind the screen of brambles that concealed it, in the pattern formed by the stones of the wall.

At last, on the fourth evening, the sky was covered with heavy black clouds and Valmeras decided that they should go reconnoitring, at the risk of having to return again, should circumstances prove unfavourable.

All four crossed the little wood. Then Beautrelet crept through the heather, scratched his hands at the bramble-hedge and, half raising himself, slowly, with restrained movements, put the key into the lock. He turned it gently. Would the door open without an effort? Was there no bolt closing it on the other side? He pushed: the door opened, without a creak or jolt. He was in the park.

'Are you there, Beautrelet?' asked Valmeras. 'Wait for me. You two chaps, watch the door and keep our line of retreat open. At the least alarm, whistle.'

He took Beautrelet's hand and they plunged into the dense shadow of the thickets. A clearer space was revealed to them when they reached the edge of the central lawn. At the same moment a ray of moonlight pierced the clouds; and they saw the castle, with its pointed turrets arranged around the tapering spire to which, no doubt, it owed its name. There was no light in the windows; not a sound.

Valmeras grasped his companion's arm:

'Keep still!'

'What is it?'

'The dogs, over there — look — '

There was a growl. Valmeras gave a low whistle. Two white forms leapt forward and, in four bounds, came and crouched at their master's feet.

'Gently — lie down — that's it — good dogs — stay there.'

And he said to Beautrelet:

'And now let us push on. I feel more comfortable.'

'Are you sure of the way?'

'Yes. We are near the terrace.'

'And then?'

'I remember that, on the left, at a place where the river terrace rises to the level of the ground-floor windows, there is a shutter which closes badly and which can be opened from the outside.'

They found, when they came to it, that the shutter yielded to pressure. Valmeras removed a pane with a diamond which he carried. He turned the window-latch. First one and then the other stepped over the balcony. They were now in the castle, at the end of a passage which divided the left wing into two.

'This room,' said Valmeras, 'opens at the end of a passage. Then comes an immense hall, lined with statues, and at the end of the hall a staircase which ends near the room occupied by your father.'

He took a step forward.

'Are you coming, Beautrelet?'

'Yes, yes.'

'But no, you're not coming — What's the matter with you?'

He seized him by the hand. It was icy cold and he perceived that the young man was cowering on the floor.

'What's the matter with you?' he repeated.

'Nothing — it'll pass off — '

'But what is it?'

'I'm afraid — '

'You're afraid?'

'Yes,' Beautrelet confessed, frankly, 'it's my nerves giving way — I generally manage to control them — but, to-day, the silence — the excitement — And then, since I was stabbed by that magistrate's clerk — But it will pass off — There, it's passing now — '

He succeeded in rising to his feet and Valmeras dragged him out of the room. They groped their way along the passage, so softly that neither could hear a sound made by the other.

A faint glimmer, however, seemed to light the hall for which they were making. Valmeras put his head round the corner. It was a night-light placed at the foot of the stairs, on a little table which showed through the frail branches of a palm tree.

'Halt!' whispered Valmeras.

Near the night-light, a man stood sentry, carrying a gun.

Had he seen them? Perhaps. At least, something must have alarmed him, for he brought the gun to his shoulder.

Beautrelet had fallen on his knees, against a tub containing a plant, and he remained quite still, with his heart thumping against his chest.

Meanwhile, the silence and the absence of all movement reassured the man. He lowered his weapon. But his head was still turned in the direction of the tub.

Terrible minutes passed: ten minutes, fifteen. A moonbeam had glided through a window on the staircase. And, suddenly, Beautrelet became aware that the moonbeam was shifting imperceptibly, and that, before fifteen, before ten more minutes had elapsed, it would be shining full in his face.

Great drops of perspiration fell from his forehead on his trembling hands. His anguish was such that he was on the point of getting up and running away — But, remembering that Valmeras was there, he sought him with his eyes and was astounded to see him, or rather to imagine him, creeping in the dark, under cover of the statues and plants. He was already at the foot of the stairs, within a few steps of the man.

What was he going to do? To pass in spite of all? To go upstairs alone and release the prisoner? But could he pass?

Beautrelet no longer saw him and he had an impression that something was about to take place, something that seemed foreboded also by the silence, which hung heavier, more awful than before.

And, suddenly, a shadow springing upon the man, the night-light extinguished, the sound of a struggle — Beautrelet ran up. The two bodies had rolled over on the flagstones. He tried to stoop and see. But he heard a hoarse moan, a sigh; and one of the adversaries rose to his feet and seized him by the arm:

'Quick! — Come along!'

It was Valmeras.

They went up two stories and came out at the entrance to a corridor, covered by a hanging.

'To the right,' whispered Valmeras. 'The fourth room on the left.'

They soon found the door of the room. As they expected, the captive was locked in. It took them half an hour, half an hour of stifled efforts, of muffled attempts, to force open the lock. The door yielded at last.

Beautrelet groped his way to the bed. His father was asleep.

He woke him gently:

'It's I — Isidore — and a friend — don't be afraid — get up — not a word.'

The father dressed himself, but, as they were leaving the room, he whispered:

'I am not alone in the castle — '

'Ah? Who else? Ganimard? Shears?'

'No — at least, I have not seen them.'

'Who then?'

'A young girl.'

'Mlle. de Saint-Veran, no doubt.'

'I don't know — I saw her several times at a distance, in the park — and, when I lean out of my window, I can see hers. She has made signals to me.'

'Do you know which is her room?'

'Yes, in this passage, the third on the right.'

'The blue room,' murmured Valmeras. 'It has folding doors: they won't give us so much trouble.'

One of the two leaves very soon gave way. Old Beautrelet undertook to tell the girl.

Ten minutes later, he left the room with her and said to his son:

'You were right — Mlle. de Saint-Veran — ;'

They all four went down the stairs. When

they reached the bottom, Valmeras stopped and bent over the man. Then, leading them to the terrace-room:

'He is not dead,' he said. 'He will live.'

'Ah!' said Beautrelet, with a sigh of relief.

'No, fortunately, the blade of my knife bent: the blow is not fatal. Besides, in any case, those rascals deserve no pity.'

Outside, they were met by the dogs, which accompanied them to the postern. Here, Beautrelet found his two friends and the little band left the park. It was three o'clock in the morning.

★   ★   ★

This first victory was not enough to satisfy Beautrelet. As soon as he had comfortably settled his father and Mlle. de Saint-Veran, he asked them about the people who lived at the castle, and, particularly, about the habits of Arsène Lupin. He thus learnt that Lupin came only every three or four days, arriving at night in his motor car and leaving again in the morning. At each of his visits, he called separately upon his two prisoners, both of whom agreed in praising his courtesy and his extreme civility. For the moment, he was not at the castle.

Apart from him, they had seen no one

186

except an old woman, who ruled over the kitchen and the house, and two men, who kept watch over them by turns and never spoke to them: subordinates, obviously, to judge by their manners and appearance.

'Two accomplices, for all that,' said Beautrelet, in conclusion, 'or rather three, with the old woman. It is a bag worth having. And, if we lose no time — '

He jumped on his bicycle, rode to Eguzon, woke up the gendarmerie, set them all going, made them sound the boot and saddle and returned to Crozant at eight o'clock, accompanied by the sergeant and eight gendarmes. Two of the men were posted beside the gipsy-van. Two others took up their positions outside the postern-door. The last four, commanded by their chief and accompanied by Beautrelet and Valmeras, marched to the main entrance of the castle.

Too late. The door was wide open. A peasant told them that he had seen a motor car drive out of the castle an hour before.

Indeed, the search led to no result. In all probability, the gang had installed themselves there picnic fashion. A few clothes were found, a little linen, some household implements; and that was all.

What astonished Beautrelet and Valmeras more was the disappearance of the wounded man. They could not see the faintest trace of a struggle, not even a drop of blood on the flagstones of the hall.

All said, there was no material evidence to prove the fleeting presence of Lupin at the Chateau de l'Aiguille; and the authorities would have been entitled to challenge the statements of Beautrelet and his father, of Valmeras and Mlle. de Saint-Veran, had they not ended by discovering, in a room next to that occupied by the young girl, some half-dozen exquisite bouquets with Arsène Lupin's card pinned to them, bouquets scorned by her, faded and forgotten — One of them, in addition to the card, contained a letter which Raymonde had not seen. That afternoon, when opened by the examining magistrate, it was found to contain page upon page of prayers, entreaties, promises, threats, despair, all the madness of a love that has encountered nothing but contempt and repulsion.

And the letter ended:

I shall come on Tuesday evening, Raymonde. Reflect between now and then. As for me, I will wait no longer. I am resolved on all.

Tuesday evening was the evening of the very day on which Beautrelet had released Mlle.

de Saint-Veran from her captivity.

The reader will remember the extraordinary explosion of surprise and enthusiasm that resounded throughout the world at the news of that unexpected issue: Mlle. de Saint-Veran free! The pretty girl whom Lupin coveted, to secure whom he had contrived his most Machiavellian schemes, snatched from his claws! Free also Beautrelet's father, whom Lupin had chosen as a hostage in his extravagant longing for the armistice demanded by the needs of his passion! They were both free, the two prisoners! And the secret of the Hollow Needle was known, published, flung to the four corners of the world!

The crowd amused itself with a will. Ballads were sold and sung about the defeated adventurer: *Lupin's Little Love-Affairs!* — *Arsène's Piteous Sobs!* — *The Lovesick Burglar!* — *The Pickpocket's Lament!* — They were cried on the boulevards and hummed in the artists' studios.

Raymonde, pressed with questions and pursued by interviewers, replied with the most extreme reserve. But there was no denying the letter, or the bouquets of flowers, or any part of the pitiful story! Then and there, Lupin, scoffed and jeered at, toppled from his pedestal.

And Beautrelet became the popular idol.

He had foretold everything, thrown light on everything. The evidence which Mlle. de Saint-Veran gave before the examining magistrate confirmed, down to the smallest detail, the hypothesis imagined by Isidore. Reality seemed to submit, in every point, to what he had decreed beforehand. Lupin had found his master.

★   ★   ★

Beautrelet insisted that his father, before returning to his mountains in Savoy, should take a few months' rest in the sunshine, and himself escorted him and Mlle. de Saint-Veran to the outskirts of Nice, where the Comte de Gesvres and his daughter Suzanne were already settled for the winter. Two days later, Valmeras brought his mother to see his new friends and they thus composed a little colony grouped around the Villa de Gesvres and watched over day and night by half a dozen men engaged by the comte.

Early in October, Beautrelet, once more the sixth-form pupil, returned to Paris to resume the interrupted course of his studies and to prepare for his examinations. And life began again, calmer, this time, and free from incident. What could happen, for that matter. Was the war not over?

Lupin, on his side, must have felt this very

clearly, must have felt that there was nothing left for him but to resign himself to the accomplished fact; for, one fine day, his two other victims, Ganimard and Holmlock Shears, made their reappearance. Their return to the life of this planet, however, was devoid of any sort of glamor or fascination. An itinerant ragman picked them up on the Quai des Orfevres, opposite the headquarters of police. Both of them were gagged, bound and fast asleep.

After a week of complete bewilderment, they succeeded in recovering the control of their thought and told — or rather Ganimard told, for Shears wrapped himself in a fierce and stubborn silence — how they had made a voyage of circumnavigation round the coast of Africa on board the yacht *Hirondelle*, a voyage combining amusement with instruction, during which they could look upon themselves as free, save for a few hours which they spent at the bottom of the hold, while the crew went on shore at outlandish ports.

As for their landing on the Quai des Orfevres, they remembered nothing about it and had probably been asleep for many days before.

This liberation of the prisoners was the final confession of defeat. By ceasing to fight, Lupin admitted it without reserve.

One incident, moreover, made it still more glaring, which was the engagement of Louis Valmeras and Mlle. de Saint-Veran. In the intimacy created between them by the new conditions under which they lived, the two young people fell in love with each other. Valmeras loved Raymonde's melancholy charm; and she, wounded by life, greedy for protection, yielded before the strength and energy of the man who had contributed so gallantly to her preservation.

The wedding day was awaited with a certain amount of anxiety. Would Lupin not try to resume the offensive? Would he accept with a good grace the irretrievable loss of the woman he loved? Twice or three times, suspicious-looking people were seen prowling round the villa; and Valmeras even had to defend himself one evening against a so-called drunken man, who fired a pistol at him and sent a bullet through his hat. But, in the end, the ceremony was performed at the appointed hour and day and Raymonde de Saint-Veran became Mme. Louis Valmeras.

It was as though Fate herself had taken sides with Beautrelet and countersigned the news of victory. This was so apparent to the crowd that his admirers now conceived the notion of entertaining him at a banquet to celebrate his triumph and Lupin's overthrow. It was a great idea and aroused general enthusiasm. Three hundred tickets were sold in less than a fortnight. Invitations were issued to the public schools of Paris, to send two sixth-form pupils apiece. The press sang paeans. The banquet was what it could not fail to be, an apotheosis.

But it was a charming and simple apotheosis, because Beautrelet was its hero. His presence was enough to bring things back to their due proportion. He showed himself modest, as usual, a little surprised at the excessive cheering, a little embarrassed by the extravagant panegyrics in which he was pronounced greater than the most illustrious detectives — a little embarrassed, but also not a little touched.

He said as much in a few words that pleased all his hearers and with the shyness of a child that blushes when you look at it. He spoke of his delight, of his pride. And really, reasonable and self-controlled as he was, this was for him a moment of never-to-be-forgotten exultation. He smiled to his friends, to his fellow-Jansonians, to Valmeras, who had come specially to give him a cheer, to M. de Gesvres, to his father.

When he had finished speaking; and while he still held his glass in his hand, a sound of voices came from the other end of the room and some one was gesticulating and waving a newspaper. Silence was restored and the importunate person sat down again: but a thrill of curiosity ran round the table, the newspaper was passed from hand to hand and, each, time that one of the guests cast his eyes upon the page at which it was opened, exclamations followed:

'Read it! Read it!' they cried from the opposite side.

The people were leaving their seats at the principal table. M. Beautrelet went and took the paper and handed it to his son.

'Read it out! Read it out!' they cried, louder.

And others said:

'Listen! He's going to read it! Listen!'

Beautrelet stood facing his audience, looked in the evening paper which his father had given him for the article that was causing all this uproar and, suddenly, his eyes encountering a heading underlined in blue pencil, he raised his hand to call for silence and began in a loud voice to read a letter addressed to the editor by M. Massiban, of the Academy of Inscriptions and Belles-Lettres. His voice broke and fell, little by little, as he read those stupefying revelations, which reduced all his efforts to nothing, upset his notions concerning the Hollow Needle and proved the vanity of his struggle with Arsène Lupin:

SIR:

On the 17th of March, 1679, there appeared a little book with the following title: *The Mystery of the Hollow Needle. The Whole Truth now first exhibited. One hundred copies printed by myself for the instruction of the Court.*

At nine o'clock on the morning of that day, the author, a very young man, well-dressed, whose name has remained unknown, began to leave his book on the principal persons at court. At ten o'clock, when he had fulfilled four of these errands, he was arrested by a captain in the guards, who took him to the king's closet and forthwith set off in search of the four copies distributed.

When the hundred copies were got together, counted, carefully looked through and verified, the king himself threw them into the fire and burnt them, all but one, which he kept for his own purposes.

Then he ordered the captain of the guards to take the author of the book to M. de Saint-Mars, who confined his prisoner first at Pignerol and then in the fortress of the Ile Sainte-Marguerite. This man was obviously no other than the famous Man with the Iron Mask.

The truth would never have been known, or at least a part of the truth, if the captain in the guards had not been present at the interview and if, when the king's back was turned, he had not been tempted to withdraw another of the copies from the chimney, before the fire got to it.

Six months later, the captain was found dead on the highroad between Gaillon and Mantes. His murderers had stripped him of all his apparel, forgetting, however, in his right boot a jewel which was discovered there afterward, a diamond of the first water and of considerable value.

Among his papers was found a sheet in his handwriting, in which he did not speak of the book snatched from the flames, but gave a summary of the earlier chapters. It referred to a secret which was known to the Kings of England, which was lost by them when the crown passed from the poor fool, Henry VI., to the Duke of York, which was revealed to Charles VII., King of France, by Joan of Arc and which, becoming a State secret, was handed down from sovereign to sovereign by means of a letter, sealed anew on each occasion, which was found in the deceased monarch's death-bed with this superscription: 'For the King of France.'

This secret concerned the existence and described the whereabouts of a tremendous treasure, belonging to the kings, which increased in dimensions from century to century.

One hundred and fourteen years later, Louis XVI., then a prisoner in the Temple, took aside one of the officers whose duty it was to guard the royal family, and asked:

'Monsieur, had you not an ancestor who served as a captain under my predecessor, the Great King?'

'Yes, sire.'

'Well, could you be relied upon — could you be relied upon — '

He hesitated. The officer completed the sentence:

'Not to betray your Majesty! Oh, sire! — '

'Then listen to me.'

He took from his pocket a little book of which he tore out one of the last pages. But, altering his mind:

'No, I had better copy it — '

He seized a large sheet of paper and tore it in such a way as to leave only a small rectangular space, on which he copied five lines of dots, letters and figures from the printed page. Then, after burning the latter, he folded the manuscript sheet in four, sealed it with red wax, and gave it to the officer.

'Monsieur, after my death, you must hand this to the Queen and say to her, 'From the King, madame — for Your Majesty and for your son.' If she does not understand —

'If she does not understand, sire —

'You must add, 'It concerns the secret, the secret of the Needle.' The Queen will understand.'

When he had finished speaking, he flung the book into the embers glowing on the hearth.

He ascended the scaffold on the 21st of January.

It took the officer several months, in consequence of the removal of the Queen to the Conciergerie, before he could fulfil the mission with which he was entrusted. At last, by dint of cunning intrigues, he succeeded, one day, in finding himself in the presence of Marie Antoinette.

Speaking so that she could just hear him, he said:

'Madame, from the late King, your

husband, for Your Majesty and your son.'

And he gave her the sealed letter.

She satisfied herself that the jailers could not see her, broke the seals, appeared surprised at the sight of those undecipherable lines and then, all at once, seemed to understand.

She smiled bitterly and the officer caught the words:

'Why so late?'

She hesitated. Where should she hide this dangerous document? At last, she opened her book of hours and slipped the paper into a sort of secret pocket contrived between the leather of the binding and the parchment that covered it.

'Why so late?' she had asked.

It is, in fact, probable that this document, if it could have saved her, came too late, for, in the month of October next, Queen Marie Antoinette ascended the scaffold in her turn.

Now the officer, when going through his family papers, came upon his ancestor's manuscript. From that moment, he had but one idea, which was to devote his leisure to elucidating this strange problem. He read all the Latin authors, studied all the chronicles of France and those of the neighbouring countries, visited the monasteries, deciphered account-books, cartularies, treaties; and, in this way, succeeded in discovering certain references scattered over the ages.

In Book III of Caesar's *Commentaries on the Gallic War* (MS. edition, Alexandria), it is stated that, after the defeat of Veridovix by G. Titullius Sabinus, the chief of the Caleti was brought before Caesar and that, for his ransom, he revealed the secret of the Needle —

The Treaty of Saint-Clair-sur-Epte, between Charles the Simple and Rollo, the chief of the Norse barbarians, gives Rollo's name followed by all his titles, among which we read that of Master of the Secret of the Needle.

The *Saxon Chronicle* (Gibson's edition, page 134), speaking of William the Conqueror, says that the staff of his banner ended in a steel point pierced with an eye, like a needle.

In a rather ambiguous phrase in her examination, Joan of Arc admits that she has still a great secret to tell the King of France. To which her judges reply, 'Yes, we know of what you speak; and that, Joan, is why you shall die the death.'

Philippe de Comines mentions it in

connection with Louis XI., and, later, Sully in connection with Henry IV.: 'By the virtue of the Needle!' the good king sometimes swears.

Between these two, Francis I., in a speech addressed to the notables of the Havre, in 1520, uttered this phrase, which has been handed down in the diary of a Honfleur burgess; 'The Kings of France carry secrets that often decide the conduct of affairs and the fate of towns.'

All these quotations, all the stories relating to the Iron Mask, the captain of the guards and his descendant, I have found to-day in a pamphlet written by this same descendant and published in the month of June, 1815, just before or just after the battle of Waterloo, in a period, therefore, of great upheavals, in which the revelations which it contained were likely to pass unperceived.

What is the value of this pamphlet? Nothing, you will tell me, and we must attach no credit to it. And this is the impression which I myself would have carried away, if it had not occurred to me to open Caesar's *Commentaries* at the chapter given. What was my astonishment when I came upon the phrase quoted in the little book before me! And it was the same thing with the Treaty of Saint-Clair-sur-Epte, with the *Saxon Chronicle*, with the examination of Joan of Arc, in short, with all that I have been able to verify up to the present.

Lastly, there is an even more precise fact related by the author of the pamphlet of 1815. During the French campaign, he being then an officer under Napoleon, his horse dropped dead, one evening, and he rang at the door of a castle where he was received by an old knight of St. Louis. And, in the course of conversation with the old man, he learnt that this castle, standing on the bank of the Creuse, was called the Chateau de l'Aiguille, that it had been built and christened by Louis XIV., and that, by his express order, it was adorned with turrets and with a spire which represented the Needle. As its date it bore, it must still bear, the figure 1680.

1680! One year after the publication of the book and the imprisonment of the Iron Mask! Everything was now explained: Louis XIV., foreseeing that the secret might be noised abroad, had built and named that castle so as to offer the quidnuncs a natural explanation of the ancient mystery. The Hollow Needle! A castle with pointed bell-turrets standing on the bank of the Creuse and belonging to the King. People would at once think that they had the key to the riddle and all enquiries would cease.

The calculation was just, seeing that, more than two centuries later, M. Beautrelet fell into the trap. And this, Sir, is what I was leading up to in writing this letter. If Lupin, under the name of Anfredi, rented from M. Valmeras the Chateau de l'Aiguille on the bank of the Creuse; if, admitting the success of the inevitable investigations of M. Beautrelet, he lodged his two prisoners there, it was because he admitted the success of the inevitable researches made by M. Beautrelet and because, with the object of obtaining the peace for which he had asked, he laid for M. Beautrelet precisely what we may call the historic trap of Louis XIV.

And hence we come to this undeniable conclusion, that he, Lupin, by his unaided lights, without possessing any other facts than those which we possess, managed by means of the witchcraft of a really extraordinary genius, to decipher the undecipherable document; and that he, Lupin, the last heir of the Kings of

France, knows the royal mystery of the Hollow Needle!

Here ended the letter. But, for some minutes, from the passage that referred to the Chateau de l'Aiguille onward, it was not Beautrelet's but another voice that read it aloud. Realizing his defeat, crushed under the weight of his humiliation, Isidore had dropped the newspaper and sunk into his chair, with his face buried in his hands.

Panting, shaken with excitement by this incredible story, the crowd had come gradually nearer and was now pressing round.

With a thrill of anguish, they waited for the words which he would say in reply, the objections which he would raise.

He did not stir.

Valmeras gently uncrossed his hands and raised his head.

Isidore Beautrelet was weeping.

7

The Treatise of the Needle

It is four o'clock in the morning. Isidore has not returned to the Lycee Janson. He has no intention of returning before the end of the war of extermination which he has declared against Lupin. This much he swore to himself under his breath, while his friends drove off with him, all faint and bruised, in a cab.

A mad oath! An absurd and illogical war! What can he do, a single, unarmed stripling, against that phenomenon of energy and strength? On which side is he to attack him? He is unassailable. Where to wound him? He is invulnerable. Where to get at him? He is inaccessible.

Four o'clock in the morning. Isidore has again accepted his schoolfellow's hospitality. Standing before the chimney in his bedroom, with his elbows flat on the mantel-shelf and his two fists under his chin, he stares at his image in the looking-glass. He is not crying now, he can shed no more tears, nor fling himself about on his bed, nor give way to despair, as he has been doing for the last two hours and more. He wants to think, to think and understand.

And he does not remove his eyes from those same eyes reflected in the glass, as though he hoped to double his powers of thought by contemplating his pensive image, as though he hoped to find at the back of that mirrored Beautrelet the unsolvable solution of what he does not find within himself.

He stands thus until six o'clock, and, little by little, the question presents itself to his mind with the strictness of an equation, bare and dry and cleared of all the details that complicate and obscure it.

Yes, he has made a mistake. Yes, his reading of the document is all wrong. The word *aiguille* does not point to the castle on the Creuse. Also, the word *demoiselles* cannot be applied to Raymonde de Saint-Veran and her cousin, because the text of the document dates back for centuries.

Therefore, all must be done over again, from the beginning.

How?

One piece of evidence alone would be incontestable: the book published under Louis XIV. Now of those hundred copies printed by the person who was presumed to be the Man with the Iron Mask only two escaped the flames. One was purloined by the captain of the guards and lost. The other was kept by Louis XIV., handed down to Louis XV., and burnt by Louis XVI. But a copy of the essential page, the page containing the solution of the problem, or at least a cryptographic solution, was conveyed to Marie Antoinette, who slipped it into the binding of her book of hours. What has become of this paper? Is it the one which Beautrelet has held in his hands and which Lupin recovered from him through Bredoux, the magistrate's clerk? Or is it still in Marie Antoinette's book of hours? And the question resolves itself into this: what has become of the Queen's book of hours?

$$\star \quad \star \quad \star$$

After taking a short rest, Beautrelet consulted his friend's father, an old and experienced collector, who was often called upon officially to give an expert opinion and who had quite lately been invited to advise the director of one of our museums on the drawing up of the catalogue.

'Marie Antoinette's book of hours?' he exclaimed. 'Why, the Queen left it to her waiting-woman, with secret instructions to forward it to Count Fersen. After being piously preserved in the count's family, it has been, for the last five years, in a glass case — '

'A glass case?'

'In the Musee Carnavalet, quite simply.'

'When will the museum be open?'

'At twenty minutes from now, as it is every morning.'

* * *

Isidore and his friend jumped out of a cab at the moment when the doors of Madame de Sevigne's old mansion were opening.

'Hullo! M. Beautrelet!'

A dozen voices greeted his arrival. To his great surprise, he recognized the whole crowd of reporters who were following up 'the mystery of the Hollow Needle.' And one of them exclaimed:

'Funny, isn't it, that we should all have had the same idea? Take care, Arsène Lupin may be among us!'

They entered the museum together. The director was at once informed, placed himself entirely at their disposal, took them to the glass case and skewed them a poor little volume, devoid of all ornament, which certainly had nothing royal about it. Nevertheless, they were overcome by a certain emotion at the sight of this object which the Queen had touched in those tragic days, which her eyes, red with tears, had looked upon — And they dared not take it and hunt through it: it was as though they feared lest they should be guilty of a sacrilege —

'Come, M. Beautrelet, it's your business!'

He took the book with an anxious gesture. The description corresponded with that given by the author of the pamphlet. Outside was a parchment cover, dirty, stained and worn in places, and under it, the real binding, in stiff leather. With what a thrill Beautrelet felt for the hidden pocket! Was it a fairy tale? Or would he find the document written by Louis XVI. and bequeathed by the queen to her fervent admirer?

At the first page, on the upper side of the book, there was no receptacle.

'Nothing,' he muttered.

'Nothing,' they echoed, palpitating with excitement.

But, at the last page, forcing back the book a little, he at once saw that the parchment was not stuck to the binding. He slipped his fingers in between — there was something — yes, he felt something — a paper —

'Oh!' he gasped, in an accent almost of pain. 'Here — is it possible?'

'Quick, quick!' they cried. 'What are you waiting for?'

He drew out a sheet folded in two.

'Well, read it! — There are words in red ink — Look! — it might be blood — pale, faded blood — Read it! — '

He read:

To you, Fersen. For my son.
16 October, 1793.
MARIE ANTOINETTE.

And suddenly Beautrelet gave a cry of stupefaction. Under the queen's signature there were — there were two words, in black ink, underlined with a flourish — two words:

ARSÈNE LUPIN.

All, in turns, took the sheet of paper and the same cry escaped from the lips of all of them: 'Marie Antoinette! — Arsène Lupin!'

A great silence followed. That double signature: those two names coupled together, discovered hidden in the book of hours; that relic in which the poor queen's desperate appeal had slumbered for more than a century: that horrible date of the 16th of October, 1793, the day on which the Royal head fell: all of this was most dismally and disconcertingly tragic.

'Arsène Lupin!' stammered one of the voices, thus emphasizing the scare that underlay the sight of that demoniacal name at the foot of the hallowed page.

'Yes, Arsène Lupin,' repeated Beautrelet. 'The Queen's friend was unable to understand her desperate dying appeal. He lived with the keepsake in his possession which the woman whom he loved had sent him and he never guessed the reason of that keepsake. Lupin discovered everything, on the other hand — and took it.'

'Took what?'

'The document, of course! The document written by Louis XVI.; and it is that which I held in my hands. The same appearance, the same shape, the same red seals. I understand why Lupin would not leave me a document which I could turn to account by merely examining the paper, the seals and so on.'

'And then?'

'Well, then, since the document is genuine, since I have, with my own eyes, seen the marks of the red seals, since Marie Antoinette herself assures me, by these few words in her hand, that the whole story of the pamphlet, as printed by M. Massiban, is correct, because a problem of the Hollow Needle really exists, I am now certain to succeed.'

'But how? Whether genuine or not, the document is of no use to you if you do not manage to decipher it, because Louis XVI.

destroyed the book that gave the explanation.'

'Yes, but the other copy, which King Louis XVI.'s captain of the guards snatched from the flames, was not destroyed.'

'How do you know?'

'Prove the contrary.'

After uttering this defiance, Beautrelet was silent for a time and then, slowly, with his eyes closed, as though trying to fix and sum up his thoughts, he said:

'Possessing the secret, the captain of the guards begins by revealing it bit by bit in the journal found by his descendant. Then comes silence. The answer to the riddle is withheld. Why? Because the temptation to make use of the secret creeps over him little by little and he gives way to it. A proof? His murder. A further proof? The magnificent jewel found upon him, which he must undoubtedly have taken from some royal treasure the hiding-place of which, unknown to all, would just constitute the mystery of the Hollow Needle. Lupin conveyed as much to me; Lupin was not lying.'

'Then what conclusion do you draw, Beautrelet?'

'I draw this conclusion, my friends, that it be a good thing to advertise this story as much as possible, so that people may know, through all the papers, that we are looking for a book entitled *The Treatise of the Needle*. It may be fished out from the back shelves of some provincial library.'

The paragraph was drawn up forthwith; and Beautrelet set to work at once, without even waiting for it to produce a result. A first scent suggested itself: the murder was committed near Gaillon. He went there that same day. Certainly, he did not hope to reconstruct a crime perpetrated two hundred years ago. But, all the same, there are crimes that leave traces in the memories, in the traditions of a countryside. They are recorded in the local chronicles. One day, some provincial archaeologist, some lover of old legends, some student of the minor incidents of the life of the past makes them the subject of an article in a newspaper or of a communication to the academy of his departmental town.

Beautrelet saw three or four of these archaeologists. With one of them in particular, an old notary, he examined the prison records, the ledgers of the old bailiwicks and the parish registers. There was no entry referring to the murder of a captain of the guards in the seventeenth century.

He refused to be discouraged and continued his search in Paris, where the magistrate's examination might have taken place. His efforts came to nothing.

But the thought of another track sent him off in a fresh direction. Was there no chance of finding out the name of that captain whose descendant served in the armies of the Republic and was quartered in the Temple during the imprisonment of the Royal family? By dint of patient working, he ended by making out a list in which two names at least presented an almost complete resemblance: M. de Larbeyrie, under Louis XIV., and Citizen Larbrie, under the Terror.

This already was an important point. He stated it with precision in a note which he sent to the papers, asking for any information concerning this Larbeyrie or his descendants.

It was M. Massiban, the Massiban of the pamphlet, the member of the Institute, who replied to him:

SIR:

Allow me to call your attention to the following passage of Voltaire, which I came upon in his manuscript of *Le Siecle de Louis XIV.* (Chapter XXV: *Particularites et anecdotes du régne*). The passage has been suppressed in all the printed editions:

'I have heard it said by the late M. de Caumartin, intendant of finance, who was a friend of Chamillard the minister, that the King one day left hurriedly in his carriage at the news that M. de Larbeyrie had been murdered and robbed of some magnificent jewels. He seemed greatly excited and repeated:

''All is lost — all is lost — '

'In the following year, the son of this Larbeyrie and his daughter, who had married the Marquis de Velines, were banished to their estates in Provence and Brittany. We cannot doubt that there is something peculiar in this.'

I, in my turn, will add that we can doubt it all the less inasmuch as M. de Chamillard, according to Voltaire, *was the last minister who possessed the strange secret of the Iron Mask.*

You will see for yourself, Sir, the profit that can be derived from this passage and the evident link established between the two adventures. As for myself, I will not venture to imagine any very exact surmise as regards the conduct, the suspicions, and the apprehensions of Louis XIV. in these circumstances; but, on the other hand, seeing that M. de Larbeyrie left a son, who was probably the grandfather of Larbrie the citizen-officer, and also a daughter, is it not permissible to suppose that a part of the papers left by Larbeyrie came to the daughter and that among these papers was the famous copy which the captain of the guards saved from the flames?

I have consulted the Country-house Year-book. There is a Baron de Velines living not far from Rennes. Could he be a descendant of the marquis? At any rate, I wrote to him yesterday, on chance, to ask if he had not in his possession a little old book bearing on its title-page the word *aiguille*; and I am awaiting his reply.

It would give me the greatest pleasure to talk of all these matters with you. If you can spare the time, come and see me.

I am, Sir, etc., etc.

P.S. — Of course, I shall not communicate these little discoveries to the press.

Now that you are near the goal, discretion is essential.

Beautrelet absolutely agreed. He even went further: to two journalists who were worrying him that morning he gave the most fanciful particulars as to his plans and his state of mind.

In the afternoon, he hurried round to see Massiban, who lived at 17, Quai Voltaire. To his great surprise, he was told that M. Massiban had gone out of town unexpectedly, leaving a note for him in case he should call. Isidore opened it and read:

I have received a telegram which gives me some hope. So I am leaving town and shall sleep at Rennes. You might take the evening train and, without stopping at Rennes, go on to the little station of Vélines. We would meet at the castle, which is two miles and a half from the station.

The programme appealed to Beautrelet, and especially the idea that he would reach the castle at almost the same time as Massiban, for he feared some blunder on the part of that inexperienced man. He went back to his friend and spent the rest of the day with him.

In the evening, he took the Brittany express and got out at Velines at six o'clock in the morning.

He did the two and a half miles, between bushy woods, on foot. He could see the castle, perched on a height, from a distance: it was a hybrid edifice, a mixture of the Renascence and Louis Philippe styles, but it bore a stately air, nevertheless, with its four turrets and its ivy-mantled draw-bridge.

Isidore felt his heart beat as he approached. Was he really nearing the end of his race? Did the castle contain the key to the mystery?

He was not without fear. It all seemed too good to be true; and he asked himself if he was not once more acting in obedience to some infernal plan contrived by Lupin, if Massiban was not for instance, a tool in the hands of his enemy. He burst out laughing:

'Tut, tut, I'm becoming absurd! One would really think that Lupin was an infallible person who foresees everything, a sort of divine omnipotence against whom nothing can prevail! Dash it all, Lupin makes his mistakes; Lupin, too, is at the mercy of circumstances; Lupin has an occasional slip! And it is just because of his slip in losing the document that I am beginning to have the advantage of him. Everything starts from that. And his efforts, when all is said, serve only to repair the first blunder.'

And blithely, full of confidence, Beautrelet rang the bell.

'Yes, sir?' said the servant who opened the door.

'Can I see the Baron de Velines?'

And he gave the man his card.

'Monsieur le baron is not up yet, but, if monsieur will wait — '

'Has not some one else been asking for him, a gentleman with a white beard and a slight stoop?' asked Beautrelet, who knew Massiban's appearance from the photographs in the newspapers.

'Yes, the gentleman came about ten minutes ago; I showed him into the drawing room. If monsieur will come this way — '

The interview between Massiban and Beautrelet was of the most cordial character. Isidore thanked the old man for the first-rate information which he owed to him and Massiban expressed his admiration for Beautrelet in the warmest terms. Then they exchanged impressions on the document, on their prospects of discovering the book; and Massiban repeated what he had heard at Rennes regarding M. de Velines. The baron was a man of sixty, who had been left a widower many years ago and who led a very retired life with his daughter, Gabrielle de Villemon. This lady had just suffered a cruel blow through the loss of her husband and her eldest son, both of whom had died as the result of a motor-car accident.

'Monsieur le baron begs the gentlemen to be good enough to come upstairs.'

The servant led the way to the first floor, to a large, bare-walled room, very simply furnished with desks, pigeon-holes and tables covered with papers and account-books.

The baron received them very affably and with the volubility often displayed by people who live too much alone. They had great difficulty in explaining the object of their visit.

'Oh, yes, I know, you wrote to me about it, M. Massiban. It has something to do with a book about a needle, hasn't it, a book which is supposed to have come down to me from my ancestors?'

'Just so.'

'I may as well tell you that my ancestors and I have fallen out. They had funny ideas in those days. I belong to my own time. I have broken with the past.'

'Yes,' said Beautrelet, impatiently, 'but have you no recollection of having seen the book? — '

'Certainly, I said so in my telegram,' he

220

exclaimed, addressing M. Massiban, who, in his annoyance, was walking up and down the room and looking out of the tall windows. 'Certainly — or, at least, my daughter thought she had seen the title among the thousands of books that lumber up the library, upstairs — for I don't care about reading myself — I don't even read the papers. My daughter does, sometimes, but only when there is nothing the matter with Georges, her remaining son! As for me, as long as my tenants pay their rents and my leases are kept up — ! You see my account-books: I live in them, gentlemen; and I confess that I know absolutely nothing whatever about that story of which you wrote to me in your letter, M. Massiban — '

Isidore Beautrelet, nerve-shattered at all this talk, interrupted him bluntly:

'I beg your pardon, monsieur, but the book — '

'My daughter has looked for it. She looked for it all day yesterday.'

'Well?'

'Well, she found it; she found it a few hours ago. When you arrived — '

'And where is it?'

'Where is it? Why, she put it on that table — there it is — over there — '

Isidore gave a bound. At one end of the

table, on a muddled heap of papers, lay a little book bound in red morocco. He banged his fist down upon it, as though he were forbidding anybody to touch it — and also a little as though he himself dared not take it up.

'Well!' cried Massiban, greatly excited.

'I have it — here it is — we're there at last!'

'But the title — are you sure? — '

'Why, of course: look!'

'Are you convinced? Have we mastered the secret at last?'

'The front page — what does the front page say?'

'Read: *The Whole Truth now first exhibited. One hundred copies printed by myself for the instruction of the Court.*'

'That's it, that's it,' muttered Massiban, in a hoarse voice. 'It's the copy snatched from the flames! It's the very book which Louis XIV. condemned.'

They turned over the pages. The first part set forth the explanations given by Captain de Larbeyrie in his journal.

'Get on, get on!' said Beautrelet, who was in a hurry to come to the solution.

'Get on? What do you mean? Not at all! We know that the Man with the Iron Mask was imprisoned because he knew and wished to divulge the secret of the Royal house of

France. But how did he know it? And why did he wish to divulge it? Lastly, who was that strange personage? A half-brother of Louis XIV., as Voltaire maintained, or Mattioli, the Italian minister, as the modern critics declare? Hang it, those are questions of the very first interest!'

'Later, later,' protested Beautrelet, feverishly turning the pages, as though he feared that the book would fly out of his hands before he had solved the riddle.

'But — ' said Massiban, who doted on historical details.

'We have plenty of time — afterward — let's see the explanation first — '

Suddenly Beautrelet stopped. The document! In the middle of a left-hand page, his eyes saw the five mysterious lines of dots and figures! He made sure, with a glance, that the text was identical with that which he had studied so long; the same arrangement of the signs, the same intervals that permitted of the isolation of the word *demoiselles* and the separation of the two words *aiguille* and *creuse*.

A short note preceded it:

All the necessary indications, it appears, were reduced by King Louis XIII. into a little table which I transcribe below.

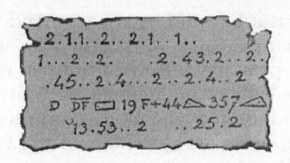

Then came the explanation of the document itself. Beautrelet read, in a broken voice:

'As will be seen, this table, even after we have changed the figures into vowels, affords no light. One might say that, in order to decipher the puzzle, we must first know it. It is, at most, a clue given to those who know the paths of the labyrinth.

'Let us take this clue and proceed. I will guide you.

'The fourth line first. The fourth line contains measurements and indications. By complying with the indications and noting the measurements set down, we inevitably attain our object, on condition, be it understood, that we know where we are and whither we are going, in a word, that we are enlightened as to the real meaning of the Hollow Needle. This is what we may learn from the first three lines. The first is so conceived to revenge myself on the King; I had warned him, for that matter — '

Beautrelet stopped, nonplussed.

'What? What is it?' said Massiban.

'The words don't make sense.'

'No more they do,' replied Massiban. ' "The first is so conceived to revenge myself on the King' — What can that mean?'

'Damn!' yelled Beautrelet.

'Well?'

'Torn! Two pages! The next two pages! Look at the marks!'

He trembled, shaking with rage and disappointment. Massiban bent forward.

'It is true — there are the ends of two pages left, like bookbinders' guards. The marks seem pretty fresh. They've not been cut, but torn out — torn out with violence. Look, all the pages at the end of the book have been rumpled.'

'But who can have done it? Who?' moaned Isidore, wringing his hands. 'A servant? An accomplice?'

'All the same, it may date back to a few months since,' observed Massiban.

'Even so — even so — some one must have hunted out and taken the book — Tell me, monsieur,' cried Beautrelet, addressing the baron, 'is there no one whom you suspect?'

'We might ask my daughter.'

'Yes — yes — that's it — perhaps she will know.'

M. de Velines rang for the footman. A few

minutes later. Mme. de Villemon entered. She was a young woman, with a sad and resigned face. Beautrelet at once asked her:

'You found this volume upstairs, madame, in the library?'

'Yes, in a parcel of books that had not been uncorded.'

'And you read it?'

'Yes, last night.'

'When you read it, were those two pages missing? Try and remember: the two pages following this table of figures and dots?'

'No, certainly not,' she said, greatly astonished. 'There was no page missing at all.'

'Still, somebody has torn — '

'But the book did not leave my room last night.'

'And this morning?'

'This morning, I brought it down here myself, when M. Massiban's arrival was announced.'

'Then — ?'

'Well, I don't understand — unless — but no.'

'What?'

'Georges — my son — this morning — Georges was playing with the book.'

She ran out headlong, accompanied by Beautrelet, Massiban and the baron. The child was not in his room. They hunted in every direction. At last, they found him playing behind the castle. But those three people seemed so excited and called him so peremptorily to account that he began to yell aloud.

Everybody ran about to right and left. The servants were questioned. It was an indescribable tumult. And Beautrelet received the awful impression that the truth was ebbing away from him, like water trickling through his fingers.

He made an effort to recover himself, took Mme. de Villemon's arm, and, followed by the baron and Massiban, led her back to the drawing room and said:

'The book is incomplete. Very well. There are two pages torn out; but you read them, did you not, madame?'

'Yes.'

'You know what they contained?'

'Yes.'

'Could you repeat it to us?'

'Certainly. I read the book with a great deal of curiosity, but those two pages struck me in particular because the revelations were so very interesting.'

'Well, then, speak madame, speak, I implore you! Those revelations are of exceptional importance. Speak, I beg of you:

minutes lost are never recovered. The Hollow Needle — '

'Oh, it's quite simple. The Hollow Needle means — '

At that moment, a footman entered the room:

'A letter for madame.'

'Oh, but the postman has passed!'

'A boy brought it.'

Mme. de Villemon opened the letter, read it, and put her hand to her heart, turning suddenly livid and terrified, ready to faint.

The paper had slipped to the floor. Beautrelet picked it up and, without troubling to apologize, read:

Not a word! If you say a word, your son will never wake again.

'My son — my son!' she stammered, too weak even to go to the assistance of the threatened child.

Beautrelet reassured her:

'It is not serious — it's a joke. Come, who could be interested?'

'Unless,' suggested Massiban, 'it was Arsène Lupin.'

Beautrelet made him a sign to hold his tongue. He knew quite well, of course, that the enemy was there, once more, watchful and determined; and that was just why he wanted to tear from Mme. de Villemon the decisive words, so long awaited, and to tear them from her on the spot, that very moment:

'I beseech you, madame, compose yourself. We are all here. There is not the least danger.'

Would she speak? He thought so, he hoped so. She stammered out a few syllables. But the door opened again. This time, the nurse entered. She seemed distraught:

'M. Georges — madame — M. Georges —!'

Suddenly, the mother recovered all her strength. Quicker than any of them, and urged by an unfailing instinct, she rushed down the staircase, across the hall and on to the terrace. There lay little Georges, motionless, on a wicker chair.

'Well, what is it? He's asleep! — '

'He fell asleep suddenly, madame,' said the nurse. 'I tried to prevent him, to carry him to his room. But he was fast asleep and his hands — his hands were cold.'

'Cold!' gasped the mother. 'Yes — it's true. Oh dear, oh dear — *if he only wakes up!*'

Beautrelet put his hand in his trousers pocket, seized the butt of his revolver, cocked it with his forefinger, then suddenly produced the weapon and fired at Massiban.

Massiban, as though he were watching the boy's movements, had avoided the shot, so to speak, in advance. But already Beautrelet had sprung upon him, shouting to the servants:

'Help! It's Lupin!'

Massiban, under the weight of the impact, fell back into one of the wicker chairs. In a few seconds, he rose, leaving Beautrelet stunned, choking; and, holding the young man's revolver in his hands:

'Good! — that's all right! — don't stir — you'll be like that for two or three minutes — no more. But, upon my word, you took your time to recognize me! Was my make-up as old Massiban so good as all that?'

He was now standing straight up on his legs, his body squared, in a formidable attitude, and he grinned as he looked at the three petrified footmen and the dumbfounded baron:

'Isidore, you've missed the chance of a lifetime. If you hadn't told them I was Lupin, they'd have jumped on me. And, with fellows like that, what would have become of me, by Jove, with four to one against me?'

He walked up to them:

'Come, my lads, don't be afraid — I shan't hurt you. Wouldn't you like a sugar-stick apiece to screw your courage up? Oh, you, by the way, hand me back my hundred-franc note, will you? Yes, yes, I know you! You're the one I bribed just now to give the letter to your mistress. Come hurry, you faithless servant.'

He took the blue bank-note which the servant handed him and tore it into tiny shreds:

'The price of treachery! It burns my fingers.'

He took off his hat and, bowing very low before Mme. de Villemon:

'Will you forgive me, madame? The accidents of life — of mine especially — often drive one to acts of cruelty for which I am the first to blush. But have no fear for your son: it's a mere prick, a little puncture in the arm which I gave him while we were questioning him. In an hour, at the most, you won't know that it happened. Once more, all my apologies. But I had to make sure of your silence.' He bowed again, thanked M. de Velines for his kind hospitality, took his cane, lit a cigarette, offered one to the baron, gave a circular sweep with his hat and, in a patronizing tone, said to Beautrelet:

'Good-bye, baby.'

And he walked away quietly, puffing the smoke of his cigarette into the servants' faces.

Beautrelet waited for a few minutes. Mme. de Villemon, now calmer, was watching by her son. He went up to her, with the intention of making one last appeal to her. Their eyes met. He said nothing. He had understood that she would never speak now, whatever happened. There, once more, in that mother's brain, the secret of the Hollow Needle lay buried as deeply as in the night of the past.

Then he gave up and went away.

It was half-past ten. There was a train at eleven-fifty. He slowly followed the avenue in the park and turned into the road that led to the station.

'Well, what do you say to that?'

It was Massiban, or rather Lupin, who appeared out of the wood adjoining the road.

'Was it pretty well contrived, or was it not? Is your old friend great on the tight-rope, or is he not? I'm sure that you haven't got over it, eh, and that you're asking yourself whether the so-called Massiban, member of the Academy of Inscriptions and Belles-Lettres, ever existed. But, of course, he exists. I'll even show him to you, if you're good. But, first, let me give you back your revolver. You're looking to see if it's loaded? Certainly, my lad. There are five charges left, one of which would be enough to send me *ad patres*. — Well, so you're putting it in your pocket? Quite right. I prefer that to what you did up there. — A nasty little impulse, that, of yours! — Still, you're young, you suddenly see — in a flash! — that you've once more been done by that confounded Lupin and that he is standing there in front of you, at three steps

232

from you — and bang! You fire! — I'm not angry with you, bless your little heart! To prove it, I offer you a seat in my 100 h.p. car. Will that suit you?'

He put his fingers to his mouth and whistled.

The contrast was delicious between the venerable appearance of this elderly Massiban and the schoolboy ways and accent which Lupin was putting on. Beautrelet could not help laughing.

'He's laughed! He's laughed!' cried Lupin, jumping for joy. 'You see, baby, what you fall short in is the power of smiling; you're a trifle serious for your age. You're a very likeable boy, you have a charming candour and simplicity — but you have no sense of humour.' He placed himself in front of him. 'Look here, bet you I make you cry! Do you know how I was able to follow up all your inquiry, how I knew of the letter Massiban wrote you and his appointment to meet you this morning at the Chateau de Velines? Through the prattle of your friend, the one you're staying with. You confide in that idiot and he loses no time, but goes and tells everything to his best girl. And his best girl has no secrets for Lupin. — What did I tell you? I've made you feel, anyhow; your eyes are quite wet! — Friendship betrayed: that upsets you, eh? Upon my word, you're wonderful! I could take you in my arms and hug you! You always wear that look of astonishment which goes straight to my heart. — I shall never forget the other evening at Gaillon, when you consulted me. — Yes, I was the old notary! — But why don't you laugh, youngster? As I said, you have no sense of a joke. Look here, what you want is — what shall I call it? — imagination, imaginative impulse. Now, I'm full of imaginative impulse.'

A motor was heard panting not far off. Lupin seized Beautrelet roughly by the arm and in a cold voice, looking him straight in the eyes:

'You're going to keep quiet now, aren't you? You can see there's nothing to be done. Then what's the use of wasting your time and energy? There are plenty of highway robbers in the world. Run after them and let me be — if not! — It's settled, isn't it?'

He shook him as though to enforce his will upon him. Then he grinned:

'Fool that I am! You leave me alone? You're not one of those who let go! Oh, I don't know what restrains me! In half a dozen turns of the wrist, I could have you bound and gagged — and, in two hours, safe under lock and key, for some months to come. And then I could twist my thumbs in all security, withdraw to the peaceful retreat prepared for me by my ancestors, the Kings of France, and enjoy the treasures which they have been good enough to accumulate for me. But no, it is doomed that I must go on blundering to the end. I can't help it, we all have our weaknesses — and I have one for you. Besides, it's not done yet. From now until you put your finger into the hollow of the Needle, a good deal of water will flow under the bridges. Dash it all, it took me ten days! Me! Lupin! You will want ten years, at least! There's that much distance between us, after all!'

The motor arrived, an immense closed car. Lupin opened the door and Beautreiet gave a cry. There was a man inside and that man was Lupin, or rather Massiban. Suddenly understanding, he burst out laughing. Lupin said:

'Don't be afraid, he's sound asleep. I promised that you should see him. Do you grasp the situation now? At midnight, I knew of your appointment at the castle. At seven in the morning, I was there. When Massiban passed, I had only to collect him — give him a tiny prick with a needle — and the thing — was done. Sleep old chap, sleep away. We'll set you down on the slope. That's it — there — capital — right in the sun, then you won't catch cold — good! And our hat in our hand.

— Spare a copper, kind gentleman! — Oh, my dear old Massiban, so you were after Arsène Lupin!'

It was really a huge joke to see the two Massibans face to face, one asleep with his head on his chest, the other seriously occupied in paying him every sort of attention and respect:

'Pity a poor blind man! There, Massiban, here's two sous and my visiting-card. And now, my lads, off we go at the fourth speed. Do you hear, driver? You've got to do seventy-five miles an hour. Jump in, Isidore. There's a full sitting of the Institute to-day, and Massiban is to read a little paper, on I don't know what, at half-past three. Well, he'll read them his little paper. I'll dish them up a complete Massiban, more real than the real one, with my own ideas, on the lacustrine inscriptions. I don't have an opportunity of lecturing at the Institute ever day! — Faster, chauffeur: we're only doing seventy-one and a half! — Are you afraid? Remember you're with Lupin! — Ah, Isidore, and then people say that life is monotonous! Why, life's an adorable thing, my boy; only one has to know — and I know — . Wasn't it enough to make a man jump out of his skin for joy, just now, at the castle, when you were chattering with old Velines and I, up against the window, was tearing out the pages of the historic book? And then, when you were questioning the Dame de Villemon about the Hollow Needle! Would she speak? Yes, she would — no, she wouldn't — yes — no. It gave me gooseflesh, I assure you. — If she spoke, I should have to build up my life anew, the whole scaffolding was destroyed. — Would the footman come in time? Yes — no — there he is. — But Beautrelet will unmask me! Never! He's too much of a flat! Yes, though — no — there, he's done it — no, he hasn't — yes — he's eyeing me — that's it — he's feeling for his revolver! — Oh, the delight of it! — Isidore, you're talking too much, you'll hurt yourself! — Let's have a snooze, shall we? — I'm dying of sleep. — Good night.'

Beautrelet looked at him. He seemed almost asleep already. He slept.

The motor-car, darting through space, rushed toward a horizon that was constantly reached and as constantly retreated. There was no impression of towns, villages, fields or forests; simply space, space devoured, swallowed up.

Beautrelet looked at his traveling companion, for a long time, with eager curiosity and also with a keen wish to fathom his real character through the mask that covered it. And he thought of the circumstances that confined them, like that, together, in the close contact of that motor car. But, after the excitement and disappointment of the morning, tired in his turn, he too fell asleep.

When he woke, Lupin was reading. Beautrelet leant over to see the title of the book. It was the *Epistolae ad Lucilium* of Seneca the philosopher.

8

From Caesar to Lupin

'Dash it all, it took me ten days! Me! Lupin! You will want ten years, at least! — '

These words, uttered by Lupin after leaving the Chateau de Velines, had no little influence on Beautrelet's conduct.

Though very calm in the main and invariably master of himself, Lupin, nevertheless, was subject to moments of exaltation, of a more or less romantic expansiveness, at once theatrical and good-humoured, when he allowed certain admissions to escape him, certain imprudent speeches which a boy like Beautrelet could easily turn to profit.

Rightly or wrongly. Beautrelet read one of these involuntary admissions into that phrase. He was entitled to conclude that, if Lupin drew a comparison between his own efforts and Beautrelet's in pursuit of the truth about the Hollow Needle, it was because the two of them possessed identical means of attaining their object, because Lupin had no elements of success different from those possessed by his adversary. The chances were alike. Now, with the same chances, the same elements of success, the same means, ten days had been enough for Lupin.

What were those elements, those means, those chances? They were reduced, when all was said, to a knowledge of the pamphlet published in 1815, a pamphlet which Lupin, no doubt, like Massiban, had found by accident and thanks to which he had succeeded in discovering the indispensable document in Marie Antoinette's book of hours.

Therefore, the pamphlet and the document were the only two fundamental facts upon which Lupin had relied. With these he had built up the whole edifice. He had had no extraneous aid. The study of the pamphlet and the study of the document — full stop — that was all.

Well, could not Beautrelet confine himself to the same ground? What was the use of an impossible struggle? What was the use of those vain investigations, in which, even supposing that he avoided the pitfalls that were multiplied under his feet, he was sure, in the end, to achieve the poorest of results?

His decision was clear and immediate; and, in adopting it, he had the happy instinct that he was on the right path. He began by leaving his Janson-de-Sailly schoolfellow, without indulging in useless recriminations, and, taking his portmanteau with him, went and installed himself, after much hunting about, in a small hotel situated in the very heart of Paris. This hotel he did not leave for days. At most, he took his meals at the *table d'hote.* The rest of the time, locked in his room, with the window-curtains close-drawn, he spent in thinking.

'Ten days,' Arsène Lupin had said.

Beautrelet, striving to forget all that he had done and to remember only the elements of the pamphlet and the document, aspired eagerly to keep within the limit of those ten days. However the tenth day passed and the eleventh and the twelfth; but, on the thirteenth day, a gleam lit up his brain and, very soon, with the bewildering rapidity of those ideas which develop in us like miraculous plants, the truth emerged, blossomed, gathered strength. On the evening of the thirteenth day, he certainly did not know the answer to the problem, but he knew, to a certainty, one of the methods which Lupin had, beyond a doubt, employed.

It was a very simple method, hinging on this one question: Is there a link of any sort uniting all the more or less important historic events with which the pamphlet connects the mystery of the Hollow Needle?

The great diversity of these events made the question difficult to answer. Still, the profound examination to which Beautrelet applied himself ended by pointing to one essential characteristic which was common to them all. Each one of them, without exception, had happened within the boundaries of the old kingdom of Neustria, which correspond very nearly with those of our present-day Normandy. All the heroes of the fantastic adventure are Norman, or become Norman, or play their part in the Norman country.

What a fascinating procession through the ages! What a rousing spectacle was that of all those barons, dukes and kings, starting from such widely opposite points to meet in this particular corner of the world! Beautrelet turned the pages of history at haphazard: it was Rolf, or Rou, or Rollo, first Duke of *Normandy*, who was master of the secret of the Needle, according to the treaty of Saint-Clair-sur-Epte!

It was William the Conqueror, Duke of *Normandy* and King of England, whose bannerstaff was pierced like a needle!

It was at *Rouen* that the English burnt Joan of Arc, mistress of the secret!

And right at the beginning of the adventure, who is that chief of the Caleti who pays his ransom to Caesar with the secret of the Needle but the chief of the men of the

242

Caux country, which lies in the very heart of *Normandy?*

The supposition becomes more definite. The field narrows. Rouen, the banks of the Seine, the Caux country: it really seems as though all roads lead in that direction. Two kings of France are mentioned more particularly, after the secret is lost by the Dukes of Normandy and their heirs, the kings of England, and becomes the royal secret of France; and these two are King Henry IV., who laid siege to Rouen and won the battle of Arques, near Dieppe, and Francis I., who founded the Havre and uttered that suggestive phrase:

'The kings of France carry secrets that often decide the fate of towns!'

Rouen, Dieppe, the Havre: the three angles of the triangle, the three large towns that occupy the three points. In the centre, the Caux country.

The seventeenth century arrives. Louis XIV. burns the book in which a person unknown reveals the truth. Captain de Larbeyrie masters a copy, profits by the secret thus obtained, steals a certain number of jewels and dies by the hand of highway murderers. Now at which spot is the ambush laid? At Gaillon! At Gaillon, a little town on the road leading from Havre, Rouen or Dieppe to Paris!

A year later, Louis XIV. buys a domain and builds the Chateau de l'Aiguille. Where does he select his site? In the Midlands of France, with the result that the curious are thrown off the scent and do not hunt about in Normandy.

Rouen, Dieppe, the Havre — the Cauchois triangle — everything lies there. On one side, the sea; on another, the Seine: on the third, the two valleys that lead from Rouen to Dieppe.

A light flashed across Beautrelet's mind. That extent of ground, that country of the high tablelands which run from the cliffs of the Seine to the cliffs of the Channel almost invariably constituted the field of operations of Arsène Lupin. For ten years, it was just this district which he parcelled out for his purposes, as though he had his haunt in the very centre of the region with which, the legend of the Hollow Needle was most closely connected.

The affair of Baron Cahorn? On the banks of the Seine, between Rouen and the Havre.

The Thibermenil case? At the other end of the tableland, between Rouen and Dieppe.

The Gruchet, Montigny, Crasville burglaries? In the midst of the Caux country.

Where was Lupin going when he was attacked and bound hand and foot, in his compartment by Pierre Onfrey, the Auteuil murderer? To Rouen.

Where was Holmlock Shears, Lupin's prisoner, put on board ship? Near the Havre.

And what was the scene of the whole of the present tragedy? Ambrumesy, on the road between the Havre and Dieppe.

Rouen, Dieppe, the Havre: always the Cauchois triangle.

And so, a few years earlier, possessing the pamphlet and knowing the hiding-place in which Marie Antoinette had concealed the document, Arsène Lupin had ended by laying his hand on the famous book of hours. Once in possession of the document, he took the field, 'found' and settled down as in a conquered country.

Beautrelet took the field.

He set out in genuine excitement, thinking of the same journey which Lupin had taken, of the same hopes with which he must have throbbed when he thus went in search of the tremendous secret which was to arm him with so great a power. Would his, Beautrelet's efforts have the same victorious results?

He left Rouen early in the morning, on foot, with his face very much disguised and his bag at the end of a stick on his shoulder, like an apprentice doing his round of France. He walked straight to Duclair, where he lunched. On leaving this town, he followed the Seine and practically did not lose sight of it again. His instinct, strengthened, moreover, by numerous influences, always brought him back to the sinuous banks of the stately river. When the Chateau du Malaquis was robbed, the objects stolen from Baron Cahorn's collection were sent by way of the Seine. The old carvings removed from the chapel at Ambrumesy were carried to the Seine bank. He pictured the whole fleet of pinnaces performing a regular service between Rouen and the Havre and draining the works of art and treasures from a countryside to dispatch them thence to the land of millionaires.

'I'm burning! I'm burning!' muttered the boy, gasping under the truth, which came to him in a mighty series of shocks and took away his breath.

The checks encountered on the first few days, did not discourage him. He had a firm and profound belief in the correctness of the supposition that was guiding him. It was bold, perhaps, and extravagant; no matter: it was worthy of the adversary pursued. The supposition was on a level with the prodigious reality that bore the name of Lupin. With a man like that, of what good could it be to look elsewhere than in the domain of the enormous, the exaggerated, the superhuman?

Jumieges, the Mailleraye, Saint-Wandrille, Caudebec, Tancarville, Quillebeuf were places filled with his memories. How often he must have contemplated the glory of their Gothic steeples or the splendour of their immense ruins!

But the Havre, the neighbourhood of the Havre drew Isidore like a beacon-fire.

'The kings of France carry secrets that often decide the fate of towns!'

Cryptic words which, suddenly, for Beautrelet, shone bright with clearness! Was this not an exact statement of the reasons that determined Francis I. to create a town on this spot and was not the fate of the Havre-de-Grace linked with the very secret of the Needle?

'That's it, that's it,' stammered Beautrelet, excitedly. 'The old Norman estuary, one of the essential points, one of the original centres around which our French nationality was formed, is completed by those two forces, one in full view, alive, known to all, the new port commanding the ocean and opening on the world; the other dim and obscure, unknown and all the more alarming, inasmuch as it is invisible and impalpable. A whole side of the history of France and of the royal house is explained by the Needle, even as it explains the whole story of Arsène Lupin. The same sources of energy and power supply and renew the fortunes of kings and of the adventurer.'

Beautrelet ferreted and snuffed from village

to village, from the river to the sea, with his nose in the wind, his ears pricked, trying to compel the inanimate things to surrender their deep meaning. Ought this hill-slope to be questioned? Or that forest? Or the houses of this hamlet? Or was it among the insignificant phrases spoken by that peasant yonder that he might hope to gather the one little illuminating word?

One morning, he was lunching at an inn, within sight of Honfleur, the old city of the estuary. Opposite him was sitting one of those heavy, red-haired Norman horse-dealers who do the fairs of the district, whip in hand and clad in a long smock-frock. After a moment, it seemed to Beautrelet that the man was looking at him with a certain amount of attention, as though he knew him or, at least, was trying to recognize him.

'Pooh,' he thought, 'there's some mistake: I've never seen that merchant before, nor he me.'

As a matter of fact, the man appeared to take no further interest in him. He lit his pipe, called for coffee and brandy, smoked and drank.

When Beautrelet had finished his meal, he paid and rose to go. A group of men entered just as he was about to leave and he had to stand for a few seconds near the table at which the horse-dealer sat. He then heard the man say in a low voice:

'Good-afternoon, M. Beautrelet.'

Without hesitation, Isidore sat down beside the man and said:

'Yes, that is my name — but who are you? How did you know me?'

'That's not difficult — and yet I've only seen your portrait in the papers. But you are so badly — what do you call it in French — so badly made-up.'

He had a pronounced foreign accent and Beautrelet seemed to perceive, as he looked at him, that he too wore a facial disguise that entirely altered his features.

'Who are you?' he repeated. 'Who are you?'

The stranger smiled:

'Don't you recognize me?'

'No, I never saw you before.'

'Nor I you. But think. The papers print my portrait also — and pretty often. Well, have you got it?'

'No.'

'Holmlock Shears.'

It was an amusing and, at the same time, a significant meeting. The boy at once saw the full bearing of it. After an exchange of compliments, he said to Shears:

'I suppose that you are here — because of 'him'?'

'Yes.'

'So — so — you think we have a chance — in this direction.'

'I'm sure of it.'

Beautrelet's delight at finding that Shears's opinion agreed with his own was not unmingled with other feelings. If the Englishman attained his object, it meant that, at the very best, the two would share the victory; and who could tell that Shears would not attain it first?

'Have you any proofs? Any clues?'

'Don't be afraid,' grinned the Englishman, who understood his uneasiness. 'I am not treading on your heels. With you, it's the document, the pamphlet: things that do not inspire me with any great confidence.'

'And with you?'

'With me, it's something different.'

'Should I be indiscreet, if — ?'

'Not at all. You remember the story of the coronet, the story of the Duc de Charmerac?'

'Yes.'

'You remember Victoire, Lupin's old foster-mother, the one whom my good friend Ganimard allowed to escape in a sham prison-van?'

'Yes.'

'I have found Victoire's traces. She lives on a farm, not far from National Road No. 25. National Road No. 25 is the road from the

Havre to Lille. Through Victoire I shall easily get at Lupin.'

'It will take long.'

'No matter! I have dropped all my cases. This is the only one I care about. Between Lupin and me, it's a fight — a fight to the death.'

He spoke these words with a sort of ferocity that betrayed all his bitterness at the humiliations which he had undergone, all his fierce hatred of the great enemy who had tricked him so cruelly.

'Go away, now,' he whispered, 'we are observed. It's dangerous. But mark my words: on the day when Lupin and I meet face to face, it will be — it will be tragic.'

Beautrelet felt quite reassured on leaving Shears: he need not fear that the Englishman would gain on him. And here was one more proof which this chance interview had brought him: the road from the Havre to Lille passes through Dieppe! It is the great seaside road of the Caux country, the coast road commanding the Channel cliffs! And it was on a farm near this road that Victoire was installed, Victoire, that is to say, Lupin, for one did not move without the other, the master without the blindly devoted servant.

'I'm burning! I'm burning!' he repeated to himself. 'Whenever circumstances bring me a new element of information, it confirms my supposition. On the one hand, I have the absolute certainty of the banks of the Seine; on the other, the certainty of the National Road. The two means of communication meet at the Havre, the town of Francis I., the town of the secret. The boundaries are contracting. The Caux country is not large; and, even so, I have only the western portion of the Caux country to search.'

He set to work with renewed stubbornness:

'Anything that Lupin has found,' he kept on saying to himself, 'there is no reason for my not finding.'

Certainly, Lupin had some great advantage over him, perhaps a thorough acquaintance with the country, a precise knowledge of the local legends, or less than that, a memory: invaluable advantages these, for he, Beautrelet, knew nothing, was totally ignorant of the country, which he had first visited at the time of the Ambrumesy burglary and then only rapidly, without lingering.

But what did it matter? Though he had to devote ten years of his life to this investigation, he would carry it to a successful issue. Lupin was there. He could see him, he could feel him there. He expected to come upon him at the next turn of the road, on the skirt of the next wood, outside the next village.

And, though continually disappointed, he seemed to find in each disappointment a fresh reason for persisting.

Often, he would fling himself on the slope by the roadside and plunge into wild examination of the copy of the document which he always carried on him, a copy, that is to say, with vowels taking the place of the figures:

```
    e . a . a . . e . . e . a . . a . .
  a . . . e . e .      . e . oi . e . . e .
   . ou . . e . o . . . e . . e . o . . e
  D  D̄F ⊏⊐ 19 F+44 ◁▷ 357 ◁▷
  ai . ui . . e          . . eu . e
```

Often, also, according to his habit, he would lie down flat on his stomach in the tall grass and think for hours. He had time enough. The future belonged to him.

With wonderful patience, he tramped from the Seine to the sea, and from the sea to the Seine, going gradually farther, retracing his steps and never quitting the ground until, theoretically speaking, there was not a chance left of gathering the smallest particle upon it.

He studied and explored Montivilliers and Saint-Romani and Octeville and Gonneville and Criquetot.

At night, he knocked at the peasants' doors and asked for a lodging. After dinner, they smoked together and chatted. He made them tell him the stories which they told one another on the long winter nights. And he never omitted to insinuate, slyly:

'What about the Needle? The legend of the Hollow Needle? Don't you know that?'

'Upon my word, I don't — never heard of it — '

'Just think — an old wives' tale — something that has to do with a needle. An enchanted needle, perhaps. — I don't know — '

Nothing. No legend, no recollection. And the next morning he walked blithely away again.

One day, he passed through the pretty village of Saint-Jouin, which overlooks the sea, and descending among the chaos of rocks that have slipped from cliffs, he climbed up to the tableland and went in the direction of the dry valley of Bruneval, Cap d'Antifer and the little creek of Belle-Plage. He was walking gaily and lightly, feeling a little tired, perhaps, but glad to be alive, so glad, even, that he forgot Lupin and the mystery of the Hollow Needle and Victoire and Shears, and interested himself in the sight of nature: the blue sky, the great emerald sea, all glittering in the sunshine.

Some straight slopes and remains of brick walls, in which he seemed to recognize the vestiges of a Roman camp, interested him. Then his eyes fell upon a sort of little castle, built in imitation of an ancient fort, with cracked turrets and Gothic windows. It stood on a jagged, rugged, rising promontory, almost detached from the cliff. A barred gate, flanked by iron hand-rails and bristling spikes, guarded the narrow passage.

Beautrelet succeeded in climbing over, not without some difficulty. Over the pointed door, which was closed with an old rusty lock, he read the words:

FORT DE FRÉFOSSÉ

He did not attempt to enter, but, turning to the right, after going down a little slope, he embarked upon a path that ran along a ridge of land furnished with a wooden handrail. Right at the end was a cave of very small dimensions, forming a sort of watch-tower at the point of the rock in which it was hollowed out, a rock falling abruptly into the sea.

There was just room to stand up in the middle of the cave. Multitudes of inscriptions crossed one another on the walls. An almost square hole, cut in the stone, opened like a dormer window on the land side, exactly opposite Fort Frefosse, the crenelated top of which appeared at thirty or forty yards' distance.

Beautrelet threw off his knapsack and sat down. He had had a hard and tiring day. He fell asleep for a little. Then the cool wind that blew inside the cave woke him up. He sat for a few minutes without moving, absent-minded, vague-eyed. He tried to reflect, to recapture his still torpid thoughts. And, as he recovered his consciousness, he was on the point of rising, when he received the impression that his eyes, suddenly fixed, suddenly wide-open, saw —

A thrill shook him from head to foot. His hands clutched convulsively and he felt the beads of perspiration forming at the roots of his hair:

'No, no,' he stammered. 'It's a dream, an hallucination. Let's look: it's not possible!'

He plunged down on his knees and stooped over. Two huge letters, each perhaps a foot long, appeared cut in relief in the granite of the floor. Those two letters, clumsily, but plainly carved, with their corners rounded and their surface smoothed by the wear and tear of centuries, were a D and an F.

D and F! Oh, bewildering miracle! D and F: just two letters of the document! Oh, Beautrelet had no need to consult it to bring before his mind that group of letters in the fourth line, the line of the measurements and indications! He knew them well! They were inscribed for all time at the back of his pupils, encrusted for good and all in the very substance of his brain!

He rose to his feet, went down the steep road, climbed back along the old fort, hung on to the spikes of the rail again, in order to pass, and walked briskly toward a shepherd whose flock was grazing some way off on a dip in the tableland:

'That cave, over there — that cave — '

His lips trembled and he tried to find the words that would not come. The shepherd looked at him in amazement. At last, Isidore repeated:

'Yes, that cave — over there — to the right of the fort. Has it a name?'

'Yes, I should think so. All the Etretat folk like to call it the Demoiselles.'

'What? — What? — What's that you say?'

'Why, of course — it's the Chambre des Demoiselles.'

Isidore felt like flying at his throat, as though all the truth lived in that man and he hoped to get it from him at one swoop, to tear it from him.

The Demoiselles! One of the words, one of the only three known words of the document!

A whirlwind of madness shook Beautrelet where he stood. And it rose all around him, blew upon him like a tempestuous squall that came from the sea, that came from the land, that came from every direction and whipped him with great lashes of the truth.

He understood. The document appeared to him in its real sense. The Chambre des Demoiselles — Etretat —

'That's it,' he thought, his brain filled with light, 'it must be that. But why didn't I guess earlier?'

He said to the shepherd, in a low voice:

'That will do — go away — you can go — thank you.'

The man, not knowing what to think, whistled to his dog and went.

Left alone, Beautrelet returned to the fort. He had almost passed it when, suddenly, he dropped to the ground and lay cowering against a piece of wall. And, wringing his hands, he thought:

'I must be mad! If 'he' were to see me! Or his accomplices! I've been moving about for an hour — !'

He did not stir another limb.

The sun went down. Little by little, the night mingled with the day, blurring the outline of things.

Then, with little imperceptible movements, flat on his stomach, gliding, crawling, he crept along one of the points of the promontory to the extreme edge of the cliff.

He reached it. Stretching out his hands, he pushed aside some tufts of grass and his head appeared over the precipice.

Opposite him, almost level with the cliff, in the open sea rose an enormous rock, over eighty yards high, a colossal obelisk, standing straight on its granite base, which showed at the surface of the water, and tapering toward the summit, like the giant tooth of a monster of the deep. White with the dirty grey white of the cliff, the awful monolith was streaked with horizontal lines marked by flint and displaying the slow work of the centuries, which had heaped alternate layers of lime and pebble-stone one atop of the other.

Here and there, a fissure, a break; and, wherever these occurred, a scrap of earth, with grass and leaves.

And all this was mighty and solid and formidable, with the look of an indestructible thing against which the furious assault of the waves and storms could not prevail. And it was definite and permanent and grand, despite the grandeur of the cliffy rampart that commanded it, despite the immensity of the space in which it stood.

Beautrelet's nails dug into the soil like the claws of an animal ready to leap upon its prey. His eyes penetrated the wrinkled texture of the rock, penetrated its skin, so it seemed to him, its very flesh. He touched it, felt it, took cognizance and possession of it, absorbed and assimilated it.

The horizon turned crimson with all the flames of the vanished sun; and long, red clouds, set motionless in the sky, formed glorious landscapes, fantastic lagoons, fiery plains, forests of gold, lakes of blood, a whole glowing and peaceful phantasmagoria.

The blue of the sky grew darker. Venus shone with a marvellous brightness; then other stars lit up, timid as yet.

And Beautrelet suddenly closed his eyes and convulsively pressed his folded arms to his forehead. Over there — oh, he felt as though he would die for joy, so great was the cruel emotion that wrung his heart! — over there, almost at the top of the Needle of Etretat, a little below the extreme point round which the sea-mews fluttered, a thread of smoke came filtering through a crevice, as though from an invisible chimney, a thread of smoke rose in slow spirals in the calm air of the twilight.

9

Open, Sesame!

The Etretat Needle was hollow!

Was it a natural phenomenon, an excavation produced by internal cataclysms or by the imperceptible action of the rushing sea and the soaking rain? Or was it a superhuman work executed by human beings, Gauls, Celts, prehistoric men?

These, no doubt, were insoluble questions; and what did it matter? The essence of the thing was contained in this fact: The Needle was hollow. At forty or fifty yards from that imposing arch which is called the Porte d'Aval and which shoots out from the top of the cliff, like the colossal branch of a tree, to take root in the submerged rocks, stands an immense limestone cone; and this cone is no more than the shell of a pointed cap poised upon the empty waters!

A prodigious revelation! After Lupin, here was Beautrelet discovering the key to the great riddle that had loomed over more than twenty centuries! A key of supreme importance to whoever possessed it in the days of old, in those distant times when hordes of barbarians rode through and overran the old world! A magic key that opens the cyclopean cavern to whole tribes fleeing before the enemy! A mysterious key that guards the door of the most inviolable shelter! An enchanted key that gives power and ensures preponderance!

Because he knows this key, Caesar is able to subdue Gaul. Because they know it, the Normans force their sway upon the country and, from there, later, backed by that support, conquer the neighbouring island, conquer Sicily, conquer the East, conquer the new world!

Masters of the secret, the Kings of England lord it over France, humble her, dismember her, have themselves crowned at Paris. They lose the secret; and the rout begins.

Masters of the secret, the Kings of France push back and overstep the narrow limits of their dominion, gradually founding a great nation and radiating with glory and power. They forget it or know not how to use it; and death, exile, ruin follow.

An invisible kingdom, in mid-water and at ten fathoms from land! An unknown fortress, taller than the towers of Notre Dame and built upon a granite foundation larger than a public square! What strength and what security! From Paris to the sea, by the Seine.

There, the Havre, the new town, the necessary town. And, sixteen miles thence, the Hollow Needle, the impregnable sanctuary!

It is a sanctuary and also a stupendous hiding-place. All the treasures of the kings, increasing from century to century, all the gold of France, all that they extort from the people, all that they snatch from the clergy, all the booty gathered on the battle-fields of Europe lie heaped up in the royal cave. Old Merovingian gold sous, glittering crown-pieces, doubloons, ducats, florins, guineas; and the precious stones and the diamonds; and all the jewels and all the ornaments: everything is there. Who could discover it? Who could ever learn the impenetrable secret of the Needle? Nobody.

And Lupin becomes that sort of really disproportionate being whom we know, that miracle incapable of explanation so long as the truth remains in the shadow. Infinite though the resources of his genius be, they cannot suffice for the mad struggle which he maintains against society. He needs other, more material resources. He needs a sure place of retreat, he needs the certainty of impunity, the peace that allows of the execution of his plans.

Without the Hollow Needle, Lupin is incomprehensible, a myth, a character in a novel, having no connection with reality.

Master of the secret — and of such a

secret! — he becomes simply a man like another, but gifted with the power of wielding in a superior manner the extraordinary weapon with which destiny has endowed him.

★ ★ ★

So the Needle was hollow.

It remained to discover how one obtained access to it.

From the sea, obviously. There must be, on the side of the offing, some fissure where boats could land at certain hours of the tide.

But on the side of the land?

Beautrelet lay until ten o'clock at night hanging over the precipice, with his eyes riveted on the shadowy mass formed by the pyramid, thinking and pondering with all the concentrated effort of his mind.

Then he went down to Etretat, selected the cheapest hotel, dined, went up to his room and unfolded the document.

It was the merest child's play to him now to establish its exact meaning. He at once saw that the three vowels of the word Etretat occurred in the first line, in their proper order and at the necessary intervals. This first line now read as follows:

e . a . a . . etretat . a . .

264

What words could come before Etretat? Words, no doubt, that referred to the position of the Needle with regard to the town. Now the Needle stood on the left, on the west — He ransacked his memory and, recollecting that westerly winds are called *vents d'aval* on the coast and that the nearest port was known as the Porte d'Aval, he wrote down:

'*En aval d'Etretat . a . .* '

The second line was that containing the word Demoiselles and, at once seeing, in front of that word, the series of all the vowels that form part of the words *la chambre des*, he noted the two phrases:

'*En aval d'Etretat. La Chambre des Demoiselles.*'

The third line gave him more trouble; and it was not until some groping that, remembering the position, near the Chambre des Demoiselles, of the Fort de Frefosse, he ended by almost completely reconstructing the document:

'*En aval d'Etretat. La Chambre des Demoiselles. Sous le Fort de Fréfossé. L'Aiguille creuse.*'

These were the four great formulas, the essential and general formulas which you had to know. By means of them, you turned *en aval*, that is to say, below or west of Etretat, entered the Chambre des Demoiselles, in all probability passed under Fort Frefosse and thus arrived at the Needle.

How? By means of the indications and measurements that constituted the fourth line:

$$D \ \overline{DF} \ \square \ 19 \ F + 44 \ \triangle \ 357 \ \triangle$$

These were evidently the more special formulas to enable you to find the outlet through which you made your way and the road that led to the Needle.

Beautrelet at once presumed — and his surmise was no more than the logical consequence of the document — that, if there really was a direct communication between the land and the obelisk of the Needle, the underground passage must start from the Chambre des Demoiselles, pass under Fort Frefosse, descend perpendicularly the three hundred feet of cliff and, by means of a tunnel contrived under the rocks of the sea, end at the Hollow Needle.

Which was the entrance to the underground passage? Did not the two letters D and F, so plainly cut, point to it and admit to it, with the aid, perhaps, of some ingenious piece of mechanism?

The whole of the next morning, Isidore strolled about Etretat and chatted with everybody he met, in order to try and pick up useful information. At last, in the afternoon, he went up the cliff. Disguised as a sailor, he had made himself still younger and, in a pair of trousers too short for him and a fishing jersey, he looked a mere scape-grace of twelve or thirteen.

As soon as he entered the cave, he knelt down before the letters. Here a disappointment awaited him. It was no use his striking them, pushing them, manipulating them in every way: they refused to move. And it was not long, in fact, before he became aware that they were really unable to move and that, therefore, they controlled no mechanism.

And yet — and yet they must mean something! Inquiries which he had made in the village went to show that no one had ever been able to explain their existence and that the Abbe Cochet, in his valuable little book on Etretat, had also tried in vain to solve this little puzzle. But Isidore knew what the learned Norman archaeologist did not know, namely, that the same two letters figured in the document, on the line containing the indications. Was it a chance coincidence: Impossible. Well, then — ?

An idea suddenly occurred to him, an idea so reasonable, so simple that he did not doubt its correctness for a second. Were not that D and that F the initials of the two most important words in the document, the words that represented — together with the Needle — the essential stations on the road to be followed: the Chambre des *Demoiselles* and Fort *Frefosse*: D for Demoiselles, F for Frefosse: the connection was too remarkable to be a mere accidental fact.

In that case, the problem stood thus: the two letters D F represent the relation that exists between the Chambre des Demoiselles and Fort Frefosse, the single letter D, which begins the line, represents the Demoiselles, that is to say, the cave in which you have to begin by taking up your position, and the single letter F, placed in the middle of the line, represents Frefosse, that is to say, the probable entrance to the underground passage.

Between these various signs, are two more: first, a sort of irregular rectangle, marked with a stripe in the left bottom corner, and, next, the figure 19, signs which obviously indicate to those inside the cave the means of penetrating beneath the fort.

The shape of this rectangle puzzled Isidore.

Was there around him, on the walls of the cave, or at any rate within reach of his eyes, an inscription, anything whatever, affecting a rectangular shape?

He looked for a long time and was on the point of abandoning that particular scent when his eyes fell upon the little opening, pierced in the rock, that acted as a window to the chamber.

Now the edges of this opening just formed a rectangle: corrugated, uneven, clumsy, but still a rectangle; and Beautrelet at once saw that, by placing his two feet on the D and the F carved in the stone floor — and this explained the stroke that surmounted the two letters in the document — he found himself at the exact height of the window!

He took up his position in this place and gazed out. The window looking landward, as we know, he saw, first, the path that connected the cave with the land, a path hung between two precipices; and, next, he caught sight of the foot of the hillock on which the fort stood. To try and see the fort, Beautrelet leaned over to the left and it was then that he understood the meaning of the curved stripe, the comma that marked the left bottom corner in the document: at the bottom on the left-hand side of the window, a piece of flint projected and the end of it was curved like a claw. It suggested a regular shooter's mark. And, when a man applied his eye to this mark, he saw cut out, on the slope of the mound facing him, a restricted surface of land occupied almost entirely by an old brick wall, a remnant of the original Fort Frefosse or of the old Roman *oppidum* built on this spot.

Beautrelet ran to this piece of wall, which was, perhaps, ten yards long. It was covered with grass and plants. There was no indication of any kind visible. And yet that figure 19?

He returned to the cave, took from his pocket a ball of string and a tape-measure, tied the string to the flint corner, fastened a pebble at the nineteenth metre and flung it toward the land side. The pebble at most reached the end of the path.

'Idiot that I am!' thought Beautrelet. 'Who reckoned by metres in those days? The figure 19 means 19 fathoms or nothing!'

Having made the calculation, he ran out the twine, made a knot and felt about on the piece of wall for the exact and necessarily one point at which the knot, formed at 37 metres from the window of the Demoiselles, should touch the Frefosse wall. In a few moments, the point of contact was established. With his free hand, he moved aside the leaves of mullein that had grown in the interstices. A cry escaped him. The knot, which he held pressed down with his fore-finger, was in the centre of a little cross carved in relief on a brick. And the sign that followed on the figure 19 in the document was a cross!

It needed all his will-power to control the excitement with which he was overcome. Hurriedly, with convulsive fingers, he clutched the cross and, pressing upon it, turned it as he would have turned the spokes of a wheel. The brick heaved. He redoubled his effort; it moved no further. Then, without turning, he pressed harder. He at once felt the brick give way. And, suddenly, there was the click of a bolt that is released, the sound of a lock opening and, on the right of the brick, to the width of about a yard, the wall swung round on a pivot and revealed the orifice of an underground passage.

Like a madman, Beautrelet seized the iron door in which the bricks were sealed, pulled it back, violently and closed it. Astonishment, delight, the fear of being surprised convulsed his face so as to render it unrecognizable. He beheld the awful vision of all that had happened there, in front of that door, during twenty centuries; of all those people, initiated into the great secret, who had penetrated through that issue: Celts, Gauls, Romans,

Normans, Englishmen, Frenchmen, barons, dukes, kings — and, after all of them, Arsène Lupin — and, after Lupin, himself, Beautrelet. He felt that his brain was slipping away from him. His eyelids fluttered. He fell fainting and rolled to the bottom of the slope, to the very edge of the precipice.

★ ★ ★

His task was done, at least the task which he was able to accomplish alone, with his unaided resources.

That evening, he wrote a long letter to the chief of the detective service, giving a faithful account of the results of his investigations and revealing the secret of the Hollow Needle. He asked for assistance to complete his work and gave his address.

While waiting for the reply, he spent two consecutive nights in the Chambre des Demoiselles. He spent them overcome with fear, his nerves shaken with a terror which was increased by the sounds of the night. At every moment, he thought he saw shadows approach in his direction. People knew of his presence in the cave — they were coming — they were murdering him!

His eyes, however, staring madly before them, sustained by all the power of his will, clung to the piece of wall.

On the first night, nothing stirred; but, on the second, by the light of the stars and a slender crescent-moon, he saw the door open and figures emerge from the darkness: he counted two, three, four, five of them.

It seemed to him that those five men were carrying fairly large loads. He followed them for a little way. They cut straight across the fields to the Havre road; and he heard the sound of a motor car driving away.

He retraced his steps, skirting a big farm. But, at the turn of the road that ran beside it, he had only just time to scramble up a slope and hide behind some trees. More men passed — four, five men — all carrying packages. And, two minutes later, another motor snorted.

This time, he had not the strength to return to his post; and he went back to bed.

When he woke and had finished dressing, the hotel waiter brought him a letter. He opened it. It contained Ganimard's card.

'At last!' cried Beautrelet, who, after so hard a campaign, was really feeling the need of a comrade-in-arms.

He ran downstairs with outstretched hands. Ganimard took them, looked at him for a moment and said:

'You're a fine fellow, my lad!'

'Pooh!' he said. 'Luck has served me.'

'There's no such thing as luck with 'him,''
declared the inspector, who always spoke of
Lupin in a solemn tone and without mentioning his name.

He sat down:

'So we've got him!'

'Just as we've had him twenty times over,'
said Beautrelet, laughing.

'Yes, but to-day — '

'To-day, of course, the case is different. We
know his retreat, his stronghold, which means,
when all is said, that Lupin is Lupin. He can
escape. The Etretat Needle cannot.'

'Why do you suppose that he will escape?'
asked Ganimard, anxiously.

'Why do you suppose that he requires to
escape?' replied Beautrelet. 'There is nothing
to prove that he is in the Needle at present.
Last night, eleven of his men left it. He may
be one of the eleven.'

Ganimard reflected:

'You are right. The great thing is the
Hollow Needle. For the rest, let us hope that
chance will favour us. And now, let us talk.'

He resumed his serious voice, his self-
important air and said:

'My dear Beautrelet, I have orders to
recommend you to observe the most absolute
discretion in regard to this matter.'

'Orders from whom?' asked Beautrelet,

jestingly. 'The prefect of police?'

'Higher than that.'

'The prime minister?'

'Higher.'

'Whew!'

Ganimard lowered his voice:

'Beautrelet, I was at the Elysee last night. They look upon this matter as a state secret of the utmost gravity. There are serious reasons for concealing the existence of this citadel — reasons of military strategy, in particular. It might become a revictualling centre, a magazine for new explosives, for lately-invented projectiles, for anything of that sort: the secret arsenal of France, in fact.'

'But how can they hope to keep a secret like this? In the old days, one man alone held it: the king. To-day, already, there are a good few of us who know it, without counting Lupin's gang.'

'Still, if we gained only ten years', only five years' silence! Those five years may be — the saving of us.'

'But, in order to capture this citadel, this future arsenal, it will have to be attacked, Lupin must be dislodged. And all this cannot be done without noise.'

'Of course, people will guess something, but they won't know. Besides, we can but try.'

'All right. What's your plan?'

'Here it is, in two words. To begin with, you are not Isidore Beautrelet and there's no question of Arsène Lupin either. You are and you remain a small boy of Etretat, who, while strolling about the place, caught some fellows coming out of an underground passage. This makes you suspect the existence of a flight of steps which cuts through the cliff from top to bottom.'

'Yes, there are several of those flights of steps along the coast. For instance, to the right of Etretat, opposite Benouville, they showed me the Devil's Staircase, which every bather knows. And I say nothing of the three or four tunnels used by the fishermen.'

'So you will guide me and one-half of my men. I shall enter alone, or accompanied, that remains to be seen. This much is certain, that the attack must be delivered that way. If Lupin is not in the Needle, we shall fix up a trap in which he will be caught sooner or later. If he is there — '

'If he is there, he will escape from the Needle by the other side, the side overlooking the sea.'

'In that case, he will at once be arrested by the other half of my men.'

'Yes, but if, as I presume, you choose a moment when the sea is at low ebb, leaving the base of the Needle uncovered, the chase will be public, because it will take place before all the men and women fishing for mussels, shrimps and shell-fish who swarm on the rocks round about.'

'That is why I just mean to select the time when the sea is full.'

'In that case, he will make off in a boat.'

'Ah, but I shall have a dozen fishing-smacks, each of which will be commanded by one of my men, and we shall collar him — '

'If he doesn't slip through your dozen smacks, like a fish through the meshes.'

'All right, then I'll sink him.'

'The devil you will! Shall you have guns?'

'Why, of course! There's a torpedo-boat at the Havre at this moment. A telegram from me will bring her to the Needle at the appointed hour.'

'How proud Lupin will be! A torpedo-boat! Well, M. Ganimard, I see that you have provided for everything. We have only to go ahead. When do we deliver the assault?'

'To-morrow.'

'At night?'

'No, by daylight, at the flood-tide, as the clock strikes ten in the morning.'

'Capital.'

★ ★ ★

Under his show of gaiety, Beautrelet concealed a real anguish of mind. He did not sleep until the morning, but lay pondering over the most impracticable schemes, one after the other.

Ganimard had left him in order to go to Yport, six or seven miles from Etretat, where, for prudence's sake, he had told his men to meet him, and where he chartered twelve fishing smacks, with the ostensible object of taking soundings along the coast.

At a quarter to ten, escorted by a body of twelve stalwart men, he met Isidore at the foot of the road that goes up the cliff.

At ten o'clock exactly, they reached the skirt of wall. It was the decisive moment.

At ten o'clock exactly.

'Why, what's the matter with you, Beautrelet?' jeered Ganimard. 'You're quite green in the face!'

'It's as well you can't see yourself, Ganimard,' the boy retorted. 'One would think your last hour had come!'

They both had to sit down and Ganimard swallowed a few mouthfuls of rum.

'It's not funk,' he said, 'but, by Jove, this is an exciting business! Each time that I'm on the point of catching him, it takes me like that in the pit of the stomach. A dram of rum?'

'No.'

'And if you drop behind?'

'That will mean that I'm dead.'

'B-r-r-r-r! However, we'll see. And now, open, sesame! No danger of our being observed, I suppose?'

'No. The Needle is not so high as the cliff, and, besides, there's a bend in the ground where we are.'

Beautrelet went to the wall and pressed upon the brick. The bolt was released and the underground passage came in sight.

By the gleam of the lanterns which they lit, they saw that it was cut in the shape of a vault and that both the vaulting and the floor itself were entirely covered with bricks.

They walked for a few seconds and, suddenly, a staircase appeared. Beautrelet counted forty-five brick steps, which the slow action of many footsteps had worn away in the middle.

'Blow!' said Ganimard, holding his head and stopping suddenly, as though he had knocked against something.

'What is it?'

'A door.'

'Bother!' muttered Beautrelet, looking at it. 'And not an easy one to break down either. It's just a solid block of iron.'

'We are done,' said Ganimard. 'There's not even a lock to it.'

'Exactly. That's what gives me hope.'

'Why?'

'A door is made to open; and, as this one has no lock, that means that there is a secret way of opening it.'

'And, as we don't know the secret — '

'I shall know it in a minute.'

'How?'

'By means of the document. The fourth line has no other object but to solve each difficulty as and when it crops up. And the solution is comparatively easy, because it's not written with a view to throwing searchers off the scent, but to assisting them.'

'Comparatively easy! I don't agree with you,' cried Ganimard, who had unfolded the document. 'The number 44 and a triangle with a dot in it: that doesn't tell us much!'

'Yes, yes, it does! Look at the door. You see it's strengthened, at each corner, with a triangular slab of iron; and the slabs are fixed with big nails. Take the left-hand bottom slab and work the nail in the corner: I'll lay ten to one we've hit the mark.'

'You've lost your bet,' said Ganimard, after trying.

'Then the figure 44 must mean — '

In a low voice, reflecting as he spoke, Beautrelet continued:

'Let me see — Ganimard and I are both

standing on the bottom step of the staircase — there are 45. Why 45, when the figure in the document is 44? A coincidence? No. In all this business, there is no such thing as a coincidence, at least not an involuntary one. Ganimard, be so good as to move one step higher up. That's it, don't leave this forty-fourth step. And now I will work the iron nail. And the trick's done, or I'll eat my boots!'

The heavy door turned on its hinges. A fairly spacious cavern appeared before their eyes.

'We must be exactly under Fort Frefosse,' said Beautrelet. 'We have passed through the different earthy layers by now. There will be no more brick. We are in the heart of the solid limestone.'

The room was dimly lit by a shaft of daylight that came from the other end. Going up to it, they saw that it was a fissure in the cliff, contrived in a projecting wall and forming a sort of observatory. In front of them, at a distance of fifty yards, the impressive mass of the Needle loomed from the waves. On the right, quite close, was the arched buttress of the Porte d'Aval and, on the left, very far away, closing the graceful curve of a large inlet, another rocky gateway, more imposing still, was cut out of the cliff; the Manneporte, which was so wide and tall that a three-master could have passed through it with all sail set. Behind and everywhere, the sea.

'I don't see our little fleet,' said Beautrelet.

'I know,' said Ganimard. 'The Porte d'Aval hides the whole of the coast of Etretat and Yport. But look, over there, in the offing, that black line, level with the water — '

'Well?'

'That's our fleet of war, Torpedo-boat No. 25. With her there, Lupin is welcome to break loose — if he wants to study the landscape at the bottom of the sea.'

A baluster marked the entrance to the staircase, near the fissure. They started on their way down. From time to time, a little window pierced the wall of the cliff; and, each time, they caught sight of the Needle, whose mass seemed to them to grow more and more colossal.

A little before reaching high-water level, the windows ceased and all was dark.

Isidore counted the steps aloud. At the three hundred and fifty-eight, they emerged into a wider passage, which was barred by another iron door strengthened with slabs and nails.

'We know all about this,' said Beautrelet. 'The document gives us 357 and a triangle dotted on the right. We have only to repeat the performance.'

The second door obeyed like the first. A long, a very long tunnel appeared, lit up at intervals by the gleam of a lantern swung from the vault. The walls oozed moisture and drops of water fell to the ground, so that, to make walking easier a regular pavement of planks had been laid from end to end.

'We are passing under the sea,' said Beautrelet. 'Are you coming, Ganimard?'

Without replying, the inspector ventured into the tunnel, followed the wooden foot-plank and stopped before a lantern, which he took down.

'The utensils may date back to the Middle Ages, but the lighting is modern,' he said. 'Our friends use incandescent mantles.'

He continued his way. The tunnel ended in another and a larger cave, with, on the opposite side, the first steps of a staircase that led upward.

'It's the ascent of the Needle beginning,' said Ganimard. 'This is more serious.'

But one of his men called him:

'There's another flight here, sir, on the left.'

And, immediately afterward, they discovered a third, on the right.

'The deuce!' muttered the inspector. 'This complicates matters. If we go by this way, they'll make tracks by that.'

'Shall we separate?' asked Beautrelet.

'No, no — that would mean weakening ourselves. It would be better for one of us to go ahead and scout.'

'I will, if you like — '

'Very well, Beautrelet, you go. I will remain with my men — then there will be no fear of anything. There may be other roads through the cliff than that by which we came and several roads also through the Needle. But it is certain that, between the cliff and the Needle, there is no communication except the tunnel. Therefore they must pass through this cave. And so I shall stay here till you come back. Go ahead, Beautrelet, and be prudent: at the least alarm, scoot back again.'

Isidore disappeared briskly up the middle staircase. At the thirtieth step, a door, an ordinary wooden door, stopped him. He seized the handle turned it. The door was not locked.

He entered a room that seemed to him very low owing to its immense size. Lit by powerful lamps and supported by squat pillars, with long vistas showing between them, it had nearly the same dimensions as the Needle itself. It was crammed with packing cases and miscellaneous objects — pieces of furniture, oak settees, chests, credence-tables, strong-boxes — a whole confused heap of the kind which one sees in the basement of an old curiosity shop.

On his right and left, Beautrelet perceived the wells of two staircases, the same, no doubt, that started from the cave below. He could easily have gone down, therefore, and told Ganimard. But a new flight of stairs led upward in front of him and he had the curiosity to pursue his investigations alone.

Thirty more steps. A door and then a room, not quite so large as the last, Beautrelet thought. And again, opposite him, an ascending flight of stairs.

Thirty steps more. A door. A smaller room.

Beautrelet grasped the plan of the works executed inside the Needle. It was a series of rooms placed one above the other and, therefore, gradually decreasing in size. They all served as store-rooms.

In the fourth, there was no lamp. A little light filtered in through clefts in the walls and Beautrelet saw the sea some thirty feet below him.

At that moment, he felt himself so far from Ganimard that a certain anguish began to take hold of him and he had to master his nerves lest he should take to his heels. No danger threatened him, however, and the silence around him was even so great that he asked himself whether the whole Needle had not been abandoned by Lupin and his confederates.

'I shall not go beyond the next floor,' he said to himself.

Thirty stairs again and a door. This door was lighter in construction and modern in appearance. He pushed it open gently, quite prepared for flight. There was no one there. But the room differed from the others in its purpose. There were hangings on the walls, rugs on the floor. Two magnificent sideboards, laden with gold and silver plate, stood facing each other. The little windows contrived in the deep, narrow cleft were furnished with glass panes.

In the middle of the room was a richly-decked table, with a lace-edged cloth, dishes of fruits and cakes, champagne in decanters and flowers, heaps of flowers.

Three places were laid around the table.

Beautrelet walked up. On the napkins were cards with the names of the party. He read first:

'Arsène Lupin.'

'Mme. Arsène Lupin.'

He took up the third card and started back with surprise. It bore his own name:

'Isidore Beautrelet!'

10

The Treasures of the Kings of France

A curtain was drawn back.

'Good morning, my dear Beautrelet, you're a little late. Lunch was fixed for twelve. However, it's only a few minutes — but what's the matter? Don't you know me? Have I changed so much?'

In the course of his fight with Lupin, Beautrelet had met with many surprises and he was still prepared, at the moment of the final catastrophe, to experience any number of further emotions; but the shock which he received this time was utterly unexpected. It was not astonishment, but stupefaction, terror. The man who stood before him, the man whom the brutal force of events compelled him to look upon as Arsène Lupin, was — Valmeras! Valmeras, the owner of the Chateau de l'Aiguille! Valmeras, the very man to whom he had applied for assistance against Arsène Lupin! Valmeras, his companion on the expedition to Crozant! Valmeras, the plucky friend who had made Raymonde's escape possible by felling one of Lupin's accomplices, or pretending to fell him, in the dusk of the great hall! And Valmeras was Lupin!

'You — you — So it's you!' he stammered.

'Why not?' exclaimed Lupin. 'Did you think that you knew me for good and all because you had seen me in the guise of a clergyman or under the features of M. Massiban? Alas, when a man selects the position in society which I occupy, he must needs make use of his little social gifts! If Lupin were not able to change himself, at will, into a minister of the Church of England or a member of the Academy of Inscriptions and Belles-Lettres, it would be a bad lookout for Lupin! Now Lupin, the real Lupin, is here before you, Beautrelet! Take a good look at him.'

'But then — if it's you — then — Mademoiselle — '

'Yes, Beautrelet, as you say — '

He again drew back the hanging, beckoned and announced:

'Mme. Arsène Lupin.'

'Ah,' murmured the lad, confounded in spite of everything, 'Mlle. de Saint-Veran!'

'No, no,' protested Lupin. 'Mme. Arsène Lupin, or rather, if you prefer, Mme. Louis Valmeras, my wedded wife, married to me in accordance with the strictest forms of law; and all thanks to you, my dear Beautrelet.'

He held out his hand to him.

'All my acknowledgements — and no ill will on your side, I trust?'

Strange to say, Beautrelet felt no ill will at all, no sense of humiliation, no bitterness. He realized so strongly the immense superiority of his adversary that he did not blush at being beaten by him. He pressed the offered hand.

'Luncheon is served, ma'am.'

A butler had placed a tray of dishes on the table.

'You must excuse us, Beautrelet: my chef is away and we can only give you a cold lunch.'

Beautrelet felt very little inclined to eat. He sat down, however, and was enormously interested in Lupin's attitude. How much exactly did he know? Was he aware of the danger he was running? Was he ignorant of the presence of Ganimard and his men?

And Lupin continued:

'Yes, thanks to you, my dear friend. Certainly, Raymonde and I loved each other from the first. Just so, my boy — Raymonde's abduction, her imprisonment, were mere humbug: we loved each other. But neither she nor I, when we were free to love, would allow a casual bond at the mercy of chance, to be formed between us. The position, therefore, was hopeless for Lupin. Fortunately, it ceased to be so if I resumed my identity as the Louis Valmeras that I had been from a child. It was then that I conceived the idea, as you refused to relinquish your quest and had found the Chateau de l'Aiguille, of profiting by your obstinacy.'

'And my silliness.'

'Pooh! Any one would have been caught as you were!'

'So you were really able to succeed because I screened you and assisted you?'

'Of course! How could any one suspect Valmeras of being Lupin, when Valmeras was Beautrelet's friend and after Valmeras had snatched from Lupin's clutches the girl whom Lupin loved? And how charming it was! Such delightful memories! The expedition to Crozant! The bouquets we found! My pretended love letter to Raymonde! And, later, the precautions which I, Valmeras, had to take against myself, Lupin, before my marriage! And the night of your great banquet, Beautrelet, when you fainted in my arms! Oh, what memories!'

There was a pause. Beautrelet watched Raymonde. She had listened to Lupin without saying a word and looked at him with eyes in which he read love, passion and something else besides, something which the lad could not define, a sort of anxious embarrassment and a vague sadness. But Lupin turned his eyes upon her and she gave him an affectionate smile. Their hands met over the table.

'What do you say to the way I have arranged my little home, Beautrelet?' cried Lupin. 'There's a style about it, isn't there? I don't pretend that it's as comfortable as it might be. And yet, some have been quite satisfied with it; and not the least of mankind, either! — Look at the list of distinguished people who have owned the Needle in their time and who thought it an honour to leave a mark of their sojourn.'

On the walls, one below the other, were carved the following names:

JULIUS CAESAR
CHARLEMAGNE ROLLO
WILLIAM THE CONQUEROR
RICHARD COEUR-DE-LEON
LOUIS XI.
FRANCIS I.
HENRY IV.
LOUIS XIV.
ARSÈNE LUPIN

'Whose name will figure after ours?' he continued. 'Alas, the list is closed! From Caesar to Lupin — and there it ends. Soon the nameless mob will come to visit the strange citadel. And to think that, but for Lupin, all this would have remained for ever unknown to men! Ah Beautrelet, what a feeling of pride was mine on the day when I first set foot on this abandoned soil. To have found the lost secret and become its master, its sole master! To inherit such an inheritance! To live in the Needle, after all those kings! — '

He was interrupted by a gesture of his wife's. She seemed greatly agitated.

'There is a noise,' she said. 'Underneath us. — You can hear it.'

'It's the lapping of the water,' said Lupin.

'No, indeed it's not. I know the sound of the waves. This is something different.'

'What would you have it be, darling?' said Lupin, smiling. 'I invited no one to lunch except Beautrelet.' And, addressing the servant, 'Charolais, did you lock the staircase doors behind the gentleman?'

'Yes, sir, and fastened the bolts.'

Lupin rose:

'Come, Raymonde, don't shake like that. Why, you're quite pale!'

He spoke a few words to her in an undertone, as also to the servant, drew back the curtain and sent them both out of the room.

The noise below grew more distinct. It was a series of dull blows, repeated at intervals. Beautrelet thought:

'Ganimard has lost patience and is breaking down the doors.'

Lupin resumed the thread of his conversation, speaking very calmly and as though he had really not heard:

'By Jove, the Needle was badly damaged when I succeeded in discovering it! One could see that no one had possessed the secret for more than a century, since Louis XVI. and the Revolution. The tunnel was threatening to fall in. The stairs were in a shocking state. The water was trickling in from the sea. I had to prop up and strengthen and rebuild the whole thing.'

Beautrelet could not help asking:

'When you arrived, was it empty?'

'Very nearly. The kings did not use the Needle, as I have done, as a warehouse.'

'As a place of refuge, then?'

'Yes, no doubt, in times of invasion and during the civil wars. But its real destination was to be — how shall I put it? — the strong-room or the bank of the kings of France.'

The sound of blows increased, more distinctly now. Ganimard must have broken down the first door and was attacking the second. There was a short silence and then more blows, nearer still. It was the third door. Two remained.

Through one of the windows, Beautrelet saw a number of fishing-smacks sailing round the Needle and, not far away, floating on the waters like a great black fish, the torpedo-boat.

'What a row!' exclaimed Lupin. 'One can't hear one's self speak! Let's go upstairs, shall we? It may interest you to look over the Needle.'

They climbed to the floor above, which was protected, like the others, by a door which Lupin locked behind him.

'My picture gallery,' he said.

The walls were covered with canvases on which Beautrelet recognized the most famous signatures. There were Raphael's *Madonna of the Agnus Dei*, Andrea del Sarto's *Portrait of Lucrezia Fede*, Titian's *Salome*, Botticelli's *Madonna and Angels* and numbers of Tintorettos, Carpaccios, Rembrandts, Velasquez.

'What fine copies!' said Beautrelet, approvingly.

Lupin looked at him with an air of stupefaction:

'What! Copies! You must be mad! The copies are in Madrid, my dear fellow, in Florence, Venice, Munich, Amsterdam.'

'Then these — '

'Are the original pictures, my lad, patiently collected in all the museums of Europe, where I have replaced them, like an honest man, with first-rate copies.'

'But some day or other — '

'Some day or other, the fraud will be discovered? Well, they will find my signature on each canvas — at the back — and they will know that it was I who have endowed my country with the original masterpieces. After all, I have only done what Napoleon did in Italy. — Oh, look, Beautrelet: here are M. de Gesvres's four Rubenses! — '

The knocking continued within the hollow of the Needle without ceasing.

'I can't stand this!' said Lupin. 'Let's go higher.'

A fresh staircase. A fresh door.

'The tapestry-room,' Lupin announced.

The tapestries were not hung on the walls, but rolled, tied up with cord, ticketed; and, in addition, there were parcels of old fabrics which Lupin unfolded: wonderful brocades, admirable velvets, soft, faded silks, church vestments woven with silver and gold —

They went higher still and Beautrelet saw the room containing the clocks and other time-pieces, the book-room — oh, the splendid bindings, the precious, undiscoverable volumes, the unique copies stolen from the great public libraries — the lace-room, the knick-knack-room.

And each time the circumference of the room grew smaller.

And each time, now, the sound of knocking

was more distant. Ganimard was losing ground.

'This is the last room,' said Lupin. 'The treasury.'

This one was quite different. It was round also, but very high and conical in shape. It occupied the top of the edifice and its floor must have been fifteen or twenty yards below the extreme point of the Needle.

On the cliff side there was no window. But on the side of the sea, whence there were no indiscreet eyes to fear, two glazed openings admitted plenty of light.

The ground was covered with a parqueted flooring of rare wood, forming concentric patterns. Against the walls stood glass cases and a few pictures.

'The pearls of my collection,' said Lupin. 'All that you have seen so far is for sale. Things come and things go. That's business. But here, in this sanctuary, everything is sacred. There is nothing here but choice, essential pieces, the best of the best, priceless things. Look at these jewels, Beautrelet: Chaldean amulets, Egyptian necklaces, Celtic bracelets, Arab chains. Look at these statuettes, Beautrelet, at this Greek Venus, this Corinthian Apollo. Look at these Tanagras, Beautrelet: all the real Tanagras are here. Outside this glass case, there is not a single genuine Tanagra statuette in the whole wide world. What a delicious thing to be able to say! — Beautrelet, do you remember Thomas and his gang of church-pillagers in the South — agents of mine, by the way? Well, here is the Ambazac reliquary, the real one, Beautrelet! Do you remember the Louvre scandal, the tiara which was admitted to be false, invented and manufactured by a modern artist? Here is the tiara of Saitapharnes, the real one, Beautrelet! Look, Beautrelet, look with all your eyes: here is the marvel of marvels, the supreme masterpiece, the work of no mortal brain; here is Leonardo's *Gioconda*, the real one! Kneel, Beautrelet, kneel; all womankind stands before you in this picture.'

There was a long silence between them. Below, the sound of blows drew nearer. Two or three doors, no more, separated them from Ganimard. In the offing, they saw the black back of the torpedo-boat and the fishing-smacks cruising to and fro.

The boy asked:

'And the treasure?'

'Ah, my little man, that's what interests you most! None of those masterpieces of human art can compete with the contemplation of the treasure as a matter of curiosity, eh? — And the whole crowd will be like you! — Come, you shall be satisfied.'

He stamped his foot, and, in so doing, made one of the discs composing the floor-pattern turn right over. Then, lifting it as though it were the lid of a box, he uncovered a sort of large round bowl, dug in the thickness of the rock. It was empty.

A little farther, he went through the same performance. Another large bowl appeared. It was also empty.

He did this three times over again. The three other bowls were empty.

'Eh,' grinned Lupin. 'What a disappointment! Under Louis XL, under Henry IV., under Richelieu, the five bowls were full. But think of Louis XIV., the folly of Versailles, the wars, the great disasters of the reign! And think of Louis XV., the spendthrift king, with his Pompadour and his Du Barry! How they must have drawn on the treasure in those days! With what thieving claws they must have scratched at the stone. You see, there's nothing left.'

He stopped.

'Yes, Beautrelet, there is something — the sixth hiding-place! This one was intangible. Not one of them dared touch it. It was the very last resource, the nest-egg, the something put by for a rainy day. Look, Beautrelet!'

He stooped and lifted up the lid. An iron box filled the bowl. Lupin took from his pocket a key with a complicated bit and wards and opened the box.

A dazzling sight presented itself. Every sort of precious stone sparkled there, every colour gleamed, the blue of the sapphires, the red of the rubies, the green of the emeralds, the yellow of the topazes.

'Look, look, little Beautrelet! They have squandered all the cash, all the gold, all the silver, all the crown pieces and all the ducats and all the doubloons; but the chest with the jewels has remained intact. Look at the settings. They belong to every period, to every century, to every country. The dowries of the queens are here. Each brought her share: Margaret of Scotland and Charlotte of Savoy; duchesses of Austria: Eleonore, Elisabeth, Marie-Therese, Mary of England and Catherine de Medicis; and all the arch — Marie Antoinette. Look at those pearls, Beautrelet! And those diamonds: look at the size of the diamonds! Not one of them but is worthy of an empress! The Pitt Diamond is no finer!'

He rose to his feet and held up his hand as one taking an oath:

'Beautrelet, you shall tell the world that Lupin has not taken a single one of the stones that were in the royal chest, not a single one, I swear it on my honour! I had no right to. They are the fortune of France.'

Below them, Ganimard was making all speed.

It was easy to judge by the reverberation of the blows that his men were attacking the last door but one, the door that gave access to the knick-knack-room.

'Let us leave the chest open,' said Lupin, 'and all the cavities, too, all those little empty graves.'

He went round the room, examined some of the glass cases, gazed at some of the pictures and, as he walked, said, pensively:

'How sad it is to leave all this! What a wrench! The happiest hours of my life have been spent here, alone, in the presence of these objects which I loved. And my eyes will never behold them again and my hands will never touch them again — '

His drawn face bore such an expression of lassitude upon it that Beautrelet felt a vague sort of pity for him. Sorrow in that man must assume larger proportions than in another, even as joy did, or pride, or humiliation. He was now standing by the window, and, with his finger pointing to the horizon, said:

'What is sadder still is that I must abandon that, all that! How beautiful it is! The boundless sea — the sky. — On either side, the cliffs of Etretat with their three natural archways: the Porte d'Armont, the Porte d'Aval, the Manneporte — so many triumphal arches for the master. And the master was I! I was the king of the story, the king of fairyland, the king of the Hollow Needle! A strange and supernatural kingdom! From Caesar to Lupin: what a destiny!' He burst out laughing. 'King of fairyland! Why not say King of Yvetot at once? What nonsense! King of the world, yes, that's more like it! From this topmost point of the Needle, I ruled the globe! I held it in my claws like a prey! Lift the tiara of Saitapharnes, Beautrelet. —You see those two telephones? The one on the right communicates with Paris: a private line; the one on the left with London: a private line. Through London, I am in touch with America, Asia, Australia, South Africa. In all those continents, I have my offices, my agents, my jackals, my scouts! I drive an international trade. I hold the great market in art and antiquities, the world's fair! Ah, Beautrelet, there are moments when my power turns my head! I feel intoxicated with strength and authority.'

The door gave way below. They heard Ganimard and his men running about and searching.

After a moment, Lupin continued, in a low voice:

'And now it's over. A little girl crossed my path, a girl with soft hair and wistful eyes and an honest, yes, an honest soul — and it's over. I myself am demolishing the mighty

301

edifice. — All the rest seems absurd and childish to me — nothing counts but her hair — and her wistful eyes — and her honest little soul — '

The men came up the staircase. A blow shook the door, the last door —

Lupin seized the boy sharply by the arm:

'Do you understand, Beautrelet, why I let you have things your own way when I could have crushed you, time after time, weeks ago? Do you understand how you succeeded in getting as far as this? Do you understand that I had given each of my men his share of the plunder when you met them the other night on the cliff? You do understand, don't you? The Hollow Needle is the great adventure. As long as it belongs to me, I remain the great adventurer. Once the Needle is recaptured, it means that the past and I are parted and that the future begins, a future of peace and happiness, in which I shall have no occasion to blush when Raymonde's eyes are turned upon me, a future — '

He turned furiously toward the door:

'Stop that noise, Ganimard, will you? I haven't finished my speech!'

The blows came faster. It was like the sound of a beam that was being hurled against the door. Beautrelet, mad with curiosity, stood in front of Lupin and awaited events, without understanding what Lupin was doing or contemplating. To give up the Needle was all very well; but why was he giving up himself? What was his plan? Did he hope to escape from Ganimard? And, on the other hand, where was Raymonde?

Lupin, meantime, was murmuring, dreamily:

'An honest man. — Arsène Lupin an honest man — no more robbery — leading the life of everybody else. — And why not? There is no reason why I should not meet with the same success. — But do stop that now, Ganimard! Don't you know, you ass, that I'm uttering historic words and that Beautrelet is taking them in for the benefit of posterity?' He laughed. 'I am wasting my time. Ganimard will never grasp the use of my historic words.'

He took a piece of red chalk, put a pair of steps to the wall and wrote, in large letters:

Arsène Lupin gives and bequeaths to France all the treasures contained in the Hollow Needle, on the sole condition that these treasures be housed at the Musee du Louvre in rooms which shall be known as the Arsène Lupin Rooms.

'Now,' he said, 'my conscience is at ease. France and I are quits.'

The attackers were striking with all their might. One of the panels burst in two. A hand was put through and fumbled for the lock.

'Thunder!' said Lupin. 'That idiot of a Ganimard is capable of effecting his purpose for once in his life.'

He rushed to the lock and removed the key.

'Sold, old chap! — The door's tough. — I have plenty of time — Beautrelet, I must say good-bye. And thank you! — For really you could have complicated the attack — but you're so tactful!'

While speaking, he moved toward a large triptych by Van der Weyden, representing the Wise Men of the East. He shut the right-hand panel and, in so doing, exposed a little door concealed behind it and seized the handle.

'Good luck to your hunting, Ganimard! And kind regards at home!'

A pistol-shot resounded. Lupin jumped back: 'Ah, you rascal, full in the heart! Have you been taking lessons? You've done for the Wise Man! Full in the heart! Smashed to smithereens, like a pipe at the fair! — '

'Lupin, surrender!' roared Ganimard, with his eyes glittering and his revolver showing through the broken panel of the door. 'Surrender, I say!'

'Did the old guard surrender?'

'If you stir a limb, I'll blow your brains out!'

'Nonsense! You can't get me here!'

As a matter of fact, Lupin had moved away; and, though Ganimard was able to fire straight in front of him through the breach in the door, he could not fire, still less take aim, on the side where Lupin stood. Lupin's position was a terrible one for all that, because the outlet on which he was relying, the little door behind the triptych, opened right in front of Ganimard. To try to escape meant to expose himself to the detective's fire; and there were five bullets left in the revolver.

'By Jove,' he said, laughing, 'there's a slump in my shares this afternoon! You've done a nice thing. Lupin, old fellow: you wanted a last sensation and you've gone a bit too far. You shouldn't have talked so much.'

He flattened himself against the wall. A further portion of the panel had given way under the men's pressure and Ganimard was less hampered in his movements. Three yards, no more, separated the two antagonists. But Lupin was protected by a glass case with a gilt-wood framework

'Why don't you help, Beautrelet?' cried the old detective, gnashing his teeth with rage. 'Why don't you shoot him, instead of staring at him like that?'

Isidore, in fact, had not budged, had remained, till that moment, an eager, but passive spectator. He would have liked to fling himself into the contest with all his strength and to bring down the prey which he held at his mercy. He was prevented by some inexplicable sentiment.

But Ganimard's appeal for assistance shook him. His hand closed on the butt of his revolver:

'If I take part in it,' he thought, 'Lupin is lost. And I have the right — it's my duty.'

Their eyes met. Lupin's were calm, watchful, almost inquisitive, as though, in the awful danger that threatened him, he were interested only in the moral problem that held the young man in its clutches. Would Isidore decide to give the finishing stroke to the defeated enemy?

The door cracked from top to bottom.

'Help, Beautrelet, we've got him!' Ganimard bellowed.

Isidore raised his revolver.

What happened was so quick that he knew of it, so to speak, only by the result. He saw Lupin bob down and run along the wall, skimming the door right under the weapon which Ganimard was vainly brandishing; and he felt himself suddenly flung to the ground, picked up the next moment and lifted by an invincible force.

Lupin held him in the air, like a living

shield, behind which he hid himself.

'Ten to one that I escape, Ganimard! Lupin, you see, has never quite exhausted his resources — '

He had taken a couple of brisk steps backward to the triptych. Holding Beautrelet with one hand flat against his chest, with the other he cleared the passage and closed the little door behind them.

A steep staircase appeared before their eyes.

'Come along,' said Lupin, pushing Beautrelet before him. 'The land forces are beaten — let us turn our attention to the French fleet. — After Waterloo, Trafalgar. — You're having some fun for your money, eh, my lad? — Oh, how good: listen to them knocking at the triptych now! — It's too late, my children. — But hurry along, Beautrelet!'

The staircase, dug out in the wall of the Needle, dug in its very crust, turned round and round the pyramid, encircling it like the spiral of a toboggan-slide. Each hurrying the other, they clattered down the treads, taking two or three at a bound. Here and there, a ray of light trickled through a fissure; and Beautrelet carried away the vision of the fishing-smacks hovering a few dozen fathoms off, and of the black torpedo-boat.

They went down and down, Isidore in

silence, Lupin still bubbling over with merriment:

'I should like to know what Ganimard is doing? Is he tumbling down the other staircases to bar the entrance to the tunnel against me? No, he's not such a fool as that. He must have left four men there — and four men are sufficient — ' He stopped. 'Listen — they're shouting up above. That's it, they've opened the window and are calling to their fleet. — Why, look, the men are busy on board the smacks — they're exchanging signals. — The torpedo-boat is moving. — Dear old torpedo-boat! I know you, you're from the Havre. — Guns' crews to the guns! — Hullo, there's the commander! — How are you, Duguay-Trouin?'

He put his arm through a cleft and waved his handkerchief. Then he continued his way downstairs:

'The enemy's fleet have set all sail,' he said. 'We shall be boarded before we know where we are. Heavens, what fun!'

They heard the sound of voices below them. They were just then approaching the level of the sea and they emerged, almost at once, into a large cave into which two lanterns were moving about in the dark.

A woman's figure appeared and threw itself on Lupin's neck:

'Quick, quick, I was so nervous about you. What have you been doing? — But you're not alone! — '

Lupin reassured her:

'It's our friend Beautrelet. — Just think, Beautrelet had the tact — but I'll talk about that later — there's no time now. — Charolais are you there? That's right! — And the boat?'

'The boat's ready, sir,' Charolais replied,

'Fire away,' said Lupin.

In a moment, the noise of a motor crackled and Beautrelet, whose eyes were gradually becoming used to the gloom, ended by perceiving that they were on a sort of quay, at the edge of the water, and that a boat was floating before them.

'A motor boat,' said Lupin, completing Beautrelet's observations. 'This knocks you all of a heap, eh, Isidore, old chap? — You don't understand. — Still, you have only to think. — As the water before your eyes is no other than the water of the sea, which filters into this excavation each high tide, the result is that I have a safe little private roadstead all to myself.'

'But it's closed,' Beautrelet protested. 'No one can get in or out.'

'Yes, I can,' said Lupin; 'and I'm going to prove it to you.'

He began by handing Raymonde in. Then he came back to fetch Beautrelet. The lad hesitated.

'Are you afraid?' asked Lupin.

'What of?'

'Of being sunk by the torpedo-boat.'

'No.'

'Then you're considering whether it's not your duty to stay with Ganimard, law and order, society and morality, instead of going off with Lupin, shame, infamy and disgrace.'

'Exactly.'

'Unfortunately, my boy, you have no choice. For the moment, they must believe the two of us dead — and leave me the peace to which a prospective honest man is entitled. Later on, when I have given you your liberty, you can talk as much as you please — I shall have nothing more to fear.'

By the way in which Lupin clutched his arm, Beautrelet felt that all resistance was useless. Besides, why resist? Had he not discovered and handed over the Hollow Needle? What did he care about the rest? Had he not the right to humour the irresistible sympathy with which, in spite of everything, this man inspired him?

The feeling was so clear in him that he was half inclined to say to Lupin:

'Look here, you're running another, a more

serious danger; Holmlock Shears is on your track.'

'Come along!' said Lupin, before Isidore had made up his mind to speak.

He obeyed and let Lupin lead him to the boat, the shape of which struck him as peculiar and its appearance quite unexpected.

Once on deck, they went down a little steep staircase, or rather a ladder hooked on to a trap door, which closed above their heads. At the foot of the ladder, brightly lit by a lamp, was a very small saloon, where Raymonde was waiting for them and where the three had just room to sit down.

Lupin took the mouthpiece of a speaking tube from a hook and gave the order:

'Let her go, Charolais!'

Isidore had the unpleasant sensation which one feels when going down in a lift: the sensation of the ground vanishing beneath you, the impression of emptiness, space. This time, it was the water retreating; and space opened out, slowly.

'We're sinking, eh?' grinned Lupin. 'Don't be afraid — we've only to pass from the upper cave where we were to another little cave, situated right at the bottom and half open to the sea, which can be entered at low tide. All the shellfish-catchers know it. Ah, ten seconds' wait! We're going through the passage and it's very narrow, just the size of the submarine.'

'But,' asked Beautrelet, 'how is it that the fishermen who enter the lower cave don't know that it's open at the top and that it communicates with another from which a staircase starts and runs through the Needle? The facts are at the disposal of the first-comer.'

'Wrong, Beautrelet! The top of the little public cave is closed, at low tide, by a movable platform, painted the colour of the rock, which the sea, when it rises, shifts and carries up with it and, when it goes down, fastens firmly over the little cave. That is why I am able to pass at high tide. A clever notion, what? It's an idea of my own. True, neither Caesar nor Louis XIV., nor, in short, any of my distinguished predecessors could have had it, because they did not possess submarines. They were satisfied with the staircase, which then ran all the way down to the little bottom cave. I did away with the last treads of the staircase and invented the trick of the movable ceiling: it's a present I'm making to France — Raymonde, my love, put out the lamp beside you — we shan't want it now — on the contrary — '

A pale light, which seemed to be of the same colour as the water, met them as they left the cave and made its way into the cabin through the two portholes and through a thick glass skylight that projected above the planking of the deck and allowed the passengers to inspect the upper layers of the sea. And, suddenly, a shadow glided over their heads.

'The attack is about to take place. The fleet is investing the Needle. But, hollow as the Needle is, I don't see how they propose to enter it.'

He took up the speaking tube:

'Don't leave the bottom, Charolais. Where are we going? Why, I told you: to Port-Lupin. And at full speed, do you hear? We want water to land by — there's a lady with us.'

They skimmed over the rocky bed. The seaweed stood up on end like a heavy, dark vegetation and the deep currents made it wave gracefully, stretching and billowing like floating hair.

Another shadow, a longer one.

'That's the torpedo-boat,' said Lupin. 'We shall hear the roar of the guns presently. What will Duguay-Trouin do? Bombard the Needle? Think of what we're missing, Beautrelet, by not being present at the meeting of Duguay-Trouin and Ganimard! The juncture of the land and naval forces! Hi, Charolais, don't go to sleep, my man!'

They were moving very fast, for all that. The rocks had been succeeded by sand-fields and then, almost at once, they saw more rocks, which marked the eastern extremity of Etretat, the Porte d'Amont. Fish fled at their approach. One of them, bolder than the rest, fastened on to a porthole and looked at the occupants of the saloon with its great, fixed, staring eyes.

'That's better,' cried Lupin. 'We're going now. What do you think of my cockle-shell, Beautrelet? Not so bad, is she? Do you remember the story of the Seven of Hearts, the wretched end of Lacombe, the engineer, and how, after punishing his murderers, I presented the State with his papers and his plans for the construction of a new submarine: one more gift to France? Well, among the plans, I kept those of a submersible motor boat and that is how you come to have the honour of sailing in my company.'

He called to Charolais:

'Take us up, Charolais — there's no danger now — '

They shot up to the surface and the glass skylight emerged above the water.

They were a mile from the coast, out of sight, therefore, and Beautrelet was now able to realize more fully at what a headlong pace they were traveling. First Fecamp passed before them, then all the Norman seaside places: Saint-Pierre, the Petits — Dalles, Veulettes, Saint-Valery, Veules, Quiberville. Lupin kept on jesting and Isidore never wearied of watching and listening to him, amazed as he was at the man's spirits, at his gaiety, his mischievous ways, his careless chaff, his delight in life.

He also noticed Raymonde. The young woman sat silent, nestling up against the man she loved. She had taken his hands between her own and kept on raising her eyes to him; and Beautrelet constantly observed that her hands were twitching and that the wistful sadness of her eyes increased. And, each time, it was like a dumb and sorrowful reply to Lupin's sallies. One would have thought that his frivolous words, his sarcastic outlook on life, caused her physical pain.

'Hush!' she whispered. 'It's defying destiny to laugh — so many misfortunes can reach us still!'

Opposite Dieppe, they had to dive lest they should be seen by the fishing-craft. And twenty minutes later, they shot at an angle toward the coast and the boat entered a little submarine harbour formed by a regular gap between the rocks, drew up beside a jetty and rose gently to the surface.

Lupin announced:

'Port-Lupin!'

The spot, situated at sixteen miles from Dieppe and twelve from the Treport and protected, moreover, by the two landslips of cliff, was absolutely deserted. A fine sand carpeted the rounded slope of the tiny beach.

'Jump on shore, Beautrelet — Raymonde, give me your hand. You, Charolais, go back to the Needle, see what happens between Ganimard and Duguay-Trouin and come back and tell me at the end of the day. The thing interests me tremendously.'

Beautrelet asked himself with a certain curiosity how they were going to get out of this hemmed-in creek which was called Port-Lupin, when, at the foot of the cliff, he saw the uprights of an iron ladder.

'Isidore,' said Lupin, 'if you knew your geography and your history, you would know that we are at the bottom of the gorge of Parfonval, in the parish of Biville. More than a century ago, on the night of the twenty-third of August, 1803, Georges Cadoudal and six accomplices, who had landed in France with the intention of kidnapping the first consul, Bonaparte, scrambled up to the top by the road which I will show you. Since then, this road has been demolished by landslips. But Louis Valmeras, better known by the name of Arsène Lupin, had it restored at his own expense and bought the farm of the Neuvil-lette, where the conspirators spent the first night and where, retired from business and withdrawing from the affairs of this world, he means to lead the life of a respectable country squire with his wife and his mother by his side. The gentleman-burglar is dead! Long live the gentleman-farmer!'

After the ladder came a sort of gully, an abrupt ravine hollowed out, apparently, by the rains, at the end of which they laid hold of a makeshift staircase furnished with a hand-rail. As Lupin explained, this hand-rail had been placed where it was in the stead of the *estamperche*, a long rope fastened to stakes, by which the people of the country, in the old days, used to help themselves down when going to the beach.

After a painful climb of half an hour, they emerged on the tableland, not far from one of those little cabins, dug out of the soil itself, which serve as shelters for the excisemen. And, as it happened, two minutes later, at a turn in the path, one of these custom-house officials appeared.

He drew himself up and saluted.

Lupin asked:

'Any news, Gomel?'

'No, governor.'

'You've met no one at all suspicious-looking?'

'No, governor — only — '

'What?'

'My wife — who does dressmaking at the Neuvillette — '

'Yes, I know — Cesarine — my mother spoke of her. Well?'

'It seems a sailor was prowling about the village this morning.'

'What sort of face had he?'

'Not a natural face — a sort of Englishman's face.'

'Ah!' said Lupin, in a tone preoccupied. 'And you have given Cesarine orders — '

'To keep her eyes open. Yes, governor.'

'Very well. Keep a lookout for Charolais's return in two or three hours from now. If there's anything, I shall be at the farm.'

He walked on and said to Beautrelet:

'This makes me uneasy — is it Shears? Ah, if it's he, in his present state of exasperation, I have everything to fear!'

He hesitated a moment: 'I wonder if we hadn't better turn back. Yes, I have a nasty presentiment of evil.'

Gently undulating plains stretched before them as far as the eye could see. A little to the left, a series of handsome avenues of trees led to the farm of the Neuvillette, the buildings of which were now in view. It was the retreat which he had prepared, the haven of rest

318

which he had promised Raymonde. Was he, for the sake of an absurd idea, to renounce happiness at the very moment when it seemed within his reach?

He took Isidore by the arm and, calling his attention to Raymonde, who was walking in front of them:

'Look at her. When she walks, her figure has a little swing at the waist which I cannot see without quivering. But everything in her gives me that thrill of emotion and love: her movements and her repose, her silence and the sound of her voice. I tell you, the mere fact that I am walking in the track of her footsteps makes me feel in the seventh heaven. Ah, Beautrelet, will she ever forget that I was once Lupin? Shall I ever be able to wipe out from her memory the past which she loathes and detests?' He mastered himself and, with obstinate assurance. 'She will forget!' he declared. 'She will forget, because I have made every sacrifice for her sake. I have sacrificed the inviolable sanctuary of the Hollow Needle, I have sacrificed my treasures, my power, my pride — I will sacrifice everything — I don't want to be anything more — but just a man in love — and an honest man, because she can only love an honest man. After all, why should I not be honest? It is no more degrading than anything else!'

The quip escaped him, so to speak, unawares. His voice remained serious and free of all chaff. And he muttered, with restrained violence:

'Ah, Beautrelet, you see, of all the unbridled joys which I have tasted in my adventurous life, there is not one that equals the joy with which her look fills me when she is pleased with me. I feel quite weak then, and I should like to cry — ' Was he crying? Beautrelet had an intuition that his eyes were wet with tears. Tears in Lupin's eyes! — Tears of love!

They were nearing an old gate that served as an entrance to the farm. Lupin stopped for a moment and stammered:

'Why am I afraid? — I feel a sort of weight on my chest. Is the adventure of the Hollow Needle not over? Has destiny not accepted the issue which I selected?'

Raymonde turned round, looking very anxious.

'Here comes Cesarine. She's running.'

The exciseman's wife was hurrying from the farm as fast as she could. Lupin rushed up to her:

'What is it? What has happened? Speak!'

Choking, quite out of breath, Cesarine stuttered:

'A man — I saw a man this morning!

'A man — I saw a man in the sitting-room.'

'The Englishman of this morning?'

'Yes — but in a different disguise.'

'Did he see you?'

'No. He saw your mother. Mme. Valmeras caught him as he was just going away.'

'Well?'

'He told her that he was looking for Louis Valmeras, that he was a friend of yours.'

'Then?'

'The madame said that her son had gone abroad — for years.'

'And he went away?'

'No, he made signs through the window that overlooks the plain — as if he were calling to some one.'

Lupin seemed to hesitate. A loud cry tore the air. Raymonde moaned:

'It's your mother — I recognize — '

He flung himself upon her and, dragging her away, in a burst of fierce passion:

'Come — let us fly — you first.'

But, suddenly, he stopped, distraught, over-come:

'No, I can't do it — it's too awful. Forgive me — Raymonde — that poor woman down there — Stay here. Beautrelet, don't leave her.'

He darted along the slope that surrounds the farm, turned and followed it, at a run, till he came to the gate that opens on the plain.

Raymonde, whom Beautrelet had been unable to hold back, arrived almost as soon as he did; and Beautrelet, hiding behind the trees, saw, in the lonely walk that led from the farm to the gate, three men, of whom one, the tallest, went ahead, while the two others were holding by the arms a woman who tried to resist and who uttered moans of pain.

The daylight was beginning to fade. Nevertheless, Beautrelet recognized Holmlock Shears. The woman seemed of a certain age. Her livid features were set in a frame of white hair.

They all four came up.

They reached the gate. Shears opened one of the folding leaves.

Then Lupin strode forward and stood in front of him.

The encounter appeared all the more terrible inasmuch as it was silent, almost solemn.

For long moments, the two enemies took each other's measure with their eyes. An equal hatred distorted the features of both of them. Neither moved.

Then Lupin spoke, in a voice of terrifying calmness:

'Tell your men to leave that woman alone.'

'No.'

It was as though both of them feared to engage in the supreme struggle, as though both were collecting all their strength. And there were no words wasted this time, no insults, no bantering challenges. Silence, a deathlike silence.

Mad with anguish, Raymonde awaited the issue of the duel. Beautrelet had caught her arms and was holding her motionless.

After a second, Lupin repeated:

'Order your men to leave that woman alone.'

'No.'

Lupin said:

'Listen, Shears — '

But he interrupted himself, realizing the silliness of the words. In the face of that colossus of pride and will-power which called itself Holmlock Shears, of what use were threats?

Resolved upon the worst, suddenly he put his hand to his jacket pocket. The Englishman anticipated his movement and, leaping upon his prisoner, thrust the barrel of his revolver within two inches of her temple:

'If you stir a limb, I fire!'

At the same time his two satellites drew their weapons and aimed them at Lupin.

Lupin drew himself up, stifled the rage within him and, coolly, with his hands in his pockets and his breast exposed to the enemy, began once more:

'Shears, for the third time, let that woman be — '

The Englishman sneered:

'I have no right to touch her, I suppose? Come, come, enough of this humbug! Your name isn't Valmeras any more than it's Lupin: you stole the name just as you stole the name of Charmerace. And the woman whom you pass off as your mother is Victoire, your old accomplice, the one who brought you up — '

Shears made a mistake. Carried away by his longing for revenge, he glanced across at Raymonde, whom these revelations filled with horror. Lupin took advantage of his imprudence. With a sudden movement, he fired.

'Damnation!' bellowed Shears, whose arm, pierced by a bullet, fell to his side. And, addressing his men, 'Shoot, you two! Shoot him down!'

But already Lupin was upon them: and not two seconds had elapsed before the one on the right was sprawling on the ground, with his chest smashed, while the other, with his jaw broken, fell back against the gate.

'Hurry up, Victoire. Tie them down. And now, Mr. Englishman, it's you and I.'

He ducked with an oath:

'Ah, you scoundrel!'

Shears had picked up his revolver with his

left hand and was taking aim at him.

A shot — a cry of distress — Raymonde had flung herself between the two men, facing the Englishman. She staggered back, brought her hand to her neck, drew herself up, spun round on her heels and fell at Lupin's feet.

'Raymonde! — Raymonde!'

He threw himself upon her, took her in his arms and pressed her to him.

'Dead — ' he said.

There was a moment of stupefaction. Shears seemed confounded by his own act. Victoire stammered:

'My poor boy — my poor boy — '

Beautrelet went up to the young woman and stooped to examine her. Lupin repeated:

'Dead — dead — '

He said it in a reflective tone, as though he did not yet understand. But his face became hollow, suddenly transformed, ravaged by grief. And then he was seized with a sort of madness, made senseless gestures, wrung his hands, stamped his feet, like a child that suffers more than it is able to bear.

'You villain!' he cried, suddenly, in an access of hatred.

And, flinging Shears back with a formidable blow, he took him by the throat and dug his twitching fingers into his flesh.

The Englishman gasped, without even struggling.

'My boy-my boy — ' said Victoire, in a voice of entreaty.

Beautrelet ran up. But Lupin had already let go and stood sobbing beside his enemy stretched upon the ground.

O pitiful sight! Beautrelet never forgot its tragic horror, he who knew all Lupin's love for Raymonde and all that the great adventurer had sacrificed of his own being to bring a smile to the face of his well-beloved.

Night began to cover the field of battle with a shroud of darkness. The three Englishmen lay bound and gagged in the tall grass. Distant songs broke the vast silence of the plain. It was the farm-hands returning from their work.

Lupin drew himself up. He listened to the monotonous voices. Then he glanced at the happy homestead of the Neuvillette, where he had hoped to live peacefully with Raymonde. Then he looked at her, the poor, loving victim, whom love had killed and who, all white, was sleeping her last, eternal sleep.

The men were coming nearer, however.

Then Lupin bent down, took the dead woman in his powerful arms, lifted the corpse with a single effort and, bent in two, stretched it across his back:

'Let us go, Victoire.'

'Let us go, dear.'

'Good-bye, Beautrelet,' he said.

And, bearing his precious and awful burden followed by his old servant, silent and fierce he turned toward the sea and plunged into the darkness of the night.

We do hope that you have enjoyed reading this large print book.

Did you know that all of our titles are available for purchase?

We publish a wide range of high quality large print books including:
Romances, Mysteries, Classics
General Fiction
Non Fiction and Westerns

Special interest titles available in large print are:
The Little Oxford Dictionary
Music Book
Song Book
Hymn Book
Service Book

Also available from us courtesy of Oxford University Press:
Young Readers' Dictionary
(large print edition)
Young Readers' Thesaurus
(large print edition)

For further information or a free brochure, please contact us at:
Ulverscroft Large Print Books Ltd.,
The Green, Bradgate Road, Anstey,
Leicester, LE7 7FU, England.
Tel: (00 44) 0116 236 4325
Fax: (00 44) 0116 234 0205